Chockolate Sauce

Smooth.Dark.Sinful

Chockolate Sauce

Smooth.Dark.Sinful

Arpit Vageria

MAHAVEER PUBLISHERS

Published by
MAHAVEER PUBLISHERS
4764/2A, 23-Ansari Road, Daryaganj
New Delhi – 110002
Ph. : 011 – 66629669–79–89
011 – 23244999
e-mail : mahaveerpublishers@gmail.com

Third Impression : February 2013

Chockolate Sauce
ISBN (10) : 8183520782
ISBN (13) : 9788183520782

This novel is entirely a work of fiction. Names, characters and incidents portrayed in it are the work of the author's imagination. Any resemblance to actual persons, living or dead, events or localities is entirely coincidental.

Distributed in India by
VAIBHAV BOOK SERVICE
e-mail : vaibhavbookservice@gmail.com

Distributed in Nepal by
BAJRANGBALI BOOK ENTERPRISES PVT. LTD.
Jyatha Mushyabahal, Ward No. 27, Kathmandu, Nepal
e-mail : bajrangbalibooks@gmail.com

Printed in India

Dedication

My Grandfather

My Parents : Mr. Dilip Vageria, Mrs. Vandana Vageria

My Brother : Mr. Ankit Vageria

Acknowledgment

I will begin by thanking my grandfather for his unconditional love and blessings; my parents, for being the loveliest couple and also for their undying support and encouragement; my elder brother, Ankit Vageria, for being my best friend, my buddy and for his unwavering faith and belief in me.

No thank you is big enough for Swapnil Kothari sir, for he not only constantly motivated me but also guided me by taking away the sting from his words, intelligently and for being with me through this arduous process of writing a book. His confidence in me gave me the strength and direction to give shape to my dreams.

A big thank you is due to 'Renaissance and Indore Indira' family for always being there with me.

Some of the names without whom I consider my life incomplete and bland are Aditi Pawar, for being the first ever person to (falsely) praise my amateur writing by making me foolishly believe me that I can write and that people will read and like it; Saloni, for partnering me in the craziest of incident in life and being the happiest human being ever; Supriti and Shreya for always believing in me and my potential; Rohit, Piyush and Romil for tolerating me and my moods and for always 'unwillingly' tagging along with me to my Lonavla escapades – 'unwilling' because they were never given an option of not coming.

I am grateful to Pankaj, Harsh, Amit, Ankit, Shruti, Ankita, Arpita, Naveen, Shreyans, Ashwini, Kunal, Sumit, Gaurav, Shubham, Mayank for always being wonderful company and available whenever I needed them either in Indore, Pune or Mumbai.

Many thanks to Kanishka for helping me with his services and making my path a lot easier; Nikita, for being a patient listener, a great friend and offering her constructive support always, without asking for anything in return; Ankit, Pramod, Prateek, Manoj, Abhishek, Himanshu Rakesh, Vinay, Rohan and Anuj for making my world better and interesting; and Rohit Sharma, for capturing my images whenever asked or not asked and giving me 'delusional realisation' that I am still handsome and can make almost all girls drool over me.

I would like to thank my publisher for accepting my story and showing huge interest in the same, especially Binay Duttaji for being ever so supportive and available for all my silly queries.

Thanks to all my friends on Facebook for their comments when I announced my novel's release. Their enthusiasm made me more confident.

And lastly to Jahnvi for being such a beautiful part of my life and understanding me always!!

Prologue

A single cigarette remaining, a last half-filled vodka glass, a dark room with a small bulb trying vainly to fight the darkness, a brand new laptop and a young gentleman with shoulder-length hair stands with his beautiful wife, while his two sons, aged five and eight years, stare into the camera. One of boys is very fair and the other has a dusky complexion. In all, they present a picture of a happy and contented family.

A completely sozzled young man, in his early 20's, tries to capture the picture in his memory in a single look. He smiles and suddenly starts searching for something on his laptop. He finds that the battery is discharged. With unsteady feet, he gets up to charge it. Luckily he succeeds in making it work. He promptly flops down on the carpet and starts searching frantically for some information on his laptop. Suddenly his eyes fall on something and he smiles before planting a kiss on the picture of someone's forehead.

What his eyes register is a picture of a beautiful girl with a fair complexion and a height of 5 feet 3 inches. He turns to the next photo, in which he himself seems to be bubbling with joy while standing with that girl. The photograph must have been clicked when he must have been enjoying his once-upon-a-time happy days.

Something dropped all of a sudden into his vodka half-emptied glass. He realises that what had fallen into his glass was nothing else but his tears. His face still shows no expression, though tears continue to flow down at a regular pace. His face registers no expression; it looks as blank as a plain sheet of paper. His face looks expressively dead.

Chapter-1

Indore or Mumbai

Yet another day, yet another hope!

Life is a mystery; hands are tied in its rope!

Dubious about the fact, is the future actually bright?

It plays its own tact, nothing seems alright!

Friends are no more same; they are moving out

When I try convincing about the same, my parents do shout!!

Life has its own surprises, to kick us again with shame

With dreams in one's eyes, who should one blame?

Lust, Love and sex have heard about this name

Frustration at apex, would like to play its game!!

Confused at what he is, confused at his identity

Life always gives me a damn, I don't expect any more serendipity!!

I am as confused as hell; just don't know who I should be?

Life fucks me without fail; don't know where I would be?

Yet another day passes, yet rises another hope

Life is a mystery; hands are tied in its rope!!

Life is full of surprises and shocks, bringing in its wake all kinds of emotions. As we are the beings of emotions, not logic, the small emotions become high-post captains of our lives, making us obey them without any questions.

In spite of having done well and having stood up to everybody's expectations, including my own, my heart was far from contented or happy. It felt as if something was a miss. The couch I sat on along with my people was, however, jumping with joy and excitement because of its other occupants, while I sat questioning myself about the reason for my lack of happiness.

My parents were happy and so were the others, as according to them I had successfully completed a chapter of my life to begin a new one. Everyone was smiling and laughing except me who had a lifeless smile pasted on the face with no one bothered about noticing or caring why it was so. Life, for me, had turned glum. Everything seemed vague and unsure. I wondered if perhaps meditation could help to ease off my uneasiness as all I felt was a sense of vulnerability at the strange ways of the universe which had different plans in store for me.

I don't generally meditate because for me, meditation brought along some very of painful memories with it and they always won, leaving me behind in a pall of nothingness.

Frustrated with everything and nothing, I switched on my laptop. Connecting device… authenticating… authenticated… and connected.

I started browsing through old files, when suddenly my fingers stopped. Time stood still as I travelled back to those beautiful days of my life five years ago. Friendship was above all and hatred didn't even exist in our life's dictionary. That was the time when a single call from a friend would send us rush out for a ride on our bikes, making us cover as much as 11 miles a day! That was also the time when a smile from a beautiful girl could enlighten us, when an extra hundred rupees in pocket money would make us jump with joy, when we would battle and argue about the importance of virginity to get off 'the small-town boy' tag.

By now, however, time had changed by leaps and bounds.

The dream of every 10+2 student in Indore was to secure admission in the best college of the city. This crowd also included those who couldn't afford to dream of such a luxury for the sake of their two brothers who harboured dreams of making it to the IIT or had three sisters waiting in the wings to get married. Though they cursed their parents and their destiny, deep within they knew and accepted that they had limited career choices and no apparent solution to their problem. Those who had rich fathers moved their base to Pune, Bangalore or Mumbai to continue their further studies.

For today's youth, the definition of the best college meant the college that attracted the largest crowd. Education for them was a mere formality; what mattered most were love, lust and sex. The undergraduate students from small towns/cities had a tough time convincing their parents to let them study in metropolitan cities or travel abroad to study and brighten their future by studying either engineering or commerce. The reason to go these big cities was not only the hype or the glitz and glamour associated with the reason, but also to overcome the unpleasant task of standing at the crossroads and wonder what to do after undergraduation. It was more about how, what and when to do!

The reasons for 'what' could be termed as the exodus from Indore had something to do with the minis or micro minis or more appropriately, a lack of them. I was certain that these being big dreams where 'the most sensitive yet vital part' of their body was to be put to use in a totally unfamiliar territory termed 'education.' I too was not left untouched by these feelings and was desperate to branch out of Indore, though I knew the mere mention of it would push my mother into tears. My dream was to go to Mumbai but it received a mortal blow, leaving me behind in a cloud of uncertainty and vagueness.

My helplessness and desperation to go to Mumbai made me shout at my mother who sat there, sobbing inconsolably, as my relatives eyed me angrily as if I was indeed the devil personified. Had there been any therapeutic approach to win over my mother, I would have used it there and then. Since I was her youngest child, she showered all her affection on me. And so, my hands were tied.

From the corner of my eye I noticed one of my aunts smile slyly at this situation. With those protruding teeth, she could have even scared the scariest of all witches. And here, my dream was getting fucked. Dad had promised that if I heeded his advice, he would secure admission for me in one of the best colleges of the city. He named a couple of government colleges from his days spent as a student, though they now looked nothing less than a porn flick theatre or worse still. My life sure had become a living hell.

Ultimately I selected my college and let my father know – it was Renaissance College, Indore.

"I have never heard about it. Where is this college? " he asked.

"Dad, this is the best college in Indore," I replied, wishing I had some statistics on my fingertips so that I could have rattled them out to convince him.

"Then why the hell have I not heard about it in the last 30 years?" he shouted. "Don't fool me. You can't always fool your parents," he muttered. There was no point in arguing with him.

"Dad, the reason you have never heard about it is because it has started commerce classes from this year only," I informed him.

"Son, then how can you say it is the best? There are dozens of colleges that start their operations in Indore every year. Education is simply a commercial business nowadays. You'd be better off at a government college as such colleges have proper affiliation. Baldev uncle is a professor there; he'll help you out with your studies." He tried to reason out with me, not to forget that he was again trying to make decisions for me.

Now who would make him understand that VMCS had no happening crowd and no sexy girls because of which it was not high on my priority list. In fact, it was not at all in my list. "Please, Dad, I have compromised enough by agreeing to study in Indore and so now allow me to join the college of my choice. Renaissance is Swapnil sir's and Sarabjeet sir's college and they were the only faculty members whom I liked. A couple of my friends will also be joining the same college, so I will have good company. I don't want to join any other government college and waste my life."

I was good at histrionics and could notice the thawing down of my parents' feelings. Dad held Swapnil sir in such high esteem that the mere mention of his name could transform him into a different person. Immediately he agreed to my joining Renaissance.

I was pleased at the way I had succeeded in winning over my father. This trick of the trade had been taught to us by none else than the esteemed Swapnil sir. A recent example of Swapnil sir's ability to tackle tacky situations was revealed when he advised a young boy, who secretly admired his next door neighbour, to approach his sister to act as the mediator. One day he purchased a red rose and had it delivered to the girl through his sister. The concerned neighbour called him the next day, asking him to meet her at a predetermined spot. Thrilled at the favourable response, the boy reached the designated spot on time, but when he neared her, she landed a stinging slap on his left cheek. The recipient was so shocked that he stood numb, routed to the spot.

This is what reality was in life. Even if you communicated things clearly, you could never hope to receive the right response. The girl went a step ahead to question him as to how he could have dared to dream of such a proposal. This was not over yet. She continued to tell him that his sister had gone a step further as to propose on behalf of her brother, using the same rose!

Swapnil Sir's lectures were great fun and we never wanted them to end. Let me take this opportunity to introduce you to Swapnil sir. He was a teacher from my CA classes and a great one at that. He was charismatic, an excellent orator and my role model. He was young; in fact he was only 28 and a very lively person. He dressed smartly and was good at everything he did. He was brilliant at *sher-o-shayari* and one could never tire of listening to his couplets which were laced with romance and never made a single moment dull.

"Ek jungle hai teri aankhon mein, mai jahaan raah bhool jaata hoon,

Tu rail si guzar jaati hai, mai ek pool sa kaanp jaata hoon."

He had brought glamour to the dull life at college which had been inaugurated by Bollywood actor Ashutosh Rana and the

Congress minister, Shrimant Jyotiraditya Singh Scindia from the royal family of Gwalior. The press would go in a tizzy when reporting about these celebrities and this could have been one of the reasons for my preference to stay behind in Indore. Three years to spend and how bad could things go than what they were then. The hope still burnt bright that Renaissance would surely draw the best and the elite girls from the city.

Chapter-2

Year-end Party @ Renaissance

'Studious' B. Com and CA students classes echoed with applause. Zeal and enthusiasm overflowed when Swapnil sir announced a treat to the CA students in Renaissance along with the year-end celebrations for B. Com students as well. Swapnil sir also used to teach at a renowned institute in Indore and this prompted many CA students who could not get admission at the said institute to opt for Renaissance. Prospective CAs are far from social; given their busy schedule, but here was an occasion which none could afford to miss or give it a go. All and sundry decided to be a part of the revelry.

The girls were thrilled and their excitement knew no bounds. They could be seen talking animatedly and discussing the dress they would choose to wear at 'the' gala event!

" What will you wear on that night?" Aditi asked her friend.

"My new red dress that I had bought last evening," replied Surbhi excitedly.

'I bet she would look her best with nothing on. Ask me!' I thought to myself.

“What about you?” enquired Surbhi.

“I just picked up a black dress from M.G. Road as it was available at fabulous discount,” stated Aditi matter-of-factly. She was a smart dresser and always waited for the seasonal sale to do her shopping of renowned brands at dirt cheap prices!!

'What cheap souls some girls could be to be surviving on fashion discard from damp factory outlets!' I thought. Aditi was my good friend, yet I never missed the chance to mock her. I could sense the excitement in the air as I entered the class, glancing surreptitiously at the pretty girls. They were reason enough for me to get distracted. I was quite vulnerable as far as the girls were concerned because it is they who brought colour and added zing to life. You could bask in the beauty of their looks, breathe in and feel relaxed. They sure were a cure for sore eyes and made you forget your worries for some time at least. Surbhi's figure was a constant source of distraction and diversion, especially from the more pressing issues at home and my Dad's dream for me.

The party that was scheduled for the year end became the talk of the campus. Almost everyone eagerly looked forward to it and the most desperate of the lot were the CA students, who were forever buried in their books with no time on hand to look up and admire the eye candy in their class. They had girls who happened to be too intelligent for them and beauty was their least concern. So this was their only chance to let their eyes rove and have their share of 'the moment'. After all commerce and management classes had one of the most sought after girls (read 'hot girls').

Amidst all the clamour, a CA student named Rohan stood up and asked, “Sir, where is the treat? And what is the amount to be paid per person?”

Everyone tuned to glare at Rohan with utter disbelief at his stupidity. Didn't this guy know that it was a 'treat'? Such a nerd he was! Soon Rohan realised his mistake as soon as he noticed some fifty-odd pairs of eyes focus on him. He immediately sat back, looking visibly embarrassed.

"It's free of cost, Rohan. Though we always appreciate the extra monetary help from our students," answered Swapnil sir with light humour.

I too had started to dream about the gala event by now. A whole bunch of excited youngsters could be seen walking and strolling in the garden. The hall was found to be packed for with almost all of them swaying to music. "What fun! Let's dance and enjoy now!" the girls would chirp and I would nod in approval. I would feast my eyes on them and Surbhi conscientiously made it a point to be sassily dressed during those days. And just as I let my eyes drool over her figure, I heard Swapnil sir call out to me, "Hey Arnab!"

I was brought back to reality by the sound of his voice and all my dreams came crashing down. "Yes, sir!" I replied faintly.

"It is your responsibility to take care of all the arrangements and also let me know the number of students that would be attending the party."

"Yes sir, sure. My pleasure," I replied.

❖ ❖ ❖

I duly began to concentrate on my duty in right earnest.

"I won't be able to come as I am going to Shimla with my boyfriend," said Ritika, giving a wide smile.

I, then approached Surbhi and Aditi.

"Hey Arnab, how are you?" Surbhi asked.

"I am good. How are you?"

"I am cool. So what's up? Seems like you are busy these days with other girls," Surbhi commented, looking sideways at Aditi.

"As if he belongs only to you," Aditi murmured under her breath and smiled wickedly with a tinge of naughtiness and flirtation in her voice.

"Who are we to ask about your personal life, eh Arnab?" somebody from Surbhi's gang asked.

"Is she in the same class? And by the way, who actually allowed her to talk?" Aditi almost yelled.

"Hey girls, listen!! I am here because Swapnil sir asked me to check out how many of you would be attending the gala event. I agreed to help him out. "

"We are on, Arnab. Let us know about the timings and also if you need some help. We'll spread the message in class as we are here for the next lecture too," Surbhi said, interrupting my dream filled with lust and desire.

❖ ❖ ❖

As I walked out of the class, I noticed Swapnil sir surrounded by several geeks discussing various theories which could be asked in the exams. So dedicated and so enthusiastic they seemed. That's why we have the best students in the entire world for we tend to suck every single piece of information for every penny that we pay for our education.

"Arnab, how are your preparations for the exam going on?"asked Swapnil sir.

“Good sir. I hope to finish revising soon,” I said unconvincingly.

“Hmm… better keep yourself busy with studies and music. Be like your brother, who was so dedicated towards his studies. His enthusiasm for CA is still unparalleled even though he didn't make it to the finals. I still appreciate his ability. Be like him.” Having spoken these words, Swapnil sir slowly walked off.

I hated my brother. I had always hated him and on hearing Swapnil sir's words I began to hate him even more. He had always been everyone's blue-eyed boy. The comparisons never seemed to cease. Come on, we were two different human beings after all. Whenever I tried being like him, I ended up faring still worse! My best efforts would always go in vain and I would become more helpless. Neither could he succeed when he tried to be like me. So it never worked really with us trying to be like each other.

“Sure sir,” I murmured to Swapnil sir's retreating back.

“Also, I look forward to seeing all of you at the gala on 31st December,” was Swapnil sir's parting shot.

❖ ❖ ❖

Come December end when both Surbhi and I decided to participate in a music competition by representing Renaissance and Indore. Nothing could beat our timing, co-ordination and music sense that we seemed to intuitively share. We had been practicing since the past couple of months to stand a good chance at the nationals and we eagerly waited to take the nation by storm.

It always was a pleasure to sing with her. I think I was in love with her figure as I could not prevent myself from staring at her boobs with lust and desire and when she sang with her eyes closed, swaying to the music, I would stare at her boobs heave up and down. She appeared alarmingly beautiful to me.

Indore in December could turn out to be astoundingly cold and irresistible. The temperature was almost as low as 2 degrees at night. People considered it the best time to be romantic and intimate, though I never underestimated the long summers.

For participating in the competition at Mumbai, we failed to get reservations on the Indore-Mumbai train; so we settled for a single ticket on the bus and decided to travel for fourteen hours, sharing a sleeper berth.

Surbhi wore a white tee shirt and a pair of pink-coloured Bermudas which matched her hair clip. Girls, I tell you, could be irritatingly concerned about co-ordination between their clothes and accessories even when travelling in discomfort at night! They could never afford to lose a single opportunity to extract a compliment from you. For us guys, it just did not matter. We were just comfortable in about anything or nothing.

"Arnab, I feel sleepy by 11. Would you like to crash too?" Surbhi asked.

"Yes, I am sleepy too but this sleeper seems not too comfortable. We might have to share it and..." saying so, my voice trailed off.

For one quarter hour or so she tried every possible position to rest, appearing like all those triangles we used to draw in our Geometry class. But after a lot of unsuccessful attempts, she boldly asked me to adjust my ass so that she could sleep beside me. Imagine my surging excitement when she lay next to me, so close to me. To ensure we had, no, I had 'my own lovely time' lying next to her, I made a make-shift curtain with her dupatta.

I tried adjusting myself for a good ten or fifteen minutes in the limited space available on the sleeper so that my damsel in distress could sleep peacefully, but failed. Half sitting and half lying down, I looked at her as she lay fast asleep in her own world. Everything about her, even when asleep, was enchanting – her soft pink lips, her slow and steady breathing, her calm and serene face and her soft sighs that made her chest heave – sending me into a trance.

Even in this uncomfortable setting, there was unexplainable comfort to see her lie next to me. Her presence in itself was hypnotic.

Seeing her thus, sleeping beautifully, something in my insides stirred, waiting to be freed and explored. Looking at her, my hands travelled down in my boxers to satiate my ever growing hunger. Slowly my legs curled around her thighs and before I could realise it, she had placed her hands on my thighs, making my insides quiver with desire. Her actions were totally unexpected and they took me by surprise. My first thought was, 'Is she dreaming?' I tried to free my legs from her hands, but feared what if she woke up and began screaming for help. But to my pleasure, all she did was draw closer to me, snuggling next to me. I dared and held her tight, my hands now supporting her back and drawing her closer to me.

I moved forward to kiss her but she suddenly jerked and I stopped. I pulled back and shut my eyes, still clasping her. I did not want to face her awkward questions. A few seconds passed and I opened my eyes only to find her eyes giving me a naughty look. And then all of a sudden, she pulled me towards herself and her lips met mine. We kissed for the first time, for a long time that seemed like eternity. Both of us were too aroused to stop now.

"Come closer," she whispered. I held her tighter, moved closer, still kissing while my hands went around her back, unhooked her bra as her hands began unbuttoning my shirt. Slowly she pulled away, her eyes full of lust. She was now biting my earlobes, slowly travelling on my neck, kissing me wildly! We both were breathing hard and heavy. The feel of her breasts in my hand was overpowering and our deeply entwined lips were saucy. The feel of our half naked and warm bodies against each other can never be put into words as it was so pleasurable. This was something I had never experienced before – the immense pleasure that overshadowed her cries of pain. The pain ceased but the feeling of ultimate pleasure continued to linger for long. I looked at her and saw that her eyes were half shut. What I noticed next was that tears were slowly trickling down her cheeks. My hands were just about to comfort her when a terrible odour overpowered my senses. I jerked up and woke up with a start. It was then that I realised that I had been dreaming, and at the end of dream the odour was of the fart that my dream girl had let out.

Soon I realised I was running late for the party. I immediately made my way to dress up for the night.

❖ ❖ ❖

"Everything that is new or uncommon raises a pleasure in the imagination, because it fills the soul with a pleasant surprise, gratifies the curiosity and conveys the sense of which it had never before possessed." I had read these lines somewhere but couldn't understand what they meant till that day of my dream.

The New Year-cum-farewell party was scheduled to begin at 4:00 p.m. in the evening, but I had to reach Renaissance College at 11:00 a.m. to finalise the arrangements.

The previous night all I had done was to dream about girls throwing themselves at me and swoon all over me, drool upon me and fight with each other for a dance with me. Agh... thank God for dreams! My yet another dream had Surbhi all over me, hugging me, kissing me and even raping me. Could it get any better? Your dream girl raping you – how did it matter if it was only in a dream? My imagination, though wild, was now in its active mode. So I rushed to the bathroom, shaved, showered and was set to rock the party.

The excitement, however, paled when Aditi messaged to inform that her grandmother had expired, so she would be skipping the party. Yet, I went ahead and reached the college. It seemed so deserted – no sounds, no lights and no trace of life. I called Swapnil sir to describe the scene. He asked me to wait until he sent someone to help out.

I wondered what Surbhi planned to wear at night.

"Hello, you must be Arnab," someone called my name from behind.

"Yes, that's me," I turned and greeted the person.

He introduced himself as D.J. Dheeraj and began to ask me about the arrangement for his sound system. After having showed him the corner where he would place his system, I turned my attention to other things that needed to be taken care of. Three hours passed and I did not even realise it. Everything was ready and set; all that was missing were the students, who were supposed to fill the hall in another hour or so. Tired of toiling the whole day, I decided to get back home, freshen up and return quickly.

❖ ❖ ❖

Going to a party without my best buddy Aditi was really boring. Still, I dressed as decently as I could and rushed for the party. No sooner did I reach the venue, than the other students started pouring in. In no time, the hall was filled with overjoyed and excited students.

"Hey, good job, man!"' Romil gasped.

"Thanks, bro," I replied.

Just as I was about to make my way out from the midst of the crowd, someone grabbed my arm. "Hey Arnab," said a sweet and melodious voice making me realise that it could be no one else but Surbhi.

"Hello!" I said, turning to face her.

I literally gasped with shock when I looked at her. Her dress was undoubtedly sexy but what with that overdose of makeup, she really gave me a fright for a moment.

"Someone is looking so handsome," she remarked, smiling naughtily at me.

"And someone is looking gorgeous," I replied, giving a fake smile.

"Are you okay? You look sick," she asked with concern in her tone.

"Yes I am fine...enjoy the party. I will be right back," I replied and almost instantly left her grip and ran outside.

I just wanted to get out of there. Nothing could hold me – neither Surbhi nor the awesome DJ.

I sat down on a chair in the garden, feeling tired and promptly dozed off into deep slumber. I woke up only when I sensed that my pocket vibrate, I mean my phone was vibrating. God our wild thoughts always make us think on similar lines.

There were four missed calls – all of them from Maya. How could I forget that she would be waiting for me at the college entrance? I ran my way to the entrance, tagging along two of my other friends with me.

"Hey guys!" Maya shouted. "Are you going somewhere?" she asked.

"Home. Not feeling too well," I replied.

"No…o…o," she cried out. "You can't leave like that. You arranged everything, so now stay for a while and enjoy yourself."

"Okay," I said, knowing too well that she would anyway drag me to the party.

"Let me introduce you to my friends. This is Neeta and this is Jahnvi," she said.

My heart skipped a beat or two. I had never believed in love at first sight before that moment. I was soon convinced that love at first sight did exist! This girl, Jahnvi looked like an angel. I could have held and kissed her then and there. Her smile lit up the whole place like a thousand-watt bulb. For once I was down, hook line and sinker.

We started walking along our way to the party. I walked with Jahnvi and caught her stealing sly glances at me. Later I invited all of them to the dance floor. We all swayed and danced to our heart's content, including Swapnil sir.

The party was a huge success. Everyone had a gala time. As the evening drew to an end, all were full of praise for not only the event but also the institution Renaissance. Everyone present cheered Swapnil sir and Renaissance. That evening was one of the best evenings I had passed and 31st December of 2006 not only brought someone special in my life but also taught me that love was more than just sex. We talked, danced and enjoyed ourselves so much that memories of that evening spend with Jahnvi are still alive in me.

Chapter-3

Love, Meet and Accident

The days are back to interesting, I have got a motive in life
One more girl at listing, again a love at dive!!
Her beautiful eyes, her innocent face
Describe her as most beautiful, yet the words sound a disgrace!!
Oh yes she smiled, and I went wild
Her cuddlesome face, she sounded like a little child!!
Her rosy lips, her wonderful cheeks
She is simply wonderful; I just want her to kiss!!
Had she been with me now, I'd bring Moon to Earth
She'll always be front in the row; I'd love her till death!!
I doubt if she's human as she rather looks like a fairy
I am sure she's the one, her eyes tell their own story!!
Hopes reach up to the sky, love is illogical
No if's or but's and whys; I am in love with an angel!!
The viral of love is spreading, through all my veins and vibe

Life never was that interesting, heartbeats again are on the dive!!

The days are back to interesting, I have got a motive in life

One more girl at listing, again a love at dive!!

In spite of how abominable and grumpy girls usually found me, this time, we started finding each other interesting with the passage of time. I was becoming obsessed with her and eventually late night parties gave way to sitting by my radio and listening to songs played by various FM stations. I was a child at heart again with the only difference being the fact that earlier I tended to catch up on cricket scores, but now I concentrated on scoring music for my girl. The late-night RJs were great to listen to because they spoke about love, romance and relationships. It all sounded crazy, awful and idiotic to those who were not in love but made complete sense to those who were.

My heart would skip a beat or two every time I would receive her call or message. Words, no more were a combination of 26 different alphabets; they surprisingly become objects to be handled with care and a mighty task it was!

The frequency of our calls increased every second of an hour and she slowly became one of my closest friends, my confidante. One day I called her but she did not answer my call. I called her again and again there was no answer. I decided to call her for the third and the final time. I was about to disconnect the call when I heard her sweet voice at the other end and my heart missed a beat.

"Hey, I am sorry, I was in class and my phone was on silent mode. I missed your calls. Anyway, tell me wassup?" asked Jahnvi.

"It's all right Jahnvi. I understand," I said, sounding contrite and mature, quite unlike me.

"Hmm...this class is really boring. I would have answered your call, but our professor, though he has one head, his ten pairs of eyes are always roving everywhere."

On visualising her facial expression at that time, I burst out laughing and asked, "What's your plan for tomorrow? It's a Sunday," I said, cooling down a bit.

"Nothing has been planned as of now. You tell me," she replied. "I have an extra class though I can give it a miss."

'How easy could it get?' I wondered.

I immediately started scanning newspapers for movies running at various theatres in the city. I had heard 'Guru' was a good movie and above all, it had wonderful music by A.R. Rehman. I offered my proposal to her and she asked, "It has to be good, Arnab. Count me in. Who all are coming, by the way?"

"Maya is out of town. I can't think of anyone else. You can invite your friends though," I offered, faintly hoping that she would not call anyone else.

"Hmm...let's just both of us go to the movie. We can have fun together by ourselves so why call others?"

"Alright, I see a point there. See you at 9:00 a.m. I'll book the tickets online for Velocity Theatre."

❖ ❖ ❖

I carefully selected my outfit, which on hindsight may have been a little inappropriate, given how cold it was at Indore in January. Then I booked two tickets for the last row corner seats. By 9:15 on Sunday morning, I was at her hostel to pick her up. She took her time getting dressed and when she stepped out, I could not help but stare at her. With her hair a bit wet and her face looking as fresh as a daisy, eyes bright and twinkling and a graceful gait, she had an apologetic grin as she approached me. I smiled and shrugged in response and we were off.

At the theatre, I parked my bike and we ran our way towards Screen Number 3, where the national anthem had just begun and everyone was up on their feet, to pay respect for the same. When it ended, we all sat down comfortably in our chairs.

It was getting cold inside the theatre and I observed Jahnvi rub her hands against each other. I would have offered her my jacket, but refrained; instead I offered her my hand.

She looked very suspiciously at me – so typical of a girl. Then she said, "A cup of coffee may help." So out I went to get her a cup of coffee.

"Thanks, Arnab," she replied, looking really grateful as she began to sip it slowly.

"My pleasure, Jahnvi," I replied. I went back to daydreaming about her. How I wished I could devour her in my dreams the way I had done Surbhi.

When the movie ended, we walked towards the coffee shop and sat down. "The movie was worth watching," she said as she ordered two café mochas for us.

"Yeah, it was. I told you Mani Ratnam is amazing," I replied.

"So is A.R. Rehman. He is a legend," she added.

And then there was silence.

"So, do you have a girl friend?" her question took me by surprise.

"No, I don't. I am taking my time to choose my girl. Not in any hurry to fall in the love trap." All I wanted to say was, 'No, I don't have one; I am keeping myself for you, only you,' but it refused to escape from my mouth.

"Are you single?" I asked, desperately hoping that she would say 'yes'.

"No, I am not single," she stated bluntly. I could have kicked myself for bringing home a girl who was already engaged.

"I stay with my parents and my brother. I have many close friends and that includes you too. So how can I be single?" she smiled innocently at me.

I smiled back, "No I meant..."

"No, I don't have a boyfriend," she said and that put to rest to all my other questions.

"Why you don't have a girl? You are a boyfriend material. You must have had girls in your life."

'Boyfriend material? What was that? So she had considered me as boyfriend material. Could she be interested in me then?' I wondered.

I had had girls in my life but it was all far from serious. There were many crushes, more than I cared to remember anyway, but I had no girlfriend.

"Oh yes, but nothing serious. Best part of being single is I have you, Aditi and all my good friends."

Neither of us mentioned Maya directly, though she did say she had one of the cutest friends.

"Oh!! She's cute," I agreed and she smiled back.

When a girl or a guy have lost all possible characteristics of being termed beautiful or handsome, there is the colourless term 'cute' that comes pretty handy.

"It's been just ten days since our first meeting and we are already going out to movies, lunches and now coffee. Seems like we have been friends for many years," she said out of nowhere.

'Years of friendship lead to a relationship,' I had the urge to say on a more optimistic note.

"You know what I liked most about you, Arnab?" she asked suddenly.

"I have so many qualities that you can select one," I said.

"Agreed, but the best part is you didn't propose to me after a couple of meetings," she said.

"What's the big deal? We are friends," I muttered. Wait, now that had been my plan. I felt lucky that she had unknowingly saved me from embarrassment.

"Yeah, but it never happens with me that often. That's the reason why girls are always my best friends," she smirked.

"I'll break that jinx," I said.

"Let's hope we can be great friends," she responded as she paid the bill, indirectly warning me.

That did not dampen my spirits though. In fact we called each other more often and enjoyed our quality time spent together. Every Sunday we would go for movies and I would not hesitate to book corner seats. She would not mind me doing that either. Hopefully she could sense that I was making a special effort, hoping that some day she would reciprocate accordingly.

We saw the movie 'Honeymoon Travels' and with every subsequent movie, I came to realise that popcorn and coffee had become a must. So I was a combo package in her life: someone who would take her to the latest movies and feed her with popcorn and coffee.

I would lie to my parents, telling them that I had tuitions on Sunday. I would also ask my mother for money and all this would get blown away on movies, popcorn and coffee. Jahnvi was happy and that made me happier. We explored many places in Indore and even tried our hand at horse riding and shooting at the polo grounds.

"I am just amazed, Arnab. There are so many things to try in this world and we don't even try one per cent of them in our life," she gushed. "I was never familiar with this part of Indore before. It's so different from the new Indore," she continued.

"I know. We have our factory just 2 kms away from here, so I have come here quite frequently. Not many people know about this place."

"What a great start to the day. Maya is also coming for a tafreeh. I just received a message from her," said Jahnvi.

I was confused, 'Is it great because we had fun here or is it because Maya is going to be a thorn in our flesh soon?' I wondered.

"Oh, is she coming?" I asked, trying to feign interest.

"Yes, she is," Jahnvi said. "You do not sound good on hearing that," she added.

"No, it's nothing like that; it's just that I have never really spoken to her. Why is she coming?" I queried.

"Is that so? She told me there was no place in Indore that you both had not been to and that you two bonded very well," she said and smiled wickedly. That only made me more uncomfortable.

"Oh, thanks for letting me know. I seriously had no idea about this before. We didn't even have a cup of coffee even once, damn it!! I have no idea why she is saying so," I commented.

"Look how angry you're getting! She's not that bad. She's just cute." said Jahnvi, thoroughly enjoying my discomfort.

"Why wouldn't I be angry? She's lying and spreading rumours at my expense."

"Why are you so pissed off, Arnab? Relax. You have something good in you and that's why people fall for you. Aah no! She was talking something of substance. You are a boyfriend material as I told you already."

As if that could placate me! "My brother always says that people actually enjoy seeing me disturbed," I said.

She seconded the statement and laughed aloud. So we waited for Maya, who arrived within half an hour, riding 'Tolu', Jahnvi's Scooty. It looked as if the scooty had bent to one side, given the 120 kg-rider. Jahnvi's eyes almost filled with tears on seeing the condition of her vehicle.

Maya was dressed horribly. Her breasts were dying to pop out of the sleeveless top.

"I thought you'd need this, that's why I didn't ask you and brought your vehicle over instead. Mine is at the service centre," she began.

"It's alright," replied Jahnvi.

"Let's go then for tafreeh," Maya said and promptly ensconced herself on my bike.

"So Jahnvi and I shall take the scooty," I said, sending across a clear message.

"Why? Can't I sit with you?" she asked playfully.

"Come on, Maya, how can both of us fit on this Pulsar?" I asked irritably.

Jahnvi gave me her 'I'll-kill-you-if-she-even-touches-my-Tolu' look. "Oh, how cute you look when you make that face!" Jahnvi said, laughing at her friend.

"Come on, Arnab, don't be that rude. Not everybody is lucky to give Maya a ride," she said and hugged Maya.

"Exactly," agreed Maya.

I sat on the petrol tank and Maya lifted her right leg first, held my shoulder and somehow managed to sit with both her bums outside the edge of the seat as I tried to kick start the Pulsar.

"Are you comfortable? Shall we move?" Jahnvi asked.

"Yes, definitely," I said and we moved.

"So Arnab, finally I get a chance to sit on your bike. I am so thrilled," Maya said.

"Oh really? Not a big deal, Maya. We are friends. Had you asked, I would have given you a ride earlier itself," I said, my eyes started searching for Jahnvi in the traffic ahead.

"Oh, that's so sweet of you. Shift back and sit comfortably. Why are you sitting on the tank? I am not that fat," she said and laughed at her own comment, which by the way was no joke. I ignored her comment anyway.

We reached the highway and I still could not locate Jahnvi. "Call Jahnvi as I think she has missed a turning," I suggested to Maya.

"Don't worry, she's not a baby. She'll manage." The response was too quick.

"Arnab, your brother too is very gentle. I saw him that day," she said, suddenly changing the topic.

"Yes, he is," I complied.

"My elder sister..." she began.

"He's committed," I said before she could finish.

"Okay, I just mentioned him generally," she said.

"And I just cleared generally," I answered brusquely.

I cursed Jahnvi for the first time for leaving Maya alone with me and disappearing on her scooty.

Maya remained quiet for a minute and I thanked my lucky stars. "Where's Jahnvi? Call her," I said again.

"Why the hell do you care so much about her? She's not a baby; she'll find her way. Its not the first time she's coming here," she yelled back.

"Do you know you are extremely irritating right now?" I said. "There's a girl who is a friend of yours and who is lost somewhere on the highway and you don't give a shit about her. Instead you are asking me about trivia and not caring a bit to contact her despite my asking you to do so." On saying this, I glanced into the mirror to await her response. What I saw was an accident happening at a blind turn ahead. I heard a girl scream and it took me less than a second to place that voice.

The guy responsible for the accident though tried running away but was caught by the patrol police car which was on its rounds. I rode my bike as fast as I could and heard Maya gasp at the speed.

The distance was quite a bit and the crowd had already gathered at the site of the accident. The scooty had become a wreck. I prayed to God as soon as I saw the crowd closing in. I pushed people aside to reach her. There was a good amount of blood all over the place. My prayers became more fervent. Jahnvi was in pain; she was neither crying, nor screaming. She had nasty cuts and bruises on her hands, face, stomach and legs.

"Is everything all right, baby?" I asked from a distance, scared and not knowing what to do.

She smiled as she saw me and luckily there happened to be a doctor passing by who stopped and attended to the minor cuts and bruises.

"Are you alright?" I asked as I held her hand and led her to the clinic close by.

"Yes, kind of...," she replied.

"Don't worry. Everything will be okay," I said.

"I know, but why are you crying, Arnab? I had an accident and now I am fine," she smiled back. By now she was sounding good too.

"I was scared, Jahnvi. I saw blood on the road and my brain worked overtime to convince me that it was the worst scenario! How I wish it had been Maya instead!"

"Shut up, Arnab!! How mean can you get? I will kill you if you say this again. Where's she?"

I pointed towards where Maya stood. Maya saw us and waved back at us.

"Your Pulsar is down on the road. Was she riding it?" Jahnvi tried her best to sound composed after the accident but her voice quivered. All the blood loss must have affected her.

We reached the doctor's clinic and I didn't explain why and how I had thrown the Pulsar with Maya on it. Maya too reached the clinic but did not utter a word. She just smiled at Jahnvi and tried to check if she was okay. I craned my neck to see if Maya was hurt. After all, I had left the engine running when I had thrown the bike down close to the spot where the crowd had gathered.

I meekly lowered my head. She gave me a scorching look and I apologised. She forgave me promptly. I smiled back to avoid further conversation.

It was my Pulsar which I was worried about, after Jahnvi. I was sure that the cops had taken care of that though.

The doctor treated Jahnvi and as a precaution took a couple of X-rays as well. "There's no need to worry. They are just bruises. She'll be fine in a week's time. Luckily, there is no fracture."

I felt good. Maya's expression changed too.

"You need to take this medicine for a week. The red one – twice a day after meals; the blue one – thrice a day and the white one – whenever you feel pain. It's a painkiller," he said and gave me the bill.

"I don't take medicines, doctor," she said and refused to take them.

"What do you mean you don't take medicines? You have to take them," I said.

"I have never taken medicines and will never do so either. I'll do the healing therapy myself. I know Reiki," she responded.

"Okay, do what you want, but just take care of yourself and take these medicines in case you need them," the doctor said, shrugging his shoulders.

I paid the bill and asked Jahnvi and Maya to wait there for the next ten minutes, as I had to take care of my bike and the men who had brought the bike to the clinic. When I reached outside, I saw my bike had been carefully parked. It was not in as great a condition as I had expected but the damage was not much. I suspected Maya had kicked it in utter frustration.

All this while, the crowd had been beating the living daylights out of the culprit, so I rescued the person and took him to the doctor as well. His bike was in a worse condition and he was in tears. He screamed as soon as he saw me approach and began to beg for mercy saying his little brother had got an asthma attack and he needed to rush.

I took that guy with me on my Pulsar to the hospital and once his injuries had been attended to, he rushed to a different section of the hospital. I saw a small boy in school uniform crying. He hugged his brother and said, "I told you not to play football. Why don't you listen to me, Aarav?"

"I have only you in my life. Why are you making it even harder for me beta? I can't do it any more, Aarav," he sobbed and hugged Aarav tightly.

Aarav noticed the blood on his shirt and asked the reason for it. The older brother dismissed it saying it was nothing.

I called Jahnvi and Maya and told them that I would take longer than I expected. "Listen, I will be late. Here the situation is slightly different and I can't leave them like this. I will send for a cab to pick you up and drop you home." Saying so, I signed off.

Meanwhile the culprit told me his name was Arpan and then proceeded to explain the tragedy of his life. His Dad had died in an accident while his mother had succumbed to cancer. His elder brother was murdered by relatives because of some property dispute and he himself worked as a cobbler, managing to eke out a living on some thousand rupees a month. I paid the bill and got Aarav attended to while asking Arpan to come to work at our factory so that he could take better care of his brother.

My day's outing had been something I had eagerly looked forward to, but it had turned out to be very different from my expectations. Nevertheless it was a day to remember. I was elated and satisfied with the day's happenings.

Arpan thanked me several times even as we serviced his bike and I took Jahnvi's scooty to the closest automobile centre.

Chapter-4

Proposal

It was raining cats and dogs. The heavy rains blurred my vision and in the haziness all I could see was a beautiful and adorable fairy in a white-laced long gown. The fairy was slowly emerging out of the cluster of clouds as though showering me with her attention and love.

Suddenly the sky turned crystal clear and a rainbow formed in the sky. I squinted my eyes to get a clearer view of the fairy's face. In an instant I knew it was her, my dream girl. She was walking towards me, coming nearer to me. Soon, she was standing in front of me, smiling! I was too paralysed to reciprocate her smile. All I did was to stand and gaze at her. Slowly she brought her face near mine, her lips closed on my ears and I thought I heard her whisper. But before I could I decipher her words, I heard a loud sound...beep...beep...beep!!

Startled, I jumped off the bed and then realised that the loud sound was my alarm; not my dream girl's whisper. Lost in a trance, I forgot to snooze the continuous blaring of my alarm. I immediately stopped it and checked the time. I cursed myself, 'Wake up dumb ass, you are late.'

It was the day I had been waiting for as it was the D-day. How could I be late on that day?

'Today I am going to propose to her,' I told myself while gargling, but how? I still was undecided on that aspect. I started rehearsing some lines to propose to her. "Hey, I love you. Will you marry me?" Boy, it sounded so obsolete and so rash. I mean marriage, seriously? "Hey, I was wondering, isn't it a coincidence that we both are single? So, what say you?" No, that sounded desperate and would have definitely left me red-faced. "Do you love me? Well, don't worry. Only if you do, shall I propose to you." Nah, what in the world was I contemplating!! She'd doubt my intentions and never wish to see my face again. "Oh! I implore you to accept my proposal or I'll cry loudly." Cry? Really? That was so gay!

I was so busy rehearsing what I would ask her that I did not even consider her rejecting my proposal. I gave myself a final surreptitious glance in the mirror and then performed all my superstitious rituals. I wore my lucky tee-shirt and jeans; my lucky watch which needed repair yet had to be on my wrist that day and of course, prayed to the Almighty. Not that I was religious but I seemed to remember God when I needed his benevolence. I am sure God too would have been taken aback at this sudden display of faith in him.

I grabbed the keys to my bike and as was about to depart when I heard mother calling out to come and have lunch. Now that could be dangerously time consuming. "Oh Ma, I won't die if I don't eat today!! I am getting late. I am not taking lunch today and I have a get together with my school friends. I will eat there. Don't worry," I said while tying the shoelaces.

"Beta, it will hardly take fifteen minutes. I have cooked your favourite food," Mom said, giving me a broad smile. "Actually it's just not you but your entire generation which is fond of junk food, that is, McDonald's, Pizza Hut and all that. It's ruining your health," and she went on and on, mentioning vague and unknown characters like Mrs. Pawar's daughter and some others who had apparently consumed large amounts of junk food and reduced to becoming vegetables. "You might be the next one, so eat properly," she warned me.

For an instant I imagined myself lying in the hospital bed next to Mrs. Pawar's daughter and pictured my mother sitting beside me and saying, "See I told you."

But one thing that actually diverted my mind from the clinical hospital dreams was the thought of Jahnvi. Would she say yes or break my heart today?

All mothers are melodrama queens as they loved blackmailing you and my mother was no exception to this rule. She persuaded me to sit and finish my lunch though I was dying to leave. Suddenly, my mobile started ringing. It was Jahnvi. What a godsend it was!

I was watching my mother from the corner of my eye. When you are in love with someone, you use a special ringtone for the person. There is no logical explanation for this, though love has its reasons. So the things that are said or done do not have relevance either. Before my mother could get in her detective mood, I answered the call.

"Hey Arnab, where are you? Are you coming or not?" Jahnvi asked anxiously.

"Yes I am very much on my way, but it's only 10:40. We were supposed to meet at 11:30. Right? What's happened? You sound tense. Is everything alright?" I asked, as Mom glared hard at me, trying to decipher the other person on the line.

"Didn't you receive my message?" she asked.

Now my phone had been on silent mode and I desisted from reading all those forwarded messages. Her query jolted me and I fumbled with my phone to check what the message had been about.

"Hmm, I shall be there in ten minutes, okay?" I asked and disconnected the call.

I checked my Inbox and noticed that her scooty Pep had to be sent for repair and she needed to reach college in about 30 minutes to get the admission forms. I immediately stood up. Like a knight in his shining armour. As I walked towards the door, my mother stared at me hard, but this was not new. She was used to my getting up and moving out in the middle of a meal, so back she went to her pet soap opera.

I started my bike and glided out of the driveway. Suddenly, out of nowhere, an auto came right beside me, splashing muddy water all over me from the puddle on the road.

"It's alright, bhaiya," I said as he looked apologetically at me.

I made my way towards Jahnvi's hostel. On reaching there, I called her. She said she would be down soon and her 'soon' lasted a good twenty minutes. Why the hell did girls take so much time to get dressed? I should have taken my time weaving through Indore's traffic; or maybe not. I saw her face and needless to say, she was looking as pretty as ever. Her smile was a thousand times sweeter than any chocolate in the world. Her hair flew carelessly in the breeze and it almost melted my heart. She wore a pink tee-shirt and dark blue denim, which made her look so cute. I loved her eyes, which were like deep pools of liquid that could make me go into a trance.

I made up my mind there and then that she was the girl with whom I wanted to spend the rest of my life. She walked slowly towards me. I could feel the fragrance of her perfume and the warmth of her voice as she said, "Hi". For an instant I went blank. It was as if she had cast her magic spell on me.

"What's up? Is something there on my face?" she asked, self-consciously touching her face.

"Oh no, no. There is nothing wrong with your face," I said, trying to cover up for my blatant stare at her. "How are you?" I asked, changing the course of our conversation.

"Not good. Today is the last day for collecting the admission forms and my scooty has got punctured."

"Don't worry. I am here now."

She smiled and added, "Shall we leave for my college? This academic year of mine is now in your hands."

I felt a sense of responsibility towards my girlfriend, but my bike decided to act up. The tire went flat just as we reached her college. Why was it that whenever I tried to impress my girl, something or the other prevented me from doing so? Was God warning me or was it his way of taking revenge for not worshipping him daily?

"Oh, now what?" she asked, exasperated.

"You don't worry. I'll find some mechanic nearby," I said calmly. "Go and get your form, quick."

"Are you sure you'll be able to handle it?" she asked.

"Yes," I replied with a smile. Why did she even have this doubt that I could not handle it!

She turned and left as I proceeded with my bike to the nearest mechanic's shop which was at a distance of one kilometre. As the mechanic took charge of my bike, I chose to pass my time by playing game on my phone. By the time she came back, I was already on my rejuvenated bike.

"Thanks, I've got the chance to study further because of you," Jahnvi said, mocking me while profusely thanking me.

"Any time," I said and held her outstretched hand as if to never let her go.

It was electrifying to hold her hand. Never had I felt thus; not even with Surbhi.

"No, seriously tell me, how can I thank you?" she asked and pulled her hand back.

"Well, seriously if you don't mind, it's been months since I've watched a movie. So how about going to a movie?" I asked.

"How can I say no to this?" she replied, smiling.

After that we went to see the movie 'Mera Pehla Pehla Pyaar.' The name in itself conveyed what the movie was to be all about – romantic and mushy. I thought the theatre would be the best place to propose or at least it would be safe even if she hit me.

The movie started and it seemed it ended pretty quickly, but I had still not proposed! 'Maybe next time,' said a small voice in my head but another voice said, 'Come on, be a man. Get on with it.' The tussle between the head and the heart commenced yet again.

After the movie, we went to Café Coffee Day. I ordered two café mocha while my heart beats increased at a fast pace.

“Jahnvi, can I ask you something?” I asked. “But promise me, you won't get angry,” I added quickly, wiping away the beads of perspiration that had gathered on my forehead. 'Man, why am I sweating? Let's get over with it,' I prodded myself.

“Sure. What is it?” she asked looking at me curiously.

“I like you, Jahnvi,” I blurted out blatantly while avoiding her steady gaze.

“So do I, Arnab. So what's the big deal?” she said making situation even more confusing. “After all, we are good friends,” she added, cautiously emphasizing the word 'friends'.

“Oh God, I can't take it any more. I will kill myself or will kill the couple sitting next to us for getting all mushy. But as they say that if it is easy, then it's not love. So I had to do it then no matter what it took.

“I mean I love you, Jahnvi,” I said, my voice trembling. There, I had said it.

“We are good friends, Arnab. The movie is making you think like this. Calm down and forget it,” she muttered, trying to put an end to the conversation.

Gosh, girls could be so rude, so difficult to comprehend. I was human, I could have feelings too and need not be influenced by Bollywood flicks. “Jahnvi, I really love you!” I emphasised. And then the words came rushing out, “I told you what I have been feeling for some time now. I didn't want myself to regret the fact that I had my chance and did not take it."

She looked everywhere, but at me. I knew she was upset at what all had just transpired. It was her turn now to reply. Ninety per cent of the girls would have said a "no" and ten per cent may have said, "don't know" when I proposed, but here there was no scope for a 'yes'. At that moment I was trying to read her expressions with a sinking heart!

It had to happen some day, might be in some or other way

The proposal did come out, I said it inside out!!

Though I tried holding back my emotions, to amount I succeed was still a question?

I did stop for once, but Gathered courage and said it all once!!

I love her to Moon and back, she's the one for me now

I hope she's not taken aback, I am the arrow and she's the Bow!!

Don't say me no, baby, try and understand the feeling

My heart is getting heavy, your one yes would do the healing!!

Every moment I spent with you are indeed forever special

Your talks, your eyes and your innocence always keep me dazzle!!

Do agree on my proposal and I won't let you down

I commit you happiness, I'll ensure it makes you drown!!

You're the one and last on the grounds we call "Love"

So many of them come and go, you're doubtlessly one in all above!!

With you I feel complete, there is much more to reiterate

Rapidly increasing heartbeats, I hope life to give me treat!!
From Monday till Sunday, always with you it's Fun day,
It had to happen someday, might be in some or other way!!

Chapter-5

Heartbreak, Music and SMS

'She must have returned home from her tour to Kashmir. I should give her a call,' I thought. That was the first thought I had in my mind. Though I had not actually called her, I was quite surprised at the fact that she and I had the same caller tune. It was the title track from MP3, the movie we had seen together the day I had proposed to her.

I called her consecutively for a week but for some unknown reason, she never answered the call. Her roommate Maya would be on the other end every time I dialled Jahnvi's number and would let loose a barrage of expletives before saying that I should never call Jahnvi again. I was disturbed. 'Why was Jahnvi behaving so strangely? Why does she not say anything? Was she putting Maya up to this?' I could not fathom the reason for her behaviour. I thought of telling her that she could always put her phone in the silent mode if she did not want to answer my calls but then, thought better of it.

After yet another round of wierd response from Maya, I began to text Jahnvi. That too yielded no response. I became all the more helpless and could not make sense of the entire story. Though my proposal had been unexpected, she seemed to have not minded it at all. She seemed quite happy that entire evening; or so I thought. But over time, I began to wonder if I had actually mistaken her silence as a response and not reaction. 'Would I ever get that happiness back? Would this girl, who I had come to dote on, be a presence in my life again?'

I knew it was love; the first above-the-belt-love as far as I was concerned; the first real love that was due to emotions and not a perverted feeling. Since the time I realised I was in love with her, I made a conscious effort to hold myself back, but things were not in my hands and I figured out that soon enough. I decided to call her from different numbers. I did it the way I planned things. I called from my Dad's number and it worked. She answered the call and I felt pure relief at it. I was hearing her sweet voice after two months and my joy knew no bounds.

"Hey, Jahnvi how are you?" I asked the moment she answered the phone. I was scared as my words were falling over each other.

"Sorry, who is this?" she asked and I felt someone had slapped me right across my face.

"It's me. Arnab. You were not responding to my calls and messages, so I called from my Dad's cell," I said, quaking in my boots by this time.

"Oh okay. Yeah on seeing an unknown number, I answered the call. But now that I know it is you, I shall not pick up the phone any more," she replied curtly.

"Why do you say that?" I asked almost reflexively.

"Because I am busy these days with my project and only respond to people who matter," her answer left me dazed and tore my heart into shreds.

"Am I not important in your life? Where has the affable chord gone that we had shared so far?"

"Bullshit, you aren't an important person in my life. Since how long have we known each other? Hardly five to six months. How can you be important to me? There are people who have been around me since the last couple of years and I consider them useless. You are just a recent addition."

That reply so depressed and belittled the rapport, the chemistry that we had built up. This was the first time I was reeling against the onslaught. The air that was entering my room could not help raising the heat within me every passing second.

"Things were great that day and what is it with you now?" I managed to somehow frame a sentence, still fumbling with words.

"Shut up. Who told you that? Nothing has been fine since then. I spoke to you because you were Maya's friend and you thought it to be otherwise and began playing games. You are pathetic. Please stop acting all innocent now," she said rudely.

"You should've stopped me that day if you thought I was out of line," I responded weakly.

"Listen Arnab, I've got many things to do in my life and I do not have time for you and your nonsensical talk. Please do not call me again and increase the hatred that I feel for you. Is that clear? Even if it's not, just get it straight into your head. I am not interested in you. Do not bother to call from your number or any other," she said with an air of finality in her voice.

I realised then why after being such a powerful country, we Indians could not stand up for what was rightfully ours; why we could not be aggressive? The simple reason was that we were emotional fools and I am one amongst the many in this country. I retreated into a shell, changed my caller tune as well to wipe away all those memories of time spent together with Jahnvi.

Rejection is perhaps the worst ever emotion as it leaves you all enervated both physically and emotionally. Though it was not new to me, this time it hit me very hard. I had flunked in my exams a couple of times earlier, but that did not get me down as badly as Jahnvi's rejection of me had done. It made my life unstable and even made me filthier. My headaches were now a constant feature and the day would just neither start nor end. Food also became a luxury now which, if avoided, made me feel better and added to the feeling of emptiness within.

I could hear my mother's footsteps as she approached my room. "Arnab, open the door, beta. It's been four hours. What's happened to you?" she called out to me.

I was sure there was going to be a major drama if I opened the door. So I refrained from doing so. "Mom, I am fine. I told you already that I just want to spend some time alone. Why are you bothering me?" I asked angrily.

"No, I won't go. You open the door or I'll call your Dad," she said. Now there was nothing more I could do but to open the door and welcome a series of unanswerable questions. She played her trump card and left me no option.

I dragged myself up from my bed and walked towards the door. As soon as I opened it, I felt a stinging slap on my cheek. I reeled for a few moments before my vision settled on my brother. "Hi," I said weakly. I began searching for my mother but could not see her around.

My mother had gone back downstairs; or rather, had been sent down by my brother.

"Your hand is bleeding again. You have bruised your knee and also broken the same mirror yet again. Can't you simply cut your hand with a 25-paisa blade once and for all? Why are you doing all this?" he asked irritably. "Did someone reject you again?"

He grimaced when I did not respond to his previous statement.

"You stay out of this," I said defiantly.

"Your knuckles are bleeding, you nutcase. Get that first-aid kit and let me bandage it. Stop this nonsense. You are not only hurting yourself but also the family. No girl who sees you act like this will be impressed by your histrionics," he thundered while trying to console and reason out with me. "And, don't worry about Mom. She's up to something, but I handled her," he said nonchalantly and I thanked him in my mind.

"Bro, I love her. I really do," I said, ignoring his now-angered glare.

"Love? You fall in love and out of it too often. This time won't be any different. Last time it was Lonika you were in love with and later on fucked up your life and ours as well. She's an old love now and it is three months already. So this time you found someone else, somebody new and with better features."

"Shut up, bro, I am already down and out. Just go away if you have nothing better to say to me and the least I expect from you is not to rub salt over my wound."

"It's true, it never hurts you much. When you hurt yourself physically, it hurts you more when you start healing yourself," he said.

Sometimes I had this irrepressible feeling of wanting to surrender myself to destiny. I would usually end up cursing my decision to stay back in Indore. Without girls everything was incomplete. You could love them; you could hate them; but you could not ignore them. They made us and they alone could break us.

❖ ❖ ❖

"She's not the one for you. Why don't you try and understand? Good that you told me, else you almost would have spoiled your life," Maya said as she hungrily gorged on the 'sizzling dazzle brownie' at Appollo Square, CCD. (Never had she sounded this arrogant. In fact on a couple of occasions she had been really sweet. I replied.) I was just not able to ignore the words she had used. "She's like that only. It's you only who took my repeated warnings to deaf ears. Don't complain now," Maya added.

"I am not complaining, yaar. I was merely explaining you what all had conspired between us and that in itself means I need a huge favour from you, as you're the only one who can bring her back into my life," I replied, sounding more than desperate.

"Shut up, Arnab. She's a bitch who can make gullible fools like you fall for her in a matter of seconds. She has used hundreds of them before you and you were amongst her latest possessions," she said, continuing to bash Jahnvi.

My cell phone beeped suddenly and after reading the message, it took less than two seconds for a smile to get plastered on my face.

The message had said: 'Where are you these days? No calls? No messages? Are you alright?'

- Jahnvi

Maya saw my cell and her snotty nose breathed hard as she finished reading the message. "Such a horrible girl she is! I mean such a bitch she is! When you proposed to her, she made you cry and when you are trying your best to forget her, she's playing her dirty games once again," Maya responded, still holding my phone and occasionally glancing at the message. "Arnab, I am really sorry to have introduced you to this girl. Nonetheless, you can still manage to get over her. You have hardly known her for long. Let's forget what all happened; forget that you both had met ever," she continued with her ranting.

"No need to console me, Maya. She must have realised her feelings for me. There is no harm in giving her one chance. After all, my proposal was totally unexpected for her."

"What is she realising now? You guys are born fuckers, aren't you? She already played with your life once and now you are ready to get your nuts cracked again by her," she almost shouted and would have hit me hard if given an option. "You're still crazy about her, and dare you lie to me about this," she threatened.

I chose to live and didn't reply to Maya on this. She, however, continued to criticise Jahnvi for the next one hour. She cried also and tried every possible trick to draw me away from Jahnvi – heated arguments, unknown facts, atrocious explanations by Maya confused me no end while I stood on an unbalanced bridge of love and hatred. Once again nobody had understood me.

It was perhaps the most difficult and trying time of my life. I realised that the best way to get rid of someone was to simply insult him the way Jahnvi had done to me. If that person possessed even an iota of self-respect, he would have automatically signed her out off his life, but I could not. After all, love too is a bitch.

My murky life started getting back on track slowly and steadily and gradually I was able to close the Jahnvi chapter. I began to drink and smoke but even these socially unacceptable activities began to bore me after a few days. Worse, they gave me no respite.

My sense of humour failed me too, so I started concentrating on music and my studies. I was highly confused and dilly-dallied between wasting my life and taking revenge. I concentrated on the latter as it always sounded better. It at least gave me kick and revenge does definitely taste sweet.

Despite all the things that had happened in my life, I began to breathe again and tried taking the preparations for the MBA entrance exam very seriously. After joining a coaching institute for it, I came to know that I was unnecessarily and uselessly blaming myself for not having been more serious about a career in chartered accountancy. The main point was that I had not been able to study anything and was too frustrated at the repeated failure in my life.

I repaired the mirror I had broken and learnt to save money, instead of spend recklessly. I matured and began to concentrate on my academics. I quit my unsocial and reclusive life and started spending more time on extracurricular activities at college. I tried to motivate myself to emerge out from the shell I had built outside me. I even turned my attention to music as it had always managed to keep me alive till now. I set up a band called 'Rooh' along with a few of my friends. I was the vocalist along with Gunny; Abhishek was on drums, Himanshu was on guitar and Sunny played the synthesiser. We were successful in coming up with quite a few chartbusters and soon began to earn some sort of fame. Our teachers were very encouraging and allowed us the use of college auditorium besides providing us with not only with instruments and workstations, but also financial backing.

My mood changed and I began to immerse myself in what I loved doing. I loved LINKING PARK and all their numbers. 'Renaissance' and 'Rooh' gave me a new lease of life. 'Rooh' went on to become a huge success and we were everywhere all at once – PR, radio bytes, fame, money and girls! We were on top of the world. We all jammed with each other and started working on our music co-ordination at a brisk pace. I selected Bryan Adams's 'Everything I do, I do it for you...' for the launch but by giving it the Rooh touch. We changed the music and gave it a desi rock flavour.

After a month-long practice schedule, we were all set for Renaissance's first ever stage show. We were all very ecstatic!

We altered our looks to suit our performance on the D-day. There were 5,000 people cheering us in the auditorium. It alleviated our confidence to new heights. We went on to the stage and started streaming in with our instruments. The Bollywood number 'Root aa gayi re...' kick started the evening, followed by Bryan Adams's numbers. We performed on a few numbers from Bryan Adams and then switched to desi music. Nothing could beat these since we wanted to see the bodies move. Himanshu mesmerised the audience with his capabilities.

Then we switched to Linking Park. Indore had never experienced such a long noisy and Musical night before. The audience went crazy and we were on top of the world. We sang, performed, danced and lit up the night sky, driving our audience crazy and wild. We were a big hit and we were savouring every moment in the spotlight. Our fan following had by now become huge.

I came back home late after celebrating our success at a party thrown by our good and close friends Aditi, Surbhi and her gang, Romil and his pals. We were the toast of the town. Girls who never used to talk with us willingly, were now readily exchanging numbers with us. My brother was so thrilled about all this development that when I got home, he hugged me with pride and contentment writ large over his face. "You look tired; you should sleep," he said in a voice filled with love and care.

"No bro, tell me if there's anything you want to talk about," I said in a slurred speech.

"No, nothing. Go to your room and sleep, you nut. Your celebration smells and you know Mom and Dad will not be happy with the stink you are emanating now."

I went to my bedroom without any further ado. The success had exhausted me no end. I slept almost immediately and snored my way through the night. I was blissfully unaware about my surroundings till I was jolted awake by my cell phone vibrations. Somebody had messaged me. I cursed the messenger. I read the text: 'Arnab, hope you are doing well. I messaged you a few weeks back, but got no response from you. I want to meet you tomorrow evening at 7. Apollo Square at CCD? I await a positive reply.' It's urgent."

I took half an hour to decide whether to respond to her message or just ignore it. I eventually decided to reply. The heart always wins when there is a tussle between the head and the heart! 'I have class tomorrow till 7:30. Let's meet at same time and same place,' I replied, feeling all the more happy.

Chapter-6

Happily Committed

I was surprised having received Jahnvi's message the previous night. 'She still wants to meet me. I should have replied to her message last time too,' I told myself, while making some effort to pay attention to the class lecture. While still deeply engrossed in my thoughts, I received a text from Jahnvi. It read:

'When are you coming? I have reached here ten minutes ago.'

'It may take ten more minutes. The faculty is in the mood to take the ongoing discussion a bit further,' I replied way too soon and eagerly.

'I am waiting,' she messaged back.

'Sir, how much arithmetic should we expect in this year's C.A.T? Please explain question number 7 for the same reason," a geek said, as he seemed to be at his most studious best even as the class went into overtime. But nobody apart from me was seen cursing him. There were those who listened to me yet ignored me with loathsome glares. I was just flabbergasted at their reaction.

'It is alright. They don't have a girlfriend waiting for them, or perhaps they are happily committed,' I told myself, trying my best to console myself. But not so secretly I was contented at making his wait.

"How long should I wait? It's been half an hour already. Should I wait or leave?" she messaged to me. I chose not to reply as I had already reached our meeting place and was parking my bike.

From a far I saw her fiddle with the newspaper. The wait was making her impatient. Her face was red with anger but it still made her look beautiful. Her big almond-shaped eyes were red with fury; her face was pink and puffed up. Even the raging anger could not hide the innocence from her face. Her slender hands now held the rolled up newspaper which she was banging on the table as if waiting to kill the very sight of me.

'Please let us not fight now; maybe over the phone, but not now. Your voice will distract me, make me blind and deaf,' I murmured under my breath.

"I am sorry! I got delayed and you had to wait for so long but some geeks in my class had yet again asked newer and smarter questions from our professors. We had to sit extra time as our great teachers were trying their best to explain the relevant concepts," I said in an explanation while guiding her to a table.

"Don't give me your sick sanctimonious smile. Five more minutes and I would have asked for the check and forgotten all about my message last night," she said bluntly, though I noticed a little frown on her face.

'What a way to start a conversation!' I thought to myself but kept quiet.

"First things first – I want to clear where we stand. I had no intention to meet you and nor do I have any desire to do so after today. I would like to thrash this out myself rather than have a mediator to do so," she said in one go, not even once hesitating.

"What are you talking about, Jahnvi? I have never said anything bad about you," I said, looking bewildered.

"Arnab, I've known you since the past eight months and unlike you, I feel I am intelligent enough to understand a person in a given time. I wouldn't have contacted you, but I did. But you crossed all your limits."

"Jahnvi, there is some misunderstanding here. Let's make everything very clear in the first instance. You don't want to talk to me? Fine. Throw me out of your life. In fact you already have done it. You have massaged your ego already. But you messaged me and here I am."

"Ego? Look who is talking about ego! You check your Inbox and see if I had not messaged you before. I am sure you must have deleted that too," she said, looking frustrated.

"No, I still have it. But yes, I didn't reply because I didn't feel like it; or because I could not," I replied.

"Then, why are you lecturing me on ego? Go and satisfy yours, a narcissist that you are. I messaged you because I realised I had been very harsh on you that day and felt that I should apologise."

"And I called you numerous times after the day I proposed to you. There's not even a single day that's gone by when I have not heard abrasive words on your behalf from your roommate, Maya. She would scream at me every time I called and I for once, could not fathom the reason for your ignorance and arrogance. And I even messaged you endlessly, only to receive no reply from you."

"I was in training and you should know that cell phones are not allowed during these sessions. I used to leave it in the hostel but I did once respond to your call. I actually considered you my… forget it… knowing your real self, who would like to talk to you? I won't pretend that I am unaware about your messages!"

"I sent messages to clear the air between us. There has obviously been a communication gap between us. You have known me since the past eight months. We have been such great friends. Why and how can a third person create a rift between us? Where did your intelligence go that you could not understand me?" I was too agitated to hold back now.

"No, Arnab I never understood you. I never knew what you really are like. Thanks to Maya who cleared your character chart that I came to know the real you. And I warn you to stay away from her too," she said it so abrasively that I was left numb and could not make sense of it.

"What the fuck are you talking about? What has she told you? We have hardly spoken ten times," I somehow fumbled through these words.

"You dare use the 'f 'word again and I'll hit you hard. And you dare say anything against Maya or me. I will do something really serious," she lashed out at me.

"Jahnvi, I am sorry. I did not mean to insult either of you, but the least you can do is hear me out. Let me reason out with you," I said, almost pleading by now.

She didn't deny me my request either. I arranged my wallet and bag on the chair next to me and started to take out thing from the bag.

"What's all this? What are you attempting to do? We are not here to play freaky games, damn it!!" she said a little too loudly. I was sure a couple of heads had turned towards our table. But I cared not even two hoots about it.

"I am not doing anything freaky. I just wanted to show you a few things – show you how much you mean to me."

I was now in full control of the situation and this could possibly help Jahnvi realise that I was not playing any games with her.

"This rough piece of small paper is nothing but the booking ticket of the very first movie we had seen together – 'Guru' and this is the parking ticket of Velocity Theatre," I said.

"What can I do if you like to accumulate junk?" she asked, sounding too irritated.

"That's what I am trying to say. I didn't throw it all off because it means a lot to me. It holds special memories for me. It makes me remember those beautiful moments we had spent together," I said it as convincingly as possible. But Jahnvi made no comment.

"I have no fucking interest in collecting pieces of paper. As it is, I have enough papers and books as junk to study," she didn't react to the 'f' word this time. "I have treasured every movie ticket, every parking ticket, every coffee bill. I've even treasured the traffic cop's receipt when we were together. All this was only because you were there accompanying me every time," I further added, showing her all the 'junk'. See my mobile – it doesn't allow more than a 100 messages. Take a look and tell me what do you find?"

"They are all my messages. Inbox and Sent Items, both," she replied, looking surprised.

"Damn it!! I've even treasured a simple 'Hi' you had sent. Look at the Call Register – all they have is your number everywhere, be it Missed calls or Received calls or Dialled calls. I don't want to allow any person other than you in my life, Jahnvi." I spoke some more only to make her see what she meant to me. "Check my Yahoo mail. There are 400 mails still unread and 50 that are read. The unread ones have the same subject. They say 'Jahnvi has left a new scrap in your scrapbook.' The ones I have read are from you.

"I got a new mobile card having the same last nine numbers as yours. I registered my bike with the same number as your vehicle '7727'. I even named my nephew after you." I might have sounded like a fool, madly in love with her, and not that it was not true, but she needed to know that she had been wrong about me and my feelings. "Brassy, you may say, but it's necessary to show how much you mean to me. So Maya or not, it's now more important that we know what we expect and what we feel. We first need to sort this out."

I took out a newspaper to further prove my love. "Look at this newspaper. Why I have been doing this rock band is not just for recognition from the world, but to be noticed by you, so that you may see me and come back. See this hand? I acted like an asshole and cut it with a mirror."

She was now intently staring at that cut.

"I didn't wait for the session to end today. Rather, I was thrown out of the class after being given numerous warnings and now have been suspended for a week because I was busy messaging you from the front row where I was sitting. Jahnvi, what else do I need to do to prove my love for you? Where have I let you down, Jahnvi? What went wrong after that day?" I was almost choking now; my eyes were all watery and any moment I could have begun to weep.

I was silent for some time then. I wanted her to get my arguments into her brain – to believe me, to trust my feelings for her. A few minutes passed and we both sat silent.

"Maya told me that you are a flirt; you are on drugs; you get into relationships just for your pleasure and you have no different intentions for me," Jahnvi said, with every word of hers piercing my heart.

"If I had the same intentions for you, I wouldn't have wasted eight months and treasured your memories," I replied.

"Does that mean you agree to the allegation that you are a flirt? Then I would not be surprised if you take drugs too. You broke your hand too, you just said. Drug addicts do that very often."

Now I was exasperated, 'What does she want?' "I have never done drugs. And you have to stop doubting me," I broke out in anger and frustration.

"In fact, she said that there's no single girl in your group with whom you haven't slept and that includes her too. She made me talk to a couple of your classmates, who told me about your insatiable thirst for them and labelled you as horny. You are rich; you can't be trusted," she said further, adding to my disappointment.

"What the fuck?" my eyes were wide with shock now.

"I told you not to use the 'F' word; it will take me less than five seconds to get up and disappear," she threatened me.

"Sorry, but what is this crap? I just have one good friend and that is Aditi. She is in my college. I don't have a group. The two of us have a good bond, but we are just friends. Getting physical is way beyond anything and more than that, it is an insult to my friendship with her.

"I still don't have a clue as to who you are talking about and why is Maya behaving like this? She's just making an obnoxious attempt to malign my character. In fact she was the one who stopped me when I was responding to your message. She maligns you every now and then. See one message in the Draft folder. I saved it but didn't message you because Maya was too adamant and asked me not to message you. She was with me when you messaged.

"I thought you would hate me more if I called you again, so I stopped communicating with you. But I really want you to know the reason. You did not want to have any contact with me. Messages are not helping us here. Can't we meet some day for coffee and get it all sorted out? I still miss and love you, Jahnvi."

She read the message that I had saved in my Drafts folder. "Hell!! If it's true..." she let the sentence linger.

"You can check the date and time I had saved my message. Jahnvi, I am not a prankster and I am not that intelligent either but I am honest. Please believe me I have always been very true to you," I said.

"Tell me everything that she has told you. What you said has left me confused and dazed. Why did she do this?" she wondered!

"I don't know the reasons for her one these things but I will tell you everything that has transpired since the day I proposed to you."

Jahnvi interrogated me for long time and I explained everything that had transpired between Maya and me to the best of my knowledge.

"I can't believe she told you all this crap and there you were, wiping her crocodile tears. And you believed her?"

Jahnvi was amazed to hear all that Maya had said about her.

"I would never believe a single word she said, not even in my dreams. I wouldn't have come today to meet you if I believed it, Jahnvi."

"Yes, I know. But how can she even say that? Then what did you do?"

"I just walked off from there and never saw her again."

"I guess I know why she did what she did. She was jealous of us being good friends and noticed us drawing closer. More importantly, I think she is in love with you," said Jahnvi.

"No, no way. Don't say that," I interrupted her, not wanting to hear any further.

"Believe it or not, but you are the only guy who speaks to her nicely. You are also rich and decent looking," Jahnvi said, putting across her point clearly.

"After you proposed, she would keep checking my messages and if ever she found your message, she would constantly badmouth you."

This made me all the more disturbed, "And you would participate in that?"

"Very actively; in fact, with great pride since I was hypnotised by Maya. She forced me to bitch about you. I thoroughly enjoyed nailing you as I was so peeved about your being a part of my life."

That just floored me completely. At that moment her eyes noticed my dejected expression and she cooled down. "But now, I really can't afford to lose you because I know how much you love me. I must have made you to go through hell. It really hurts when I remember the time I literally cursed you."

"Let us just flush it down the toilet, okay?" she said excitedly and I nodded in acceptance.

"I know she gave us a lot of trouble by behaving like a nut, but we should be thankful to her because of what she has unwittingly done for us. Now our love, our bond has only got stronger," I said.

"That we will never do. This is history and so is she!!" she replied.

And that marked the end of Maya and her presence in our lives. We flushed out everything that was ill and evil. We let go off Maya and her devilish attitude. Now all we had with us was our love, our feelings for each other. That day we spoke out our hearts to each other. We said everything that we had been holding back deep within us. We cried; we laughed; we hugged and kissed. It was now 'us' together.

I was happy at the fact that Jahnvi, through all this conversation, had realised that I was still a virgin.

Chapter-7

First Salary and Precious Gifts

And so our journey of love began. We would meet daily and spend the greater part of our day together at Café Coffee Day outlet and later in the evenings, we would be glued over the phone. We were together 24/7 like magnets. We had become insomniacs and a cup of coffee was just about enough to aid that. She looked even more beautiful now and her beauty made me all the more in love with her. Love was in the air; it was all around us and fluttering like a butterfly.

It was a usual day, yet there was an unusual feel about this usualness, perhaps because I had seen a disturbing dream the previous night. I don't know how, but it was a sequential dream which began with the time. I met Jahnvi for the first time, our subsequent misunderstanding, our blossoming of love and ending with our marriage. The dream stirred something within me and I was tempted to act on an impulse. I had an overpowering desire to let her know that I loved her insanely and make her feel the depth of my feelings; to let her enjoy the feeling of being loved by someone. I immediately decided to make the day special, and what could have been a better way than to gift her something that would make her feel all the more special.

"A rose and a feather diary? Wow!" Jahnvi exclaimed with excitement. "What is this for? Am I missing something here? Why this, all of a sudden?" Jahnvi went on and on with confusion writ large over her face.

"Firstly, it is; secondly, I don't think I need an occasion to gift my girlfriend and thirdly, why don't you read it yourself?" I replied.

She opened the diary and started reading it. I could see her expressions change from curiosity to thrill, to happiness, to contentment and finally to tears of joy and love. It had a record of all the discussions that we had engaged in right from the time of meeting at Renaissance.

"That's astounding, Arnab! I am so impressed," she smiled wide, her eyes glistening. "I did not know that you maintained a diary! That's quite a girly thing to do!" she joked and winked.

"And here is another gift for you." I took out a gift-wrapped box from my bag and presented it to her.

"What's this?" she asked, sounding more than surprised.

I had 'it-could-be-anything' expression on my face. So she shrugged. She opened it slowly and found a 'Kelly doll' inside it.

"Oh, she is so cute! Thank you. But you know what, Arnab? I will not accept it," she said.

"Why?" I was flummoxed. "I bought it especially for you as I thought you would love it," I said, unable to hide my disappointment.

"I accepted your diary only because it was your way of expressing your love. I loved the gift from the bottom of my heart because you invested your days in it and more than that, it is your heart that you poured out in this diary. That's what makes it special," she explained and held my hand. "But you are buying me an expensive and superfluous doll which costs a thousand rupees at least. And the worst part is, you are using your Dad's money for all this," she complained.

Now I was confused.

"Look Arnab, I totally respect your emotions, gifts and your love for me. I am like any other girl in that sense, but I would love it even more if you were to spend the money earned by you to buy me these gifts rather than using your Dad's money because the former would be really special for me," she explained.

"You're right!" I was surprised at the way she put forth her point and I loved her for it though it did make me a little sad.

"Now there is no reason to be sad. I just wanted you to know how much you mean to me and how I wanted 'us' to work out in the future," she said while ruffling my hair. "And another thing," she started talking in all seriousness, "I would like to state now is that..." she paused for few seconds and my heart began to beat faster. "I am feeling very hungry, so can we grab a bite?" she asked very innocently, patting her tummy and winking.

I was initially hurt at her response as I had spent a whole lot of time and effort in finding a way that could best convey my feelings. I thought gifting her a doll that she so loved would make her treasure the moment, but she plainly refused to accept it. That dejected me no end. I began sulking and felt very low. Sensing my dejection, she did accept the doll but on the condition that I would never gift her anything bought with Dad's money. After having given a thought to what she had said, I capitulated. She was right in making me realise my mistake at the right time and it struck me that Dad would have been grateful for saving his money if only he had known. I promised myself that I would work towards what she had asked.

❖ ❖ ❖

I startzre you?" I called her, knowing too well she must be in her class.

"In college; in fact at a lecture. I will call you later," she whispered hurriedly.

"No, no, listen, it's urgent. Meet me now," I said, faking urgency in my voice.

"You sound tense. I hope everything is alright?" she said. I loved it whenever she very lovingly asked me if everything was alright.

"Everything is just okay. I mean it umm... just uh...meet me now and I'll explain to you." I left the sentence incomplete so as to make her anxious.

"Okay, I'll meet you, once I am done with my lecture," she said.

"Now Jahnvi, it's serious," I said.

"Right now? I just can't, Arnab!! Tell me what has happened?" she pleaded.

"Let it be then. Well, I just have to tell you that I am waiting for you outside your campus near gate no. 2," I said and disconnected the call.

After a couple of minutes, I saw her running towards me. I smiled to myself and opened the car door for her.

"Before you say anything, you should know this that I almost risked a semester by running away from class in between a lecture. It better be something worth it," she said on seeing a big grin pasted on my face.

"Of course I do," I said and blindfolded her.

"Are you raping me?" she said angrily.

"I wish I could," I sighed.

"Shut up, idiot and tell me why am I being treated so inhumanely?" she asked, trying to extricate her hands from my firm grip.

"It's a surprise," I said and held her tight.

"Use your brains, you jerk. This is my college. What if someone sees us?" she demanded angrily.

"Love is blind, baby," I said and drove the vehicle to the destination.

"The suspense is killing me," she said in frustration.

"Have patience, sweetheart" I replied, smiling to myself.

"Come here and please open this blindfold for a minute, sweetheart," she implored. I couldn't resist her tone and gave in almost too quickly.

No sooner did I touch her face to open the blindfold that she grabbed me hard, hugging and kissing me on my chin, assuming that it was my lips I guess, given that she was still blindfolded. I sought her lips then and we kissed, we floated and we swam in the pool of our emotions.

I unknotted her blindfold, cupped her face with my hands, brought her closer and kissed her on the lips, slow and gentle at first, before the volcano within me erupted and I bit her hard on her lips while her fingernails scratched my chest. The hunger to have more and do more took over my senses. I slowly unbuttoned my shirt and drew her closer to me. Our bodies collided with each other, making the moment very ecstatic. Our intimacy levels had risen to higher levels and even the hitting and bumping with various things inside the car did not bother us. I could feel the sugary lip gloss all over me even as she kissed my body and I almost experienced heaven. My hands were slowly making their way inside her tee-shirt and caressing her belly, before moving upward and cupping her breast tightly. Just as I was about to unhook her bra, she stopped me.

"Sssshhhh, not now. It's been just a month to our relationship," she said, preventing my hand from venturing any further.

"It hardly matters. Let's make this day all the more special," I said and kissed her again, holding her tightly.

"Behave yourself. I am not like the ones who make out in the back of the car. Please understand, Arnab or it's the last time we will come so close," she warned me rather naughtily.

"Close your eyes as they speak a lot. The next time you had better not stop me or I'll rape you mercilessly," I said, backing off. She kissed my forehead and smiled.

It was 6.30 p.m., dark enough for us to be romantic. I blindfolded her again and guided her to the place where I had planned our evening.

"You may open your eyes," I said as I gently let lose the blindfold.

An open ground with lush green grass, an open hut, a luminous sky filled with stars, a light breeze and some light showers completed the ambience. A beautiful cake was placed right on a dinner table in the centre of the hut and the room was filled with the fragrance of scented candles. I had promised myself that this would be an evening Jahnvi would cherish all her life.

"Surprise!!" I said.

Jahnvi was struck speechless and kept on staring at the place. "Arnab!" she shrieked with joy. "I am enthralled, astonished, pleased by your efforts to surprise me. That's incredible and really, really special," she whooped with joy and hugged me tight. "But Arnab, didn't I tell you that day… "

"Shush!! Listen to me," I covered her lips with my fingers, gazed into her eyes and said, "Dear girl, your boyfriend is neither stupid nor rigid in his habits. Here is the official letter which I got after working at the institute as a proof. And believe me, it's really hard to earn this kind of money. So please enjoy it for my sake even if you don't like anything."

"Why wouldn't I like it, Arnab? I loved it. In fact, I have seen all this happening in movies only. It makes me feel more special because you are spending your hard-earned money on me to make me feel special, to show me your intense love. I bet that none of my friends could have ever experienced this before. I am speechless. I am euphoric. I am in seventh heaven. I am so fortunate and I still can't believe you did all this for me. I am overwhelmed," she said it in one breath, looking and sounding completely overwhelmed at my effort. I could also see that she was teary-eyed with tears of happiness. I started the music and we danced to make the evening more romantic. However, we both had two left feet. We collided and fell down a couple of times but she looked deep into my eyes and I gave myself completely to her that very moment. When the music became one with the slower tempo, I lay down on the ground and Jahnvi rested her head on my chest.

"I owe it to you. Whatever you wish and dream of here tonight, you'll get more than that. That's a promise and I'll keep my word," I said.

"Thanks for everything, Arnab," she said and kissed me on the cheek. "You know I never believed in the adage that 'relationships are made in heaven', but after meeting you, I've started believing in it."

"Don't thank me again and again or that will be the end of the surprises." I said in mock irritation.

We danced again and came closer – so close that we could feel each other's breath. We spoke about almost all our grievances and beautiful moments in our relationship.

"You know Arnab, initially I was not willing to accept your proposal but gradually I realised that your love, your feelings for me were true and I saw how crazy you were about me, how you treated me with extra care and the way you kept all those things like tickets, bills and other such memoirs, it was truly amazing. I am truly lucky and today I feel that I am the happiest person in the world," she confessed.

"Is your essay over?" I said and she nodded, grimacing.

"Now, can I give my love a vote of thanks by kissing you gently?" I asked and moved forward.

She looked around warily to see if anyone else was there and then nodded her head. Our heads moved towards each other and our lips met. I moved down to her neck and as I nuzzled my face against her slender neck, I began to feel excited. I unbuttoned my tee-shirt, but she was made of iron, I guess, as she strictly stopped me from going any further.

"Some day...some day...restrain yourself till then. Let us understand each other a bit more till the right time comes. Let us be a bit more familiar with each other," she said. I had no other option but to agree as I didn't want to spoil her mood. We kissed each other again, though I could not get enough of her.

"How much money did you spend on all this?" she asked.

"Does that matter?" I said.

"Not at all," she replied.

"Then it's worthless to ask."

"It's priceless rather. Okay tell me, how did you zero in on this place?" Jahnvi asked.

"I booked this place for an hour given that both of us love Nature. I considered it the best option and I had to do it, otherwise you would have underestimated my potential," I said and took a sharp turn.

"Arnab. I never underestimated you. I just wanted you to be responsible but I never knew you could do it so fast. Sorry, if that hurt you," she apologised.

"Don't be. In fact I am happy because you are not like the other girls who fake emotions. Instead, you are very frank and that makes me fall more for you and I feel more confident about our future," I said.

"Exactly, that's how I am too," she said and bent her head to let it rest on my shoulder. She put her hands on mine and I brought my car to a sudden halt to gaze at her for a few minutes.

❖ ❖ ❖

"I didn't mean to do that," she said, expecting me to be strong again.

"Neither did I," I laughed, holding her hand. I pointed at a church some distance away before saying, "I come here often. It is quiet and beautiful and I wanted to end this day here."

"You are becoming a habit," she said and clasped my waist tight.

"Okay, now, can we unhook ourselves? The Father is waiting for us, and please don't say anything to him," I said and took her inside the church to meet the priest.

"Father, this is the girl I am in love with," I confessed to Father.

"She's God's child, son. You both are meant for each other," Father smiled and bestowed his blessings on us.

"Thank you, Father," Jahnvi said and smiled back.

"But son, I can sense complexities in your relationship, though don't be disheartened by the same. You have a long life ahead. Never spy on each other. You two are pure souls and can't live with any other person. However, you need to trust each other completely. Never let even a seed of doubt enter your relationship. This fairy will always guide you," Father said.

"I am always with him. I will never leave him and will be with him through thick and thin. I love him and moreover, respect the love he has for me," Jahnvi said and held my hand tighter.

"God bless both of you," Father said and offered me the ring I had purchased for her.

"Take your ring, child," Father said, offering me the ring.

"Arnab..." Jahnvi said in surprise.

"May I ask you for your hand in front of the Almighty and with his due permission present you this ring as a token of my commitment?" I asked.

"It's so beautiful," she said and her eyes became wet with disbelief and joy.

"I wish I could bring a ring for you too," she said with a hint of regret.

"Don't worry, I have planned everything. I bought one for myself too," I said and took out another ring from my pocket.

"You are quite a planner and don't you dare look at any other girl now that we are committed. Right, Father?" she asked.

"Of course, in front of God, my child!!"

"May this day be one of the best days of your life, my children. God bless you both with love and give you strength to stand by each other and fight against all the odds that you might face in your relationship. Be committed and convicted to your decisions. One wrong decision can change your life forever. I shall be happy to see you both as a married couple soon," Father said and walked away.

'You bet!' I thought.

Chapter-8

Anything, Anytime, Anywhere for Love

Date: 23rd November

"Arnab beta, I can't make it today and I am sorry I couldn't receive your call as I was busy in a meeting," Jahnvi's Mom said.

"That's all right, aunty, I concluded that. So I didn't call you for the third time."

"In case I reach Indore tomorrow morning, would I be able to clear my exam?" she asked anxiously.

"You don't worry, aunty, I'll teach you. We'll hone in on the basic concepts and you'll clear the exam. Believe me, a day is enough to prepare. You just inform me a couple of hours before you reach here and in the meantime I'll prepare myself to teach you," I responded.

"Thanks, I'll reach Indore tomorrow morning at 11. See you there," Jahnvi's Mom said.

Date: 24th November

Time: 8:00 p.m.

My mother and I happen to be very similar. We love making people wait for us and seldom care for the unlucky soul who would be waiting.

"Look at yourself as you are not worried about your performance and getting late, though the teacher is more worried," Jahnvi said.

"I am not worried about her performance, Jahnvi; rather, I am worried about mine. It's about mutual welfare. If she passes, I pass. God forbid, if she fails, I don't even want to think about that because I don't want to be blamed for the rest of my life. Ask her to be docile and obedient," I said half tense and half jokingly. But only I knew how nervous I was.

She burst out laughing. I gave a loathsome glare as she was laughing at my helplessness.

"Don't worry, I trust you. That's why I have you trapped for the rest of my life," she smiled and kissed my chin.

"And what about your Mom? Should I trust her as a good student in her mid-40's?" I asked.

"You have to deal with her. She is not my concern. I didn't ask you to take it on. You yourself agreed to teach her, but is it okay with you to teach her so late?" she queried.

"Well, I don't think there is anything wrong. Mommy and Daddy are going to Mumbai today. If they call me late at night, I'll handle it somehow. You just ask aunty to make it a bit quick," I replied, thinking of some possible excuse to put up in such a situation. I did not want to let down either my parents or Jahnvi's for that matter.

10:00 p.m.

"Are you sure, uncle and aunty won't mind if you come with me on my bike at this time?" I asked, as Jahnvi held me tight from the back and rode pillion.

"Don't you worry. You are here to teach my Mom and anyway, I am coming with you to show you my brother's flat. My Tolu is getting serviced; why would they mind?" Jahnvi said nonchalantly.

"Okay, if you are sure about it," I said, somehow not at all sure about it or anything.

"Take a right and the house on the corner with the white and red combination is my brother's," Jahnvi directed me and pointed towards the house before I could take a right turn.

"Here we are, but where are your Mom and Dad?" I asked as I didn't see their car in the parking lot.

"Here they are," she said smiling.

My heart began to race and I was sure they could hear it beating wildly. I was certainly nervous. Time slowed down or came to a standstill, I don't know, but I was frozen.

Her Mom and Dad stepped out of the car. Aunty looked beautiful in a blue silk sari. Jahnvi smiled at her parents.

Her Dad was wearing a printed T-shirt which said, 'Cuter than the kids'. Now this was difficult to answer but he was certainly cute and cuddly and seeing him somehow, my nervousness evaporated. It was difficult to believe that he was in his early fifties. He looked quite dynamic and sharp.

Jahnvi moved towards her parents and they hugged each other. In the midst of all this hugging and loving emotions, they seemed to have forgotten my existence. I almost felt like a villain in the midst of this happy family. Jahnvi's mother noticed me fidgeting and called out my name, gesturing me to join them. Secretly for a moment I felt like I was being invited by them as their son-in-law. The thought in itself made me blush.

"How are you beta? Thanks to you, I now have some help," she said, patting my shoulder.

'I had to. It is better if I impress you asap,' I thought within my mind.

"I am doing great, aunty, No need to thank me. I am looking forward to a treat once you clear the exams."

"Definitely Arnab, I owe you a treat," she smiled.

'You owe me the beautiful girl standing beside you,' I wanted to say but good sense prevailed and I did not.

Jahnvi interrupted my thoughts and introduced me to her Dad.

"Yes, I know. She talks a lot about you," he replied as we shook hands. His handshake was firm and his stare, deadly and scary. I could imagine him strangling me.

"Uncle, I so wanted to meet you," I replied with a nervous smile. I was sure he had got the hint that I was trembling out of nervousness. I could see it in his eyes, or was it all just my imagination?!

"Why? Anything special?" asked her Dad, giving her a suspicious look.

Jahnvi shrugged as her Dad kept on looking from me to his daughter and back again at me and I guess I even saw Jahnvi's Mom smile slightly or was I imagining things again?!

"I mean she talks a lot about you too and I had already met aunty once before. So I was looking forward to meeting you," I said and could sense Jahnvi sigh in relief.

"Then you must meet Jahnvi's elder brother Aabhas too. You have not met him, have you?" he asked.

"No, I haven't." I said. I did not want to either. I was not too thrilled with the dirty looks he had given us the couple of times we had bumped into him at CCD.

"I'll meet him for the very first time," I said, completing my answer after having paused for few seconds.

Just then a cute male version of Jahnvi opened the door. How could this guy harm me? Seeing Aabhas, I heaved a sigh of relief, maybe a bit too audibly, I guess, because I saw Jahnvi's parents and brother look at me intently. Jahnvi gave me a dirty look.

"So, what do you do, Arnab?" That was the first thing Aabhas asked me.

"I am a B. Com student from Renaissance College and I am also preparing for CAT," I said, hoping that this could bring some respect and seriousness to their evaluation of me.

"Okay. CAT 08?" he asked.

"Yes, Jahnvi told me that you too are preparing for it."

"Yes, second attempt for me though," he replied morosely.

"Anyway, you carry on. Mom is already late, so let's not waste more time," Jahnvi said and thus rescued me. My eyes thanked her and she smiled.

Aabhas asked his father and Jahnvi to accompany him for a walk. Jahnvi smiled, said her farewells to me and her mother and walked out of the door with her father.

❖ ❖ ❖

I opened the book to the chapters I had a fair knowledge of and we started the session without further delay.

"Aunty, the current ratio=current assets/current liabilities. You just need to add the assets given in the trial balance after excluding the fixed assets and same is the case with the current liabilities. Just take a ratio of that. So simple!"

"What is meant by fixed assets and how can I identify them?" aunty asked me, confusion writ large over her face.

"Aunty, assets which are not purchased on a regular basis or generally purchased once when you initiate a business are called 'fixed assets'. It could be machinery, plant, etc."

"Okay, let it be. I need practical questions to be done fast. Can we do it in an hour or so?" aunty asked.

"No, Aunty it will take more time," I replied.

"But my paper is tomorrow morning and I am hardly able to make head or tail about it. Don't mind, beta, you people are in touch with the subject and also good at it, but it's tough for people who have left studies years ago. That's why I may be sounding a bit irritating, kindly bear with me," she pleaded.

We progressed well till my Dad called and that almost ended my attempts to impress Jahnvi's mother.

11:00 p.m.

"Where are you?" Dad asked sternly.

"I will take a while to reach home," I said hesitatingly.

"How much time and where are you?" Dad repeated.

"Half an hour more and I'll tell you afterwards," I replied.

"I am going outside. Call me once you get home," Dad shouted and disconnected the call.

Aunty had been watching me while I was talking and must have wondered why I was acting like a half wit. She could not help but ask, "If there is any problem, you can go back home, Arnab!!"

"No, aunty, I'll go after some time," I replied, avoiding her gaze.

11:30 p.m.

"I just now called your brother and discovered you have still not reached home, Arnab!! I warn you, you had better reach home soon, else I'll take a sharp turn to Indore right now. Go home and call me from the landline. Your Mom is worried. You must be out with Manish and Tejas for sure. I am warning you to stay away from those drunkards," Dad threatened, fuming with anger. I could almost see his face go red. What if he had been in Indore? I am sure I would have been dead meat by now.

"Dad, I am just leaving. Relax now. I will call you in fifteen minutes after reaching home. I was studying with one of my friends," I lied.

"Sorry aunty, but I need to leave now," I apologised profusely and collected my stuff.

"It's alright, beta. I had in fact asked you if it was fine for you to come over and help me out. There was no need to lie to your parents," she seemed upset.

"No, aunty it's okay. I had to lie because my father is a heart patient and he's getting tense as I have got delayed and my mother is worried."

"It's alright, but still, I think you could have handled it in a better way without being dishonest. Let it be. Drive slowly and reach safely," she said, displeased at my behaviour.

"Aunty, if you don't mind, I'll come tomorrow morning and teach you at 5 a.m. before dropping you at your exam centre. Is that alright with you?" I asked as if begging.

"Are you sure?" she asked me, wondering what was prompting me to do so.

"Yes, aunty. I'll come here at 5."

She acquiesced and I departed. Aabhas gave me a suspicious look as he entered the house but I brushed past him in a hurry.

I reached home and immediately called Dad and also spoke to Mom. I hardly could sleep that night. I woke up before time and got ready to leave for Jahnvi's place. I did not want to leave any stone unturned to turn the tide in my favour, especially after the previous day's fiasco.

It was difficult locating Jahnvi's flat early in the morning but I managed to reach there on time.

I rung their doorbell three to four times when Aabhas finally answered the door and gave me a dirty and loathsome glare.

His mother was surprised to actually see me that early. "You actually managed to come, Arnab?"

Everyone seemed to have been disturbed.

"Who's it, Aabhas?" uncle asked from inside his room.

"Mom's teacher, Arnab," he replied sharply.

"Oh, okay. Let him in and you go back to your studies," he said groggily.

Aunty prepared tea and we hit the books promptly. She had nearly covered 75 per cent of the syllabus. Uncle's snores did not distract us either. We reached the exam centre a little early. I wished her luck and prepared myself for the next three anxious hours.

❖ ❖ ❖

"Why didn't you go out and talk to your Dad? It could have been a better option, Arnab," she said yawning. I had called Jahnvi to kill the three hours, but I failed to realise that she was still asleep.

"It would have given her a wrong impression, Jahnvi. Going out of the flat just to talk to my Dad at 11:30 in the night could have been risky."

"Let it be. Don't worry. My Mom doesn't react to such small things. She is cool. Now let me sleep," she said, sounding sleepy. I would have asked her to talk to me, but her yawns and lack of enthusiasm made me give in and let her go back to sleep.

Jobless, I passed three hours in the same restaurant and after eight cups of tea, a heavy breakfast and having listened to a number of bawdy songs, I reached the centre to pick up Jahnvi's Mom. Somewhere in my heart, I felt uncomfortable at acting like a teacher-cum-driver and taking so much pain for her Mom.

Had I done half as much for my own Mom, only God knows how happy she would have been. Instead to win over the hearts of my beloved's parents, I had to do something unusual much as it added to my discomfiture.

Her Mom seemed happy as she came out of centre. A smile was pasted on her face as she walked towards me.

Seeing her happiness, I promptly congratulated her!!

"I missed it by 5 marks, Arnab," she said elatedly.

"Oh, I am sorry. Seeing you happy and smiling, I presumed you had cleared the exams," I said, biting my tongue over my haste.

"I am happy because I missed it only by 5 marks. It is because of your assiduous attempts to tutor me that I could reach here. I think if only I had got one more hour to study, I would've definitely cleared my exams," she said happily. She seemed more than contented with her result. I did not see even a hint of regret in her eyes or voice. In fact, she was thankful to me and my feeble attempts at coaching her.

"Come on, aunty, no need for all this. Jahnvi too would've done the same for my Mom. In fact, somewhere I too felt good that I could help you, though I want you to clear the exam next time."

"Aah, that's a promise," she said, giving me a thumbs up.

She enquired about my family while we walked back to the car and in turn told me how special her children were to her and how much she missed them when they were away. We talked for the next half an hour till we reached their home.

"Come in, let's have lunch together," she suggested.

"Thanks, aunty, but I need to leave now. My brother will be waiting for me," I replied.

"Okay. Thanks, Arnab. Bye."

"Bye aunty, nice to have met you!!" I expressed my regrets at my Dad's call to me when I had been teaching her as I was rather embarrassed at the incident. I was not convinced by what Jahnvi had said to me, though deep down in the corner of my heart, I was confident that at least Jahnvi's Mom did not harbour any anger at me. This thought made me smile and very happily I drove back to home.

Chapter-9

Jahnvi's Birthday and Empty Bank Balance

I was pacing up and down, thinking hard as to how I could make Jahnvi's day very special. It was not just any other day; it was her birthday; my Jahnvi's birthday. 'Something special, something different, something exuberant, something out of the box, something that she would never have dreamt of is what I want to do', I thought, my mind coming up with all kinds of possibilities to please her.

While I was lost in my thoughts, my friend Rishi kept on calling out my name desperately. I missed it few times, but it caught my attention when he almost shrieked aloud, venting his guts out. "Arnab!!! Which world are you in? I have been calling; no shouting your name for what seems like ages now," Rishi shouted, sounding angry and frustrated. "Anyway, let's go out and play cricket at the net" he suggested.

"Huh? Yeah, wait for some time, bro!" I replied, completely lost in my thoughts.

"What has happened to you? What are you so serious about? God knows what?" Rishi asked.

"Yes, I am fine. It's Jahnvi's birthday and I am nowhere close to planning something," I sounded dejected. "I just don't want her birthday to be like any other birthday she might have had. I want to make it memorable; make it different, extravagant and yet personal," I said, sharing my plans with him.

Rishi was initially curious, then surprised, then speechless before turning blank. "Arnab, let's go out and play. Then we shall have a brainstorming session and see what unique idea we can come up with," Rishi suggested, sounding quite exasperated.

"Yes, Rishi! Better ideas come when we play and that's the only venue apart from the bogs!" I said jocularly, though frankly, I had always felt that whenever one tried to plan or decide on something special, the best place was the pot. It alone could offer peace and solitude to think. Spending a considerable amount of time there surely helps us to release all the dump of worries and other things before emerging with a fresh mind and new ideas. Now, I seriously don't know the logic behind this, but I have observed it happening with me quite often.

Anyway, we reached the nets and I chose to bowl to Rishi. "Arnab, I warn you, I am taking an aggressive stance," he said, glaring at me very hard.

"Take whatever stance you want. Had I been in your shoes, I would have chosen a defensive one and planned something exciting for Jahnvi."

Rishi moved ahead, hit the first shot real hard as the ball rolled off to the boundary. "So, what surprise you want to give to Jahnvi?"

"The only thing I know is that there is no birthday party," I replied in frustration as he hit my second ball for a six.

Rishi was now grinning at me.

"Stop it, you bastard!! I was actually trying to plan something for her birthday and you came in between saying, 'Let's play'. You fucker, you are now playing with my two balls. Fuck your ass," I swore hard because neither could I decide on something for Jahnvi nor could I concentrate on the game.

Rishi's brother came out on hearing us swear and began to laugh. Rishi joined in too. "Great, Arnab!! Your balls are safe in the nets," Rishi said, laughing loudly. And then he saw my face and came running to me. He put his hands on my shoulder and said, "Arnab. Don't worry, yaar, we will plan something out. Let me think," his voice softened down.

"Plan a trip to Goa. It would be a wonderful surprise; it would be romantic and beautiful. Can you manage that?" he asked excitedly.

"Hey, relax!! It needs a budget of at least Rs. 15,000. I don't even have half of that money. My savings of the last few months will not be enough," I said morosely.

"Okay, how much do you have? Now do not tell me you are planning a bash and have money only to finance a fifth-standard birthday party!" Rishi said angrily.

"I have about 5000," I replied proudly as this much I had manage to save with lots of trouble. It was a considerable sum especially for two people to have a good time in Indore – at least that is what I had thought.

"Arnab, the amount is not less, but we need more in order to make the occasion grand!!"

"Yeah I know!! It is not considerable if I want to plan a birthday befitting my girl."

Ultimately we discarded the plan for a party. So we had to start planning afresh as we were back to square one. So we began thinking, planning, discarding and rethinking.

"Let us do one thing. We will reserve a table for both of you in a 5-star hotel, maybe at the Sarovar Portico and plan an evening full of surprises. Nothing beats a candlelight dinner. It's great and most probably it will fall within your budget."

"Yet, how much will it come to?" I was still unsure and undecided.

"Close to Rs. 4,500, maybe. Anyway you need to book just a table and not the entire hotel. And this will be inclusive of everything – music, cake, dinner…so that should be good."

"Are you serious?" I could not believe my ears.

"No, I am not. Just screwing my head, asshole," Rishi joked. He hit the next ball just above my head and I fell down at the response.

"Okay, Arnab, I know you're tense about this whole surprise thing and want a solution. Let us at least go there and see what they have to offer us!! They would not charge us for that anyway."

I was now more sure of myself and threw a fulltoss at him. The bails flew off the stumps and Rishi stood there at the crease, looking shocked at what had just happened.

"I give you a brilliant idea and this is what you do?" Rishi asked in mock anger.

"It's wonderful, baby! And now you are coming with me to Sarovar to discuss everything. Let's go," I started off without waiting for his response.

❖ ❖ ❖

We parked the bike in the parking lot and made our way to the hotel. A huge hall full of diamond art on the walls and Arabian carpets greeted us as we entered the lobby. The receptionists glanced at us and smiled. The concierge and the doormen saluted us and the respect they showed us elevated us to a different level. All of a sudden we began to feel important.

"May I help you, sir?" asked one of the receptionists.

"We would like to meet the restaurant manager of portico with regard to arranging a private birthday party for a couple," I said.

"Sure, sir, her name is Shakti. She is the Event Manager and her office is right through that passage and next to the elevator," said the receptionist, pointing in the direction of the office.

I turned back towards the elevators when I heard Rishi ask directions to the washroom. Now why was he doing that? I wondered.

The Receptionist merely smiled and pointed the markers on the walls which would guide him to the washroom. He thanked her but made no effort to move. I wanted to get through with the planning and was not in the mood to flirt or watch him strut his stuff.

"You are Priya, right?" he asked, glancing at the name plate on the desk.

"No sir, Priya is on leave today. I am just filling in for her," the young lady replied calmly, still smiling.

I tried to control myself at his gaffe. We were just about to turn when the receptionist said, "I am Anvesha, Mr. Rishi."

We turned back instantly and Rishi seemed to be glued to the desk. He smiled at me and turned to Anvesha. He went and stood in front of her, keeping both his hands on the desk before asking excitedly, "Do you know me?"

"When did I say that?" Anvesha smiled and replied.

"But you just called me by my name! Do we know each other?"

"Oh, did I..?" she pretended to have forgotten.

Very soon Rishi started his guessing games and Anvesha too played along, enjoying the undivided attention from Rishi. She seemed completely in awe and smitten by him. He named a few more colleges and then finally, Anvesha uncovered the source.

"It's Cambridge International, Indore. Do you remember the girl you would always stand with during the assembly? The girl who always shared your bus seat? Yes it was some time ago...the tenth standard."

"Hey, hey Anvi...is that you?" Rishi went close to her. I was by now itching to move away and plan the party I wanted.

"You have changed a lot. I would not have recognised you at all."

"Oh, thanks!! And you're as hot as ever," Anvesha said, smiling shyly. I gestured to her that we would be back soon and pulled Rishi away from the desk. We headed towards the passage Anvesha had pointed out and turned towards the elevator.

Rishi was lost in thought. "Oh man, I had a huge crush on her. She was a year junior to me in school. I was the one who made her realise how sexy she was. How can I forget her?" he said with a long pause. "Did I fuck her?" Rishi suddenly blurted out. I stopped short in my tracks.

"What?"

"Really. I am not sure if I fucked her or one of her pals."

"You'll be accused of sexual harassment some day, lifelong imprisonment if this is the way you behave," I said.

"Shut up."

"You shut up," I said.

Our argument ended abruptly as we spotted Shakti Mehta's office. We knocked and entered the office. It was a very pleasant space. She seemed to be in her mid thirties and was seated at her desk. She glanced up as we walked in.

"Have a seat, please," she said, smiling.

"Thanks. We are actually looking for…."

"Yes, I just got a call from the reception saying you are wanting to organise a birthday party for just two people," she said, cutting me mid sentence, but not rudely.

I briefed her about my plans and revealed my budget too.

"As far as your ideas are concerned they are terrific and grand. And your budget is a little low for everything that you wish to have and do for the surprise. Perhaps, if you could increase your budget to Rs. 7500, we could easily accommodate all of this."

I quickly agreed in excitement and ended up making a cash advance of Rs. 3,500. Rishi was by this time glaring at me. How had I decided on this so fast? Where would the rest of money come from? I had not given a second thought to any of this. We left the place. "You know what? You are a big nut, Arnab. The nut who just got crushed by its own madness. Could you have not bargained a little? And where is the balance amount coming from? I did not know you had hidden financial sources!" he said sarcastically.

"You know what, Rishi?" I replied.

"What?" he said.

"I am not sure about where the balance is going to come from but I shall arrange the money. Of that I am certain," I said.

"Seriously? Well, love can make a person do anything. I just saw Mr. Arnab ruin his own life," Rishi said. "And now you may go to hell. I am going to meet my sexy lady at the reception," he said and went ahead excitedly. Unfortunately no one was present there.

"But where is she?" Rishi asked me.

"How would I know? I didn't fuck her," I replied.

"Shut up." His disappointment was pretty clearly seen in his face. We left and were saluted again. Just then Rishi spotted the Concierge holding a few boxes of visiting cards. He stopped the man and checked the boxes. It was his lucky day. Anvesha's card was also there. A smile spread across Rishi's face as he took out one card from the box. "Okay, Ramcharan, thank you. And please keep this," he said, handing over Rs. 100 to the surprised Concierge, who stared at Rishi but took the currency note gladly.

"Thank you, sir," he said and was off dancing and grinning like a mad man.

'Happiness can also make a person go mad,' I thought.

❖ ❖ ❖

Now that the hotel had been fixed, my basic worry was to organise the balance Rs. 4,000 for party. I had already paid up an advance and that was non-refundable!

"Dad, how are you today? Let's go to the temple," I said, racking my brains as to how best to tap this source.

"I am fine, but what's with you? Temple? With me? Is it the exam results or something else that' bothering you?" Dad asked, surprised by my behaviour.

"No, nothing like that, Dad. Just ..uh..." saying so, I shrugged.

"Oh okay, son. What do you want?" my Dad asked me point blank.

I asked him to loan me Rs. 1,500 for petrol and as pocket money. I then clarified why I needed this extra money, citing reasons like petrol, extra classes leading to the need for more food and juice outside and a couple of other things. It was not easy to give him excuses but somehow I managed to do so, almost fearing he would slap me any given moment.

"So, how much do you actually need?" he asked, perplexed.

"Rs. 2,000 in all. I won't ask for anything else, I promise."

"Young man in the midst of all this, do take time out to learn to manage your finances. It will certainly help you out in future."

I manage to more or less sort out the gap, but I was still Rs. 2,000 short. How would I arrange that now?

My eyes fell on some books which Dad had bought for me some time ago. I felt a bit uneasy doing so, but that feeling passed pretty fast. I headed with the books to the nearest bookstore. Therein lay the solution, just in front of me.

❖ ❖ ❖

A girl stood in front of the counter, asking for a book. "Uncle, do you have Shivani for OOPS and electronics and instrumentation?"

"I don't have it now. Please check the day after tomorrow," the man replied.

"Uncle I do not have the time. We have exams in three days," she answered.

"Hey, why don't you go to K. Bhushan? Tell him that I am Arnab's friend and he'll arrange it for you," I butted in.

"Hey, thanks. I'll do that," she said.

"My pleasure," I replied.

"Uncle, these are first year B. Com books. I want to sell urgently," I said.

"Go to K. Bhushan as he'll give you a good price for these," he said. "Harming my business, aren't you?" he raved looking at me. And I realised the mistake I had made.

"Oh, uncle, sorry. I just wanted to help her out as the engineering exams start from tomorrow. There is hardly any time left for preparation."

"Forget it! Tell me, what books do you have?" he asked.

"I have economics, accounts and auditing with me," I said.

He suddenly started searching for something.

"What are you looking for?" I asked.

"Calculator," he said.

"It's there, next to your bill book," I said, pointing to the shelf on the wall to his right.

He smiled at his own mistake and said after counting, "It's 400+155+125. Total Rs. 780."

I counted and saw the man had made a mistake. It was actually Rs. 680. I decided to point him his mistake and see his reaction at that. "Uncle count it once more please," I said.

"We are good at our maths. We are not useless like you guys," he said sarcastically.

"Still uncle, count it again."

He counted it again on his calculator now showed the figure Rs. 680. "Oh, I just don't know how I missed it," he said.

"It's alright, uncle." I took the amount from him and left.

❖ ❖ ❖

Once I had this amount in hand, I went to Rishi who was kind enough to help out with the balance and make my dreams come true.

❖ ❖ ❖

"Happy b'day to you, happy b'day to you, happy birthday, happy birthday, happy birthday to you!" I played the tune on the synthesiser and wished Jahnvi by singing along on it.

"Love you, Arnab!! Even this time you are the first person to wish me."

"And I'll always be so, my love," I said.

"But you wished me the same old way," she complained.

"I don't know much about musical instruments. Gift me a guitar on my birthday and I'll play it and sing next time," I said.

"That is so materialistic, Arnab. Can't you buy it yourself?"

"No dear, no chance. I won't get an increment so soon and without the pocket money that my parents give, I shall not be able to afford the pleasures of life," I replied.

"Arnab, I have a number of calls waiting. So I will call you back."

"Alright birthday girl! I shall see you tomorrow," I said and disconnected.

❖ ❖ ❖

She looked stunning in her white, knee-length sundress and I re-adjusted the black Louis Philippe blazer I had exclusively borrowed from Rishi to wear on her birthday.

"You are looking great, Arnab!" she said.

"Not as great as you. I am feeling like...like..."

She hugged me in excitement, saying, "I know I am looking beautiful. But I won't kiss you till you give me my gift."

"Then who gifted you this beautiful sundress?"

"Arnab, you did. But I know you well. There is more to this than this sundress," she said.

"Really?"

"Yes and there's no doubt in that."

"Let's not waste more time and go to Sarovar, Jahnvi."

"Arnab, It's my birthday treat, so I shall decide the venue and not you," she said.

"Sure Jahnvi, but some other time. Right now, Arush bhaiyya and Amita di are waiting for us."

"Then why didn't you tell me so before?"

"Because I wanted to give you a surprise and as usual, you don't have patience."

She smiled and I felt like hugging her.

"Shall we move?" she asked.

Due to a last minute booking, the portico had been fully reserved by someone else. Shakti Mehta had been kind enough to upgrade me to the terrace on the tenth floor and I was more than glad to be accommodated there – open air and candlelight dinner with your beloved! It could not have been more romantic.

I was still worried about the arrangements – worried if everything would go as planned. I smiled as the door of the terrace opened and Jahnvi looked at me questioningly.

"Why is no one here? Where are Arush bhaiyya and Amita didi?" she asked, stopping near the door. Then her eyes spied the lone table with candles, the streamers and balloons all over the terrace and the plates and cutlery arranged for two.

"Let's sit there. They will come for sure. I think we are early," I said. I was not sure if she could read my mind at that point, but she played along.

"Happy birthday to you, happy b'day to you, happy b'day happy b'day. Happy b'day to you..." and the Sarovar Italian Froza 'Vacanza 94' serenaded her to the accompaniment of guitars and banjo.

"Is that for me??" she asked as the song ended.

I didn't respond, instead I led her to the terrace's greenroom and as we opened the doors, the lights came on and ribbons and streamers were flung from all directions with "happy b'day, Jahnvi" written on the glass panes.

Shakti Mehta was at hand with her staff to oversee the things and she wished Jahnvi too.

"Oh, thank you so much. I knew there was something on, but I never knew it could be this special, Arnab! You're unbelievable and so romantic. You are always beyond my expectations. I love you. I so, so, so love you," she shrieked in excitement and kissed me.

I was overwhelmed. I had surpassed her expectations and made her extremely happy and joyous. The serenading by the Italian quartet went on for quite some time. After that they left us to ourselves. The cake arrived and her eyes became wet on seeing the amount of thought that had gone into planning this. A dark chocolate cream 'Titanic' ship cake with a cute picture of her on the deck made her smile. Once the cake had been cut, the Italian quartet was back and they sang some slow and fast numbers to which Jahnvi and I danced, as no one was watching us. As if it was just the two of us. Nothing existed, not even the music. It was just sound to our ears and we were swaying to it.

We were still dancing, lost in each other when suddenly the door of the terrace opened wide and what followed surprised Jahnvi all the more. She was too overwhelmed and excited. Everything that she saw made her dance and shriek with joy and love – lots of love. A bouquet of flowers came up, then came a vintage pocket watch, silver coloured and round-shaped with a button to open its upper part and a silver-coloured pendant attached to it, making the watch a beauty to behold. Then arrived the teddy bear, a pair of Ray Ban sunglasses, a sketch of the two of us and the very first picture we had clicked of us together in a silver frame.

"Arnab, no one has ever done anything close to this ever before. Thank you so much for everything. I don't know if I can ever match the amount of love you shower on me. I am so lucky to have you as my lover." Saying so, she buried herself deep in my arms and all I could do was to stand there, holding her securely, caressing her back and kissing her forehead. What she said moved me from within. How I wished I could even be verbal with what I felt for her, but I knew that she knew I loved her insanely and that she meant the world to me.

In all this humdrum of activity, dinner was forgotten. No sooner did we almost come out of the romantic trance than we placed the order, still completely unaware of what were we ordering. Dinner seemed trivial and unimportant to the upsurge of our feelings and depth of our emotions, which were vast and never ending like a sea.

It had been a beautiful evening and every penny spent seemed too less in comparison to the happiness my ladylove felt. We got a picture mug from the 'Sarovar' portico staff with a picture of the two of us dancing together.

Jahnvi did not ask me about how much all this could have cost or even where the money had come from. She assumed it must have been financed through my savings or earnings.

When we were in the elevator, we hugged and kissed each other passionately. We grabbed each other and could not let go of either. If given a choice, I would have never let her go, but held her forever.

Finally we did reach the basement and were walking towards the car when suddenly Jahnvi stopped, clutching my arms and looking at me intently. Suddenly she hugged me tight and kissed me. After we parted, I saw her wet eyes. I was about to ask her as to what had happened when she shushed me and I did not probe, realising she was overcome with emotions. While driving her back, I held her hand throughout the journey. The drive back home was silent, but even that silence in itself spoke so much that words could have never conveyed.

After dropping her home, I drove home, recalling my conversation with Dad about needing more money and how he had said I should learn to manage money better. The next day however, he surprised me when he said that he had overheard me and Rishi plan a party for Jahnvi.

"Don't you want money for that?" he asked. I nearly fell off my chair. I was so shocked at it that I could not respond for a couple of minutes. "It's fine if you don't want it," He continued.

"No, Dad, I want it. I want it badly," I said too quickly, almost snatching the money from him. I desperately needed Rs. 3,000 that he was offering. "Thanks, Dad," I said and touched his feet.

Dad smiled, blessed me and said, "Now do well in your studies too. Jahnvi is a pretty girl and I hope you two stay together forever and I also hope that this is not just any other affair for you like what we see around us these days."

"I won't let you down, Dad."

"I see a future for you with her, so you'd better not."

I was so relieved when Dad spoke to me that way. I was happy and so was he. The tension of where I could get the extra money from was finally off me.

Driving back home, I smiled to myself. Dad was happy. Jahnvi was happy. And that summed up to making me very happy. To move pune for some years and further education was next on cards for us now.

Chapter-10

Mission Pune Accomplished

Beep...beep...beep...beep...

Aditi had been honking the car's horn for a couple of minutes because she had reached my apartment and not seen me. "Are you ready?" she asked when she saw me standing at the balcony.

"Yes, wait. I am coming."

"Hurry up."

I grabbed my bag and ran to the main gate where Aditi was busy trying to convince my Mom that it was her birthday and she was taking me to her farmhouse where she had organised a party for all her close friends. Mom wished her and we drove off at jet speed the very next minute.

From the moment the car started, none of us exchanged a word. I was hopelessly staring out of the car window, thinking about nothing and everything, whereas Aditi was time and again gazing at me and keeping track of the road ahead. She did try to initiate the conversation a couple of times, but I guess, seeing my indifference towards everything around me, she gave up. But she could help not saying something. "Your Mom is cool. She didn't ask too many questions. She just asked when I'll drop you back," Aditi casually stated.

"Hmmm...,"my reply was almost inaudible.

"Come on, Arnab, don't sound so hopeless. You're a fighter. You'll surely win this one too. Bad times just don't stay forever with brave souls," Aditi said, trying her best to make me feel good and make me see the positive side.

"Are you reading too much of philosophy or has the spiritual-cum-motivational urge bitten you," I asked out of irritation. I did not want to be consoled by anyone. I knew she meant good for me, but still... "It's already been two years Aditi and I don't know how I am going to respond or react," I said, sounding helpless.

"Despite what happened, there have also been some good things in the past two years; times that you can cherish for life. How can you forget that?" Aditi's attitude was always positive and she has been very encouraging.

"Oh, they never were," I said gloomily.

"Or it is it that you just don't want to consider it?" her counter question did leave me fazed.

I didn't reply.

"Anyway, forget it. Just check the tickets and let's talk of something else; something good. How about your time in Pune? You consider it the best time of your life, don't you?"

"Remembering the good times you've lived, often hurts you during bad times," I replied. Saying this, I recollected a few beautiful chapters of my life again.

❖ ❖ ❖

Swapnil sir called me into his cabin after my interview with the OUTLOOK INDIA group. "You've so far lived up to our expectations, Arnab. It's now time to work on these expectations. The company's national head is visibly impressed with your performance and has decided to select you for a six-month internship," he said, smiling big. He seemed so happy and contented.

"That's great sir. I never ever in my dreams expected this."

"Aren't you happy?" he asked, not seeing the glint in my eyes.

"No sir, I definitely am. This is a moment of mixed emotions for me as I shall be leaving Indore for the first time as I have got selected for what I had always dreamt of. It's all happened so suddenly. I am overwhelmed," I said. I had received the offer letter for the internship that I so badly wanted, but felt sad at the thought of having to leave my parents, my friends, my life here at Indore.

"You still have one month to leave and this internship will certainly give you an edge in terms of choosing a college for your PG. You're getting a good start, my boy; a good brand, a decent pay as an intern and exposure that will help you in future. This experience will count later at the professional level. Besides, you are going to a metro city where life would be different."

"Sure sir," I said and shook hands with him.

"You've always wanted to move out, isn't it? Pune is a beautiful place to stay. Destiny has knocked on your door and is giving you an opportunity to live your life, your dreams. Go grab it. We'll miss you here."

I looked at Swapnil sir and realised how firm his conviction was in me. I had worked hard in achieving my dreams; performed well and was on my way to fulfil them. The first hurdle was to reach Pune, which Jahnvi and I had cleared that. We both had managed to find something of our interest in the same city - to live together in the same city, 600 kms away from home and family and every other trouble.

I reached Apollo Square CCD and saw Jahnvi waiting for me. "Sorry baby, I couldn't answer your call as I was with Swapnil sir," I said as I hugged her.

"Blazer and all, huh!?" she said, raising an eyebrow. Hundreds of questions danced in her head.

"It is a sad one," I replied, pointing at the blazer.

"Okay, then. You tell me what's the occasion?" she said, making a face so typical of herself.

I waved the offer letter in front of her. She grabbed the letter from my hand and enthusiastically started reading it. "Is this for real?" she questioned, her eyes wide with disbelief.

"No, I have recently started making fake certificates and fooling my girlfriend these days," I mocked fake anger. "Obviously, they are for real! Why? Do you doubt my intentions or potential?" I asked, a little disappointed.

"Now, now, I never said I doubted your intentions and potential. But it's awesome, Arnab. I can't believe it. It's just been a week since we were planning about Pune and here you are, telling me that we are going." She was so glad and happy; her eyes were glistening with joy.

"Come on, give me a hug," I pulled her towards me.

"Okay now, let's first make a plan for Pune since there is a lot that needs to be looked after – your college, accommodation and a few other things."

"Yeah, but how shall we go and when?"

"The sooner, the better. How about this weekend? I have already posted queries on pagalguy.com and various other online query sites. I am getting good responses too. I'll make a list of the places to visit and then there's Rishi too in Pune now. We can count on him to help us with the rest of the things."

"Let's get the reservation done first or else we'll end up with no tickets, like the previous time."

"We'll fly to Pune and take back the last flight, the same night," Jahnvi suggested.

"We'll need a lot of money; at least Rs.15000 and we don't have it."

"Don't worry about that. I will be getting a cheque today from the engineering college where we performed. It will be enough for our plan."

June 4th;

Time 6:30

Actual plan: We are still in Indore

For her parents in Volvo with Shruti (her college friend)

June 5th Actual Plan, 6 a.m: Board the flight to Pune

For her parents: They are in a dream world, so nobody will call Jahnvi.

7:00 a.m.

Actual Plan: We'll reach Pune Airport and Rishi along with his girlfriend Resha will come along to pick us up.

For her parents: Reached Pune, going to friend's hostel.

10:00 a.m.

Actual Plan: We'll have breakfast with Rishi and Resha.

For her parents: This was true and there was nothing to hide except for the fact that Rishi and I were with her.

12 p.m.

Actual plan: Hunt for a college begins with DY Patil.

For her parents: They will be busy with their jobs from 10 a.m. to 6 p.m., which lessened our tension.

2 p.m.

KVP PUNE and Suryadatta college to take Admission forms for Jahnvi.

3 p.m.

Resha will help Jahnvi book a room in the same hostel.

4 p.m.

Exploring Pune.

6 p.m.

Submit my acceptance form to Outlook India.

For her parents: Completed all formalities and also booked a room in the hostel of Shruti too. Just boarded the bus for Indore.

9 p.m.

We'll take a flight to Indore after dinner.

Parents: They think their daughter is still in Volvo.

At times, when we were in Pune, during a call, when her parents asked Jahnvi to give the phone to her friend, it was either Resha who was with us the whole day or Aditi in a conference çall that saved our lives. Technological advancements were still unknown to the older generation. They never could figure out our 'Plan Pune' and we heaved a sigh of relief after a long day.

After a week full of emotional drama at home, I finally started my journey from Indore to Pune, leaving behind the beautiful moments I had spent with my family, friends at Renaissance and of course, Jahnvi. I had never before felt so attached to Indore. The traffic of Indore was now suddenly not as frustrating as it used to be. The typical attitude of people around me was now not an issue. Everything had changed in and around me in my last week at Indore and so did my perspective to look at things and people's behaviour towards me. All of a sudden, everybody had certain respect when they spoke to me. My arguments and fights with my elder brother now seemed silly. My Mom's constant jabbering and involvement no longer irritated me but was sweet which I could hear all my life. My friends were the lifelines I was leaving behind.

I reached the station and looked at my ticket, Indore-Pune Express, Berth No. 28, lower berth. I found my seat and arranged my luggage.

"Hey baby, tomorrow shall be your first day away from home. I am a little worried about you, though I know you will manage everything very well. Take all the necessary things along with you, like your towel, brush, charger and headphones. Take the common medicines too. Don't talk to strangers. Eat well and make good friends. I'll try my best to come there soon. Work well. I am missing you already. Love you.

P.S. Stay away from the bitches out there in Pune!"

I read Jahnvi's message again and again, smiling to myself. 'I am missing my family very much. Please come soon,' I messaged her.

"Welcome to my world, honey!" she replied.

I went to the washroom and cried like a child, not only for Jahnvi, but also for my family and my hometown that I was leaving behind for the first time.

I tried my best to kill time during the journey. I tried conversing with the girl sitting next to me and on Seat Number 30; also with the uncle from the middle berth and also with other two guys in the other berths, but it seemed like everybody present there wanted to catch up on their lost sleep. Since I was bored to the hilt, I sat down to analyse the attitude of people from different classes and realised that this was how it went: First Class AC: People were too dignified to talk to each other or even acknowledge the other's presence. Two Tier AC: People had an attitude problem and therefore never talked much beyond what was asked and even then, their responses were equal to reactions. Three Tier AC: People tried to talk and talked but would suddenly stop talking for no reason. Sleeper Class: They were like a mobile encyclopaedia, ready to discuss anything and everything under the sun. Everybody's business was their business. They were real blabbermouths. I belonged to this category, especially with respect to the talking aspect, but unfortunately, I was not there. I was stuck in the middle of a desert where nobody other than the T.T.E. was interested in talking to me. My luck was not in my favour.

'I should sleep now,' I thought and closed my eyes shut. I connected my headphones and started listening to music. I was grateful to Jahnvi for reminding me to take this 'magical' connector, called headphones. It surely could take you to your own dream world without needing anyone's company. I don't know when I dozed off. Suddenly I felt someone poking me. I ignored it once but when I was poked again, angrily, I opened my eyes and saw my co-passenger, the boy on Seat No. 30 standing in front of me with both his hands on his butts.

"Are you planning to go back in the same train?" he asked.

I was confused. Was I to be angry that he had woken me up or be happy that he had finally chosen to talk to me? I decided to be neutral. "Why? What's happened?" I asked.

"It's the last stop, Pune," he announced condescendingly and picking up his luggage, left.

"Oh! We have reached? Thanks for waking me up. This is my first visit here," I said excitedly to his retreating back.

"You are welcome. Bye," he called out before adding, "Welcome to Pune."

I disembarked from the train and could already feel the difference between Indore and Pune. The climate was cooler, roads better, youth trendier and greenery all around. This meant an amazing start, I thought. I called Rishi, who recently shifted to Pune and was already outside, waiting. He came and hugged me tight and I loved him for making me feel at home instantly. He took me to Cumsum, Pune's 24×7 Café for breakfast. After breakfast, we left for his room in his car.

"Finally, you're here. Everything you planned is falling in place," Rishi said, while driving.

"Yes, so far it has, from my side at least. Let's see how things work out for Jahnvi," I replied.

"Don't worry, everything will be fine. You guys will definitely enjoy it here. This is a dream city. It has its own charm," Rishi said, beaming. I could see he was already a part of this city.

Pune was quite different from Indore; it had its own uniqueness. The population consisted mainly of young and energetic people, coming mostly from other cities, states and countries to make their career, to work and earn a living.

My day began with jogging at the BMCC College ground, followed by checking offline messages at a cybercafé, having breakfast at 'Vaishali,' lunch at I.L.S. mess and doing my internship with the Outlook media group till evening. Then it was dinner, again at I.L.S. mess and a long chat with my family, before I could finally call it a day. But one thing that had a permanent occupancy in my mind was Jahnvi and anything I would do to get her off my mind would not succeed for more than a few minutes.

I could explore almost all the peripheries in and around Pune in a week's time, including Lonavla, Khandala, Pune-Bangalore highway, Durga Coffee House, Koregaon Park, Osho Ashram, German Bakery, F.C. Road among others. It was more than a week since I had arrived in Pune but there had been no news from Jahnvi; no offline messages either. Shankar, the cyber cafe guy, too had stopped taking money, saying, "It's okay, Arnab bhaiyya. You check for less than 30 seconds. You don't need to pay anything," and I stopped arguing any further.

I curtailed my visits to the cyber café as I was growing mad day by day. Despite sharing, what I felt was a healthy relationship for the last one year, I started doubting Jahnvi's intentions. I felt as if she had left me alone in the middle of nothing. What would I do without her in the next six months? She was the sole reason for my being in Pune. All kinds of questions clouded my mind.

Nobody was in the flat. It was the third day in a row that I hadn't been to office nor had I received any of their calls. Absolutely 'nothing' was what I had done in the last few days. I did not go for my regular jogging sessions. I would eat once in two days. My body was in a deplorable state. I would sleep all the time and not take a bath. The only time I would get up from my bed was to relieve myself. My day was spent doing nothing; it was as if I had become modern-day 'Devdas'. Everything around me, including myself had become useless, hopeless.

Then suddenly one day, I got a call from Jahnvi. I could feel my heart racing at jet speed. I picked up the phone with trembling hands, like a patient of Alzheimer's. So excited was I to hear her voice again, but all I heard from the other end was a mournful cry. It was certainly not the best of ways to break the silence of twenty-one long days.

"What has happened Jahnvi? Are you alright?" I asked. The tension was apparent in my voice.

The next ten minutes seemed never ending for she did not utter a single word. She kept on crying like a baby and the reason was still a mystery to me. "Would you please tell me what happened? Is everything alright?" I asked again.

She continued to be in what I called 'the moods of the great Mona Lisa.'

"We have been caught. Aabhas found out about our Pune plan and he's very angry with me. He is threatening to leak it out to my parents. I am worried, Arnab. Please do something," she began to sob more loudly.

I was stunned. I saw everything crashing right before my eyes. This news scared the hell out of me. I saw my world come crashing down in front of my eyes, but I did not want to add to Jahnvi's worries and fear. So I tried to sound calm and composed. I gathered my wits and said, "Relax Jahnvi. No matter how difficult it sounds, there has to be a way out. Tell me how did it all happen?"

"I don't know. He said that he received an anonymous mail saying that we went to Pune together for two days in a Volvo," Jahnvi said, still sobbing uncontrollably. "And guess what? He wants to talk to you now," she continued.

"And what did you say?" I asked.

"I said, 'Okay.' I had no other choice. I have given him your number. He may call you any time," she said. Her words struck me like a thunderbolt.

"Give me his number. Let me see how and what I can do," I said. My brain had already started ticking on what my next step I could take.

"Okay, here you are. Take down the number, but please do not lose your cool if you want to reduce our problems," she replied.

"Don't worry. Everything will be fine. You take care of yourself. Trust me," I consoled her.

"I do. Now I have to hang up. Love you."

"Love you too. Bye."

❖ ❖ ❖

"What happened?" Rishi asked when he saw me looking worried.

"Jahnvi called. I am going to the terrace," I said and asked him to go back to sleep.

"Any problem?"

"Yes, a major one. I'll tell you later," I said and climbed the ladder to go to the terrace. Would this be the right time to call him or would it be better to wait till tomorrow, I debated!

I tried to put myself into Aabhas's shoes and began to think what would be going on in his mind. 'Is my sister going around with this guy? Is he making fake promises? What kind of intentions does he harbour?' All these questions were enough to make me get up and beat up the culprit mercilessly. Given a chance, he would definitely throttle me, I thought. It had to be now or never. I decided to call him right away. I rehearsed the script before making my bold move. I focused on all the alternatives which could make a difference to the situation.

Tring…tring...disconnected... tring…tring...disconnected. This happened for the next ten minutes before he finally answered, "Hello?" I heard a grumpy voice at the other end.

"Hi Aabhas! It's me, Arnab, Jahnvi's friend," I said. "She told me that you wanted to talk to me," I added with a sinking heart. He disconnected the call even before I could ask something further or say something. That was something I had not expected nor thought about.

What should I make out of this? I thought. Will he call back? Will he never let Jahnvi come to Pune? Will he tell his parents and put an end to our relationship? Anxiety over the situation made me lose sleep for the night.

I never gave up but called Aabhas numerous times thereafter. He would disconnect sometimes or never respond most of the times. I messaged him to call me back when free. I messaged Jahnvi about the uneasiness I was going through.

She replied, 'Try calling again tomorrow. I trust you.'

The next morning I began the ritual of calling Aabhas from seven in the morning. I had no choice. After numerous unanswered calls, he finally messaged me: 'I am in class. I'll call you at three in the afternoon. Stop irritating me now.'

I didn't reply and waited for the said time. The clock struck three but he didn't call. I called him instead and he answered this time. "Yeah, tell me what is it?" asked Aabhas.

"It was you who was supposed to call me. Why are you not answering any of my calls?" I asked.

"What's going on between you and Jahnvi?" he asked me, completely ignoring my previous statement.

"Nothing; we are good friends."

"Then why did you guys go to Pune together for two days?"

"We never did. Who told you so?"

"An anonymous mail."

"And you trust that more than your sister, whom you have known since the last twenty years? By the way, how does this anonymous person know me?" I was more than keen to know who that guy/girl was who was trying to break my relationship with Jahnvi.

"Why would anyone send me a hoax mail? Everybody has noticed you both spending hours together at Apollo Square CCD."

"Listen Aabhas, first of all it's none of my business to sort the problem out between you and your sister. Secondly, why I called you is because Jahnvi is a good friend and she asked me to do so. I would say it's better to trust somebody you know rather than anonymous e-mails. I am a reasonably decent guy. It's just not in my nature to lie and run away for a couple of days to any place without intimating my parents. In fact, you shouldn't have asked that question. Your parents know me too well. I often talk to them. I wouldn't do anything to hurt anybody's sentiments," I clarified.

"Anyway, you're sure that you guys are not going around?" he asked.

I wished I could tell him exactly what it was, but that would lead him to doubt my intentions. It was not the right time. Maybe sometime later, I thought.

"Yes, I am sure. You shall be the first one to know if something like that happens. I promise."

"And I wish I don't hear from you any more henceforth. Bye!" he said and disconnected the call.

I narrated the whole conversation to Jahnvi. She sounded better than the previous night. "I don't think he should create any problems now. Thanks for handling it so well."

"You just take care of yourself. You're still not sounding good. Take good rest. Relax and come to Pune soon. Love you."

"I will. Love you too. I'll call you as soon as I can. Bye."

I narrated everything to Rishi later, but he didn't react much. To him it was one of the many goof ups in my life.

❖ ❖ ❖

Days passed and I resumed going to office. My daily routine began as usual, though I never heard from Jahnvi again after that day. But it was not as worrisome, since this had become common now. I confirmed her admission in college. It was to begin twenty days from hence. I was excited about being together again.

Then one night my cell phone buzzed and it was enough to make me sleepless and restless. 'Don't call.'

Sender: Jahnvi's Dad

(Number)

Received:

01:45 a.m.

03/06/2008

This message made me hold back my nerves again. It raised umpteen unrealistic queries in my mind. It was like a calamity that had hit me and I turned numb again. Why would she send me a message like this from her Dad's number and that too in the middle of the night? There was a fair possibility that Aabhas had told his parents about us. I imagined her locked up in her room after a heated argument with her parents following lots of melodrama. She must have taken a chance and sent a message from her father's number in his absence.

Now that they knew everything about us, they would not waste any time in finding a groom for their daughter. I'd be alone once again. What could I do now? Should I ask Mom to call her parents? Should I threaten Aabhas? Should I go to her house and try some heroics to impress them? Or should I wait for her to call me?

I decided to wait for Jahnvi's call; for a few days at least. Once again I retreated into my shell. Once again there were no jogging sessions. I lost my appetite. Nights became longer. I would be in bed till nine in the morning. I would go late to office. My appearance became more sloppy and dull. I would check my mobile every few minutes, hopelessly hoping at least a message from Jahnvi.

It was disheartening to simply see the Airtel network showing the coverage area and info display. No missed calls. No 'smses'; no offline messages. Every time my mobile buzzed, I would pray it to be from Jahnvi, but what I would receive was either recharge plans or some forwarded messages from somebody. That made matters even worse for me. The wait was too long and frustrating. I visited KNP and Osho Ashram to kill time.

Swapnil sir called me to check how things were and to congratulate me on my decent performance in the first month. He told me how much Renaissance and 'Indore Indira had missed me in the last performance of the 'Renaissance Rooh'. I so wanted to talk my heart out to him, but I held back and let the tears flow only when I was alone. Rishi and Piyush (My Roommates) began to get worried on seeing my condition. They took me to Sinhgad and Lonavla over the following weekends. Resha introduced me to the sexiest of her friends, yet that could not distract me for long. They made all possible attempts to cheer me up and put some life into me. Soon, even they gave up. It was a hopeless situation. I was hopeless! My love life was hopeless! All the consoling made me go more mad and pessimistic.

"Get well soon. Nothing is irreparable in this world," Piyush said as he left for college.

I realised how difficult I was making life for myself as well as for others. There was a volley of questions I wanted to hurl at Jahnvi, but I could not and that made my situation worse. I was upset. All I wanted to do was to go back to her and make one more attempt to figure things out. Yes, I would go to her house, convince her parents and take her to Pune with me. The worst that could possibly happen was that they'd hit me or get me arrested. Even that would be better than dying out of guilt for not talking to her, one last time. I packed my bags. Without any second thoughts I headed for Ujjain, for Jahnvi's home. I boarded the 'Pune-Indore Express', arranged my luggage and went off to sleep. Suddenly, I was awakened by a call.

"Hello."

"Hello, who is this?"

"Are you nuts? Jahnvi here, stupid. Sleeping during daytime?"

I couldn't believe my ears. It took me some time for this to sink in – the joy, or the shock, to hear her voice so unexpectedly silenced me and my senses went numb. "Where the hell have you been, Jahnvi? What had happened? Why did your brother reveal the Pune incident to your parents after all went well? Anyway, don't you worry. I am coming to your place to settle things. You just don't worry." I was worried she might disconnect the call at any moment and therefore lost no time in speaking out my mind to her.

I said it all in one breath and checked whether the call was still on. Time was flying. I was relieved to see that the call was still on.

"What the hell are you talking about?" Jahnvi asked with confusion.

"About what happened during the last few days, because of which you didn't call me. Why are you so surprised?"

"Why shouldn't I be surprised? Your presumptions are hilarious?

"Jahnvi, don't kid me. Didn't you send me a message that night from your Dad's number saying, 'Don't call'."

"Yes, I did, but that didn't mean that things conspired the way you thought."

"What else did it mean when you suddenly messaged me from your Dad's mobile? Don't tell me now that you weren't locked up in a room by your parents after being hit hard, after Aabhas told them everything?" I knew I was talking too much, but I had been scared for so long and this sudden call from Jahnvi, excited me besides numbing my senses. So it made me indulge in insensate conversation.

"Certainly not. They are not jailors. They have never hit me and they never will. Neither has Aabhas told them anything. He just warned me to steer clear of you; nothing else. You're sounding crazy, Arnab. I didn't know you would interpret that message this way. Didn't you get any of the previous messages of mine?"

"Did you send any?" I asked, perplexed.

"Yes, quite a few times from my Dad's number, telling you that the internet connection was unavailable and the landline at home was not working, because the telephone wires had got accidentally cut. But you never responded."

"I don't understand. Why didn't you message me from your mobile?"

"Because it got washed with the clothes about twenty days back. Hey, but you were supposed to know about it."

"How would I know unless you tell me? I don't see visions, Jahnvi."

"I had messaged you that too, Arnab. I couldn't call you because my cousin had been here since last month. I wonder why you didn't get any of my messages other than the one saying, 'Don't call'."

"Don't know. Maybe your Dad needs to change the service provider," I said in utter frustration for not having received her previous messages.

"But what was the need to send that message? I wasn't going to call you, anyway." I further added before Jahnvi could respond.

"I presumed that after reading all the messages, you might call back. That's why I messaged you not to call."

"And as luck would have it, only that message reached me, as if to make my condition even more critical!"

"You're just a volcano of hypertension, waiting to erupt any moment. Why can't you think simply that everything would be well and that I would be coming to Pune soon?"

Jahnvi's words brought back life into me and my heartbeats became more regulated than what they had been for a week now. I so felt like arguing with her, listing out the better alternatives she could have tried to keep me informed, such as calling from a PCO, checking the delivery reports, sending me offline messages from a cyber café, but I held back. This was not the right time. I was extremely happy to hear her sweet voice. I was relieved and breathing normally. Everybody around saw me smiling for the first time in the day. They too smiled back. All changed in a matter of few seconds. The sun began to shine again for me. Flowers were blooming again. I was in love again and with Jahnvi.

"And what all were you saying? You are coming to my place to settle things?"

"I am on my way to Ujjain. I will be joining you tomorrow for breakfast."

"Don't tell me!" she screamed in terror.

"You can check my tickets online. The train has just reached Mumbai."

"You've gone mad. You're not coming now," her voice became louder and she seemed to be shrieking with every sentence.

"I am coming."

"No, you're not."

"Okay, not this time. But if you ever happen to do something this silly, be sure I am coming to your place and spending the whole day with you, with your parents around and Aabhas around," I laughed loudly and I heard her chuckle at this. I was relieved to see her happy again.

"It won't happen again. They'll agree to see you. Mom was just a little disappointed because of your lie."

"Oh no, she still remembers it? This is certainly not good for my image," I laughed after a long time.

"Not really. I made her understand your point of view. In fact, she quite likes you."

"I hope so too."

"Don't worry. And now, just extend your route till Indore and surprise your parents by spending a beautiful weekend with them."

"Yes, that's the only alternative I have now."

"And don't worry even if you don't hear from me for a few days. Don't sweat and make a big fuss out of everything. I am with you and will always be, no matter what happens. You're my sweetheart. Always smile because you look your best when you do so. Mom is expected any time, so I must hang up now. Love you," she said all in one breath.

"Love you too. Bye."

❖ ❖ ❖

Mom and Dad were pleasantly surprised to see me arrive unannounced and I enjoyed the look on their faces. Tears started rolling down Mom's cheeks and she hugged me as if to never let go, ever. Those three days with my family were seemingly refreshing and loving. I had never enjoyed life as much as I did in those three days. We all were happy being together and I was more than joyous because I now knew that Jahnvi was still with me and will always be there. When it was time for me to depart from Indore, we hugged each other. There were emotional moments, as I left. Tears rolled down once again. I reached Pune after a refreshing three days at home.

My problems never seemed to end, but nothing was new to me. I had better ways of handling things.

"Hey Arnab, I am from KVP Institute, Pune and this call is regarding Jahnvi's admission status," a female voice said.

"Yes, please go ahead."

"25th is the last date for submitting the documents. Please ask her to do it soon, or else her admission will be cancelled."

"Why didn't you inform earlier?" I asked.

"We e-mailed her a number of times and tried calling her too. There was no response."

"Oh, yes, there is some problem with the internet connectivity at her place."

"I understand. Kindly inform her as soon as possible since there are only four days to go. Ask her to courier the documents to our postal address."

"Yes sure. I'll certainly do that."

I asked Aditi to request Jahnvi's Dad to convey the information to Jahnvi's home, pretending to be the administration department officer of KVP Institute, Pune.

She did the same and Jahnvi sent the documents through the deluxe service of a local courier, named 'Samay Swaroop'. The service of the group was worse than its name. The courier did not reach the institute till the morning of the last day, even after opting for the deluxe service.

"Mr. Arnab, today is last day to receive the documents. If we don't get them before 5 p.m., we will have to cancel her admission and give preference to somebody from the wait-listed candidates," said the lady from the administration department of KVP Institute.

"But she has couriered it to you already. Haven't you received it?"

"No. Please check with their local office in Pune."

I wondered if there was any. Nevertheless, I made numerous attempts to search for a local office of 'Samay Swaroop' in Pune, on the internet. I luckily got an Ujjain number. I called them up and took the number of their distributor in Pune.

"Do you have any parcel sent by Jahnvi Sharma, addressed to 'KVP Institute', Tilak Road?" I asked the person on the line, hoping for a positive response.

"Yes, we do. Who are you?"

"I am her friend. The courier is urgent and I am coming there to collect it."

"Okay, come to our office. We are near the Bharti Vidyapeeth city office."

I reached the place and asked for the parcel. He started questioning me for security reasons. I hesitantly replied and tried to convince him that I had no intentions of misusing the parcel. He then proceeded to call the number written at the bottom left of the parcel, to get the approval.

"Hello. There's a guy who has come here to collect the courier on behalf of KVP Institute. He says it's urgent," I heard him say on the phone.

I watched the number he had dialled, carefully. Oh no! It was Jahnvi's Mom's number.

"She wants to talk to you," he said to me, handing over the phone to me.

What the hell? She'll easily identify my voice. We had spoken over the phone a number of times before. I tried to change my accent and my voice as far as possible, lest my identity got revealed.

When her Mom asked who I was, I replied, "I am from KVP Institute, ma'am. It was urgent, so I personally came here to collect the documents. Today is the last day for Ms. Jahnvi to submit her documents. if they are not submitted by today evening before 5, then it may lead to cancellation of her admission, without a fee refund." I made matters sound as bad as possible to her.

"Oh, you don't worry. I'll ask him to hand it over to you. Thanks for coming all the way and taking so much trouble." Her words reminded me of an earlier incident when she had thanked me the same way.

Luckily I didn't get caught. I was able to submit the documents on time. Jahnvi got her admission and I hoped that things would run smoother henceforth. It was party time. I had just emerged victorious in one of the battles. The occasion called for a table full of booze bottles and snacks, the cool breeze heralding autumn, Bryan Adams' evergreen numbers playing in the background. It was an awesome night on which we were celebrating the success of 'Mission Pune'.

Rishi, Piyush and Resha joined me for the big night and we got drunk as though there was no tomorrow. It all started and ended in the best possible way. We spoke our hearts out that day over thirteen bottles of beer, two bottles of vodka and wine. It was later that I realised that I was completely lost my senses. I was talking whatever came to my mind. Everybody was laughing at the cost of my openness and frankness. The drinks were playing their trick. We ended up paying a steep bill of Rs. 3,000. I sponsored half of it.

Jahnvi arrived in Pune with her Dad in a week's time. Resha made it easier for us as she personally took care of all the arrangements that were to be made while her Dad was around. Jahnvi got her hostel accommodation, visited her college and paid the fees. They fixed up a mess too and at the same place where Resha went. Resha acted her part well and was successful in being obedient that day and Jahnvi's Dad was visibly impressed. I maintained a safe distance of 200 metres. After completing all the formalities, Jahnvi's Dad took the flight back to Indore from Pune the same evening. Jahnvi shed a few tears of mixed emotions.

No sooner did her Dad leave that I ran to meet her. She was standing near the British library and looking as cute as she always did. Her cheeks were a vibrant strawberry pink. Her eyes were red after shedding tears on her Dad's departure, but were still shining bright, looking for the love they had missed over the last month. Seeing her stand with her hands crossed on her chest and her lips smiling big was like a dream come true. All the hurdles were over. We had won after having surpassed so many obstacles. Every step was getting me closer to her and I was confused as to whether to kiss her or just hug her. She looked like she had gained some weight. She pounced on me with excitement and held me like a little baby. Everybody around was wondering what was happening? I could feel her weight. Earlier, I could easily hold her, but now it seemed I couldn't do so for long; certainly not more than ten seconds. But I did not mind this weight because it was better than the 'wait' I had gone through for so many days.

Having her so close to me I wanted to tell her much, do so much. I wanted to grab her into my arms, but didn't do so out of fear of upsetting her. The feeling was lovely. The position a little awkward, though. I kissed her forehead. She put her feet on the ground. We exchanged a few words about how life had been the past few days. I was already dreaming about the next some months together, in Pune. We thanked Resha and left. We were off to a beautiful start in Pune from the same position where it had all ended in Indore. Yes, C.C.D it was and C.C.D it had to be and here we chose F.C. Road to start with.

"Your plan worked successfully. You're a mastermind," Jahnvi said.

"Thank you. It was a high pressured one. Life was at a knockout stage. One mistake and we would have lost everything forever," I said and we smiled.

"And here's the beginning of 'phase two', where we expect a totally different life. Let's see what Pune has to offer us."

Saying so, we both cheered up and started talking about everything, anything and nothing in the face of the world. Both of us were smiling and felt contented; both were in love, yet again.

Chapter-11

Lonavla, Sinhgad and KNP

It was the same routine, the same situation, the same me and the same her. It was 'us'. Time was repeating itself while we were traversing the same path. The only difference lay in the year and place. I was once again waiting outside a girl's hostel for my girl, my life for more than ten minutes and this feeling of wait and anticipation revived me. I sure did hate to wait, but my love for her always won and I would smilingly wait for my ladylove. I saw her coming from a distance in a long green tee and a faded pair of jeans. I noticed that she had put on weight and she always did so when she went home, but that only added to her prettiness. She was the only girl in the world who could put on a thousand kilos and yet manage to look beautiful and breathtaking. The sight of her from a distance itself gave me a kick. I was so lost in admiring her beauty that I never realised she had come and stood in front of me. Her touch gave me jitters and I was back in the world of real dreams. Jahnvi held my hands tight and smiled.

"How do I look?" she asked, making a cute face.

"You have lost weight and you look beautiful as always," I replied. Now if I'd said the truth, I'd have been dead.

"You liar! I have ballooned like an inflated tyre," she said, making a sad face. Now how was I to tell her the truth but still not hurt her. I was figuring out a suitable response when she herself added," You know what? We should be honest with each other at least," she declared and signalled me to reframe my response.

"Well, yes, you have gained some weight, but you still look cute," I said truthfully. "Love is blind you know," I joked.

"Oh yes, see how flawlessly you lie. You don't love me any more. Now you feel I am bloated and clumsy," she screamed. My truth had hurt her and I felt miserable.

"No baby, I love you," I said holding her by her waist. Her response perplexed me but I have become more diplomatic than ever in the face of these bouts that she tended to through at times. It was best to lie but she could catch a lie so fast! The truth, I was sure would have led to my strangulation. She had mastery over confusing anyone.

"Okay, then, prove it. Get off your bike and dance," she shot back.

"What!! Dance here? On the road?" I said horrified.

"Yes," she nodded and God, she sounded serious.

"But..." I was not able to find any words.

"See? What did I tell you? You don't love me any more. Then, why did you say that love is blind when you are afraid of people?" she asked, turning her back to me.

"Okay wait," I said and got off my bike and to my own amazement, I started dancing with my eyes closed. When I opened my eyes I saw Jahnvi standing in front of me and laughing her guts out. How I wished I could stop and just gaze at her laugh so happily. I could dance right there forever, do anything to see her smile. She held me by my arms, still laughing and hugged me tight.

"I know you love me, baby. You didn't have to prove it. I was just kidding," she winked at me and showed me the video clip she had recorded of my dance.

"What the hell!" I smiled back. I was looking miserable in the video, like some joker dancing for entertainment. I was lucky that there weren't many people around, but at the end of it all, I did not care. I had got what I wanted – my love and not to forget my first hug in Pune from her. We sat astride the bike.

"So what's the plan?" she asked.

"We are going to Lonavla," I said and geared up.

"On the bike? is it safe?" she asked, turning tense.

"Oh! Come on baby. We are not in Indore any more! And here we go," I said and accelerated the engine.

It had rained the previous night. Dewdrops covered the grass which seemed a lot greener and the sky seemed to shimmer as I set my gaze on the horizon. The clouds had acquired an added fluffiness and the wind seemed to be chirping a mesmerising tune. Pune had its own ways to make the moments romantic. Someone had said it was true that pleasure did not lie in the destination, but in the path one traveled, and my path for the day was heavenly. She put her arms around my waist and her chin on my shoulder. I knew she had the same thoughts and the same feelings that I had that very moment.

"What are you thinking about?" Jahnvi asked.

"About you," I said and smiled naughtily.

"Stop the bike," she ordered. I hit the brakes and just prayed she would not get angry. She jumped down and stood there in front, her hands on her hips. Then she walked closer to me, put her hands on my cheeks, pulled me towards her and kissed me. She was still an enigma to me. No matter how hard I tried, I just could not ever fathom her next step.

"What do you want now? You boys are all same," she bawled.

"No baby... I was... I was just lost. You are a surprise package for me every time!" I said, steering clear of my intentions.

"You are a devil. There is more to come from this package," she said and got back on the bike. "Shall we move?"

I kick started my bike and suddenly from nowhere a traffic policeman stopped us. He was huge and dark. His white teeth gleamed against his dark skin and his moustache seemed well-oiled and shiny. "Show me your licence," he demanded

"But what has happened, officer? What did I do?" I resisted.

"It's routine checking, lad. Who is this girl with you?" he asked and extended his hand to take the licence.

"I am his sister," Jahnvi said.

"Sister! I see," said the officer, raising an eyebrow. I knew he would not believe us but he did not ask us anything further. I gave him a copy of my licence.

"What is this? Where is the original licence?" he thundered.

"It's at home. I don't carry it," I replied.

"Then be prepared to pay a fine of Rs. 1,200," he said without looking at me.

“What the…!!! But why? Isn't it obvious that the copy is made from the original? I swear I have a licence for this bike,” I protested.

“Lad, know that an original is an original,” he said, wielding his stick threateningly. “Rs. 1,200 right now or a visit to the police station - choose quickly.”

“Okay,” I said and signalled to Jahnvi to hold me tight and as soon as the policeman turned around, I accelerated my bike and disappeared.

“Are you mad, Arnab? He has your licence,” Jahnvi shouted.

“The original is the original,” I replied and we shared a good laugh. We stopped for a break at 'Joshi Wadewale' which was famous for local sweetmeats and snacks and then resumed the journey to Lonavla. We reached there before the stipulated time.

“It's cold here. I want tea,” Jahnvi said. She loved tea! I wondered sometimes what she would do if offered a choice between tea and me and I never could be sure about it.

“Yes, even I can have hot masala tea along with onion pakodas,” I replied.

We had tea at a local teastall and roamed about the hotspots of the hill station till early evening. While returning to Pune, it started raining and since we both had no raincoats, we were soaked to the skin. We stopped the bike at a local shop and asked them for two polythene sheets to cover our heads. It soon began to pour and after a point I was unable to see anything ahead. So I stopped the bike. Luckily there was a bus stand which seemed deserted. We went and stood under the roof and waited for the rain to subside.

“It's very cold,”Jahnvi said, rubbing her hands.

"Do you want me to give you some warmth?" I asked slyly.

"Monster, demon!!" she shouted and blushed, encouraging me to make the next move.

"I am glad we agreed," I said and held her tight. She closed her eyes and I drew her to me, let her feel my breath and kissed her. I kissed her some more and got so carried away that my hands automatically pressed her hard against me, bringing her as close as possible.

"Hey, control yourself, Arnab. We are in a public place, at a bus stand!" she said and pushed me away.

"And we are the only public here. Please Jahnvi don't spoil the moment," I begged and held her again.

"No means 'no.' See the rain has slowed down; we should move," she said and stood up.

"Fine ma'am, after you," I bowed and gestured towards the bike.

The one-day trip was coming to end and it seemed to have ended too quickly. We felt like a retro couple from the 60s, on a bike and singing romantic songs, while driving our way through the panoramic scenery, ensuring that we did not hit the herd of cows we passed.

"Tea, tea, tea!!" Jahnvi said in a singsong manner. I was more tired than her, having driven all the way but her voice refreshed me.

"Do kadak chai dena, bhaiyya," I said to the teastall lad as we seated ourselves on a broken bench.

"Isn't this awesome?" Jahnvi chirped.

"Yes it is and it's all because of you," I acknowledged her.

"You bet," she smiled.

We had our tea and commenced our journey. I dropped her back at her hostel, which was followed by a long chat over the phone. That night's talk was one of the most loved and romantic chats we could have ever had. The aura of romance was whirling all around us.

I remember her telling me, "My roommates are nice but I wish you were my roomie."

"You bet," I had replied.

She was adept at adjusting with anyone. I had never heard her fight with anyone and was good to all. Though her social skills were a little forlorn and I particularly did not like her inability to maintain a long-term relationship with her friends. Since I had entered her life, I had taken all the responsibilities of maintaining contact between her and her friends and eventually many of her friends had become my friends who rarely seemed to keep in touch with her.

This reminds me of our 'couple friends,' Pankaj and Ankita. We would be the awesome foursome and go everywhere and do everything together. Ankita was Jahnvi's childhood friend but they had separated in the sixth standard. They met again when Jahnvi came to Indore, and one of her friends Gunjan from her hostel happened to be Ankita's friend too. The day Jahnvi and Ankita bumped into each other was something to see. That day I had come to drop Jahnvi at her hostel and we had been standing at some distance, outside the gate, fighting about something and suddenly Jahnvi went all quiet. It seemed as if she had seen a monster as her mouth flew open and eyes opened wide in disbelief. I turned around and saw the same expression on the girl standing in front of her.

"Anki," Jahnvi shouted in excitement.

'Should I hide myself somewhere?' I wondered. Jahnvi's upbeat, high decibel voice had attracted attention and had turned few heads in our direction.

"Jahnvi!" shouted the other girl with almost equal excitement.

They ran towards each other and hugged tight, laughing, smiling, surprised and bewildered.

"Oh my God, what a surprise! How come you are here?" Jahnvi exclaimed.

"I.. I.." the other girl uttered and started crying there and then on the road. More people started to gather around. I saw a boy standing in a corner, feeling quite left out. He must be this girl's boyfriend as he seems to be as overjoyed about this chance encounter as I, I thought.

"Arnab, she is Ankita, my childhood friend! We are meeting after so many years!" In her excitement Jahnvi was screaming into my ears.

"Seven damn years!" Ankita shouted back.

I didn't know how to respond. Should I be happy for them or ask them to calm down and make them realise that they were embarrassing the others. I decided to favour the former.

"Wow! That's incredible," I said smiling. "Hey, I am Arnab," I introduced myself.

"Very nice to meet you, Arnab. Let me introduce Pankaj, my boyfriend," she said and called him over. A good looking guy came forward and introduced himself. What the hell is going on! We shook hands and since that day Pankaj and I began to share a strong telepathic bond with each other. I just hoped to make some more friends like them in Pune.

Their arrival in our life changed things for good. A new phase of life began for us. What had happened in Pune may just have been a precursor of things to come. In a week's time, before Jahnvi's college reopened, we explored most of the tourist attractions within and outside Pune.

The 'foursome' was good but we sure did need the 'us' time. So we, Jahnvi and I decided to plan another one-day trip. We went to a place called Sinhgad, which was situated on top of a mountain and was famous for the monument which was part of the territory of a local king. The path to it was very slippery and zigzag and covered with shrubs. We had somehow managed to find the way. Even this half journey had tired me a little. I was still thinking if I should stop by for a few minutes.

"I need to go to the loo," Jahnvi said abruptly.

"What! Now?" I asked in shock.

"Yes, now! I have been controlling myself since the last half an hour. I thought I would make it till we reached, but I can't. The pressure is at its epic," she replied.

"Okay wait, I'll do something," I said, searching for some place to pee and I found an old shop which lay deserted. I stopped the bike there and inspected the area. " It's safe; you can go," I told Jahnvi.

"Oh! Thank God."

"Hello! I found the place, thank me," I said.

"Oh! Shut your mouth and your eyes and don't you dare look this way," Jahnvi warned me.

"Anyways I don't entertain some girl peeing in front of me," I taunted.

"Oh! So now am I some girl for you, you pervert?" she said. I can't understand girls. Just a few seconds ago she was hollering at me because she wanted to go to the loo and now that I had located an apt place, instead of being grateful, she was fighting with me. What about your pressure, ma'am! I thought.

"Baby, can you hurry up before anyone comes?" I requested.

"Okay, but I am not finished yet. It is to be continued," she said, proceeding to relieve herself.

While standing and waiting for Jahnvi, I kept a strict eye on the road.

"I am done. Thank you for your loyalty," Jahnvi said and kissed me on the cheek.

"Anything for you, ma'am!" I bowed and kissed her hands and then her cheek.

We continued our journey. The nearer we got to our destination, the more we found ourselves gaining height. Though the view was breathtaking for the height, it started to become foggy and cold. It was yet again a perfect romantic setting. How I wished I could just stand there, look at nothingness with Jahnvi besides me, her head buried in my chest. In this romantic setting could be seen local vendors selling hot buttered corn in cups, onion pakodas and tea and coffee.

"Tea, tea, tea," Jahnvi screamed with excitement as soon as she espied a teastall. We had tea and then explored the place. It was very peaceful and we visited a small temple where we sat awhile on the ground in front. We sat there for some time, deprived of words and absorbing the beauty of nature.

"I am getting bored now. Let's dance," Jahnvi said after fifteen minutes of having surveyed the place.

"Here! Now?" I asked, appalled.

"Do you have only these two words in your dictionary?" Jahnvi asked and slapped me lightly. I smiled.

My princess wanted to dance with me in such a lovely place, then how could I deny her wish? Her wish had always been my command and this time it was no different. I complied and started the music on my mobile phone. I selected the most romantic songs and bowed down in front of her to ask for her hand. I then pulled her towards me. With her hands around my neck and mine around her waist, I pulled her closer and moved slowly, swaying to the music. When dancing, I would occasionally brush my hands on her cheeks and she would smile and shut her eyes for a moment or two, as if registering this and savouring the moment deep in her heart. Our movements were slow, but they were intense and passionate. Our gaze never left each other for a fraction of second. We were so lost in each other that we did not even care for the fact that there were people who were intently staring at us, some with a smile on their face, some with disgust, some with shock and some without any concern. Whatever it was, we did not care as long as we were together.

We left Singhad in the evening and returned to Pune, refreshed after our short trip.

After a week of back-to-back trips, Jahnvi's college started. We fixed a schedule where I would come in the morning at 8 to drop

Jahnvi to her college, then I would go to the Outlook office, and at 11 a.m., would return and pick her up from college and go to some place to have lunch together. She would then sleep till 5, while I would put in a few hours at the gym and at 6 p.m., we would meet again and walk around Kamla Nehru Park (KNP). We would then have dinner at some place before parting and going our own way at night. We had the consolation that after a few more hours, we would meet again to undergo the same routine.

Days passed and so did weeks. No sooner it was November and I was over-excited for many reasons. My internship had been going much better than I had expected. My boss loved my work. Jahnvi was more than happy in Pune with me and my birthday was approaching. Everything was a bliss – Jahnvi and internship, Jahnvi and our love, Jahnvi and my routine life, Jahnvi and me – all of it was a dream and I was more than glad to live this dream.

Chapter-12

Birthday Surprises

I was all excited and eagerly awaiting the next day to arrive, imagining how it would be spent. I knew for sure that Jahnvi was planning something for me and that itself was enough to make me anticipate the permutations-combinations of the plan. I tried hard to find out what Jahnvi had planned for the day but she had one answer, "Didn't your teacher teach you the meaning of a surprise?" and I would have nothing to reply but simply comply and wait.

'Surprises' are always astounding and amazing. I have always been pleasantly surprised by surprises, even if I knew that a surprise was being planned for me. Sometimes they were good but sometimes they could be really bad and I had tasted the flavours of both and I knew there many more surprises to come. It was my first birthday in Pune and I could hardly conceal my excitement. After dropping Jahnvi off at her hostel, I came back to my flat around 11 p.m. All of my friends were already waiting there for me.

"So dude, when are we opening the bottles?" Piyush asked, holding a bottle of beer in his hand.

"My birthday is tomorrow, brother. Save it," I said with a smile and went to my room, fully aware that they would soon follow me to my room.

"You got to be kidding me! Come on, man, what's the matter with you?" asked Rishi, following me into the room. I could not help but smile at this. "And don't you dare delay the celebrations for tomorrow, you rascal. We all know you'll spend the whole day with Jahnvi," Rishi said and called everyone into my room. We sat down on the floor and drank our hearts out.

❖ ❖ ❖

The next morning I got up early, had a bath, said my prayers, wore my brand new tee-shirt and jeans, grabbed the bike keys and left my flat. It all seemed so pleasant – the breeze, the trees, the weather, even the street dogs. I say so because the bark of the dogs sound different as though playing a lovely symphony. I reached Jahnvi's hostel and to my surprise, she was already waiting there with something in her hands. Never had she been on time for any of our meetings; she would always be at least fifteen minutes late, if not more. So I used to tell her that I had reached even before I started from my place. I would thus spare myself the long wait, but that day, there she stood right in front of me.

"Good morning, sweetheart!" I greeted her with a broad smile and expecting a long lecture since my 'secret of waiting' had been revealed. To my utmost surprise, she was calm and wore a sweet smile on her face.

"Good morning, darling. Wish you a very happy birthday," she wished me in her sweet voice and came closer to me. I thought she would hug me, but she did not.

"So, are you not angry with me because I am late?" I asked in surprise.

"Why should I be angry? I have made you wait every day for so many years. And anyway, it's your birthday today, so I have decided to follow your decisions for the day. Whatever you want to eat or wherever you want to go, I will follow. So, shall we move from this place?" she asked and handed me an envelope. My first surprise for the day was Jahnvi's absence of anger at waiting for me. How I wished my birthday came every day! I know...I know... it was wishful thinking.

"What's in it?" I asked, scanning the envelope.

"Why don't you see for yourself, baby?" she replied ever so cutely.

I opened the envelope and found a small hand-made, leaf-shaped greeting card. On it were written the words, 'First Meeting'. I opened the card and read it. It was a brief story about our first meeting, when we were in Renaissance College. It was indeed very touching and brought back many memories, not only of Jahnvi, but of all my friends there and Swapnil sir too.

"Thank you very much, Jahnvi. I am deeply touched," I said and I meant it because she had given me an opportunity to relive my memories.

"And guess what? This is just the beginning. There is more to come," and she handed me a gift-wrapped box on which was pasted a sticker. I held it closer to read. On it was written a riddle.

"What is it?" I asked.

"Read it and solve it. You will come to know what it is," Jahnvi replied.

'You will use me in the morning and night; I will help to make you capable to fight,' I read. Many thoughts started passing through my mischievous mind but I didn't get the answer.

"I give up," I admitted. "Can I open it now please?" I asked humbly.

"Of course, you can. It's your gift after all," she replied sweetly. She was definitely acting weird. On many other occasions she might have humiliated me by saying, "You can't solve this simple riddle. What a shame?" But this response was totally different and quite unlike the Jahnvi I had known.

I opened the gift like a small child and discovered a mug in it. I was still confused.

"From now on, you are going to drink milk in this mug. It will make you strong," Jahnvi explained the riddle and I smiled to myself. God damn it. I loved this girl, I thought.

"Thank you very much, baby. This is the best gift I have ever received," I said, beaming.

"Such a liar you are. Shall we go to the college now? I am getting late," she said and came near and sat behind me on the bike. I started the engine and dropped her off to college.

She got off from the bike and stood there for a few minutes, smiling at me. "There," she said and pulled out another card from her bag. The card was heart shaped and on it was written: 'The Proposal.' I opened the card and read. It had a brief description of how I had proposed to her and her reaction, which when I was reading was really funny, but only I knew how much it had shattered me. It also reminded me of the goose bumps and nerves that were troubling me then.

"This is really awesome!" I said excitedly. "How many more are there?" I asked.

"Two thousand or something like that. I haven't counted them," she said and made me realise how foolish my question was. Hearing her reply, I lightly hit my forehead with my hand.

"I'll wait for all of them," I said sheepishly.

"Take this also," she said, handing me a pen drive.

"What is it?" I asked puzzled. I could not fathom the surprises I had in store for the day.

"Discover it for yourself, baby! This is all what you are going to do today," she said and left for her classes. "See you at 2," she waved from the college corridor.

I gave her a flying kiss and ran back home to see what was in store. I connected my laptop and plugged in the pen drive. There was only one video file in it named 'Happy Birthday.' I clicked the file. It had both our pictures floating on the screen with a slow romantic music playing in the background.

It was a ten-minute video clip, which first began with Jahnvi singing, 'Happy birthday' at her sweetest, chirpiest and loudest possible. After the wishing and singing part was done, she started a small, lovely speech where she confessed her undying love for me, where she poured out her heart. The videos that followed were that of my other friends: Pankaj, Ankita, Rishi and Resha with some messages from them as well. I really became emotional after seeing the video. I promised myself that come what may, I would always keep Jahnvi more than happy. With this video, she had made me madly, insanely in love with her.

Now I just waited for the clock to strike 1. I lay down and started daydreaming without realising the time as I was so lost in them. After a while, my mobile started ringing. It was Jahnvi calling. I saw the time – it was 1:15 p.m. Oh my God, she is going to kill me for making her wait. I picked up the call and told her I'd be there in ten minutes. Only God knew how.

I rode my bike as fast as I could and reached her college by 1:40 p.m. She was sitting alone under a shade, outside the college.

"I am really very sorry, honey," I said apologetically as I approached her.

"Oh, it's okay, Arnab. You are human after all and that too an Indian!" she said calmly. "I am really feeling very hungry now," she said and sat down on the bike. It was weird to see her like this but somehow I was enjoying being given a dominant role to play. We went to our patent mess and had lunch.

"The small video clip made by you was fantastic," I began, expecting the next of the card chain series.

"I know," she said and continued to eat. Her response was so cool that she confused me again.

"So where is the next card?" I asked enthusiastically.

"What next? Did you seriously think I made two thousand cards for you? No baby, that was the last one," she said seriously.

"Oh, I just thought...," I said and tried to smile, but then I was disappointed as my expectations came crashing down.

We finished our lunch and I dropped her at the hostel. She got off the bike and kissed me on my cheek and made her way to the hostel. After having walked a few steps, she suddenly stopped, looked at me and smiled again before making her way back to my bike. She came closer to me, held out my right hand and handed me an oval-shaped card with the word 'Accepted' written on it. I was more than happy after seeing the card. I would have hugged her tight and kissed her like mad, but refrained. Anyway, the card mentioned the time when Maya had created all our misunderstandings and we had had a rift and also of the time when we cleared all the misunderstandings before she accepted my proposal. I must say that day was one of my best days in my life.

"This is great, Jahnvi. You really are very creative," I said and held her hand. "I love you. Will you marry me?" I proposed to her again.

She smiled and said, "Yes."

Then she went back to the hostel and we promised to meet at 5 'o'clock in the evening. I was so excited that I wanted to share everything that had happened during the day with Rishi. But when I reached home, he was not there. I called him and he said he was with his friend and would be home in an hour or so.

I watched the video again and again. It was a coincidence that we had met and then begun our friendship which later turned to attraction and then something beyond love. It was mutual respect for each other, something rare in other relationships which people called an 'affair'. I respected and adored her a lot. She was the best and the only girl in this whole world who could and had cast a spell of love on me. I was getting obsessed with her thoughts day by day. She was ruling my heart. I remembered once when we used to be 'just friends', we were out in a garden one evening, talking about our lives, past and future. Jahnvi asked me what was the one thing I could die for? Passing the final exams was what I had said at that time, but now I was sure that she was the one I could die for.

My phone rang. It was Jahnvi. I quickly answered it.

"Where are you? I am ready," Jahnvi said. I could hear the traffic in the background.

"Where are you?" I asked.

"I am standing right in front of your flat! Now come down fast," she ordered and hung up.

What was she up to? I wondered. May be she was playing a prank. I ran down and was shocked to see her standing in front of me. She was dressed in pink. I wondered how girls were so particular about matching everything they wore! She was holding a bouquet in her hands.

"What a surprise! How did you come here?" I asked.

"I booked a flight," she jested.

I smiled and accepted the bunch of red roses. "So where to now?" I asked.

"Wherever you would like to throw a party," she replied.

"Well, wherever you want to go," I said.

"Can we please stop this game?" she grunted. "Let us go to the most special place," she smiled.

We went to CCD and as we entered, I noticed many familiar faces singing and wishing me 'happy birthday'. I was pleasantly surprised.

I saw Jahnvi's roommates and my flat mates. Resha too wished and asked "surprised?" I had no words to explain.

"Where is Rishi?" I asked.

"He will be here in some time. He's gone to meet his friend," Resha said.

I was so surprised at everything that was happening that I was astounded. Jahnvi had made my day so special and made me feel in seventh heaven.

The waiter brought the cake which I cut and shared with everyone. We hit the floor with dance music. Rishi finally joined us. We danced till we were exhausted. Everybody left by 8 p.m.; all except Jahnvi.

"Liked it?" Jahnvi asked.

"Loved it and love you, baby. It was really the best birthday of my life. Thank you very, very much," I said and realised that my eyes were wet.

"Oh, my dear sentimental boy friend," she wiped my tears and kissed me.

"You know I am emotional about you," I said and held her tight.

"I know your emotions flow from every part of your body," she smiled naughtily. We felt the warmth of each other's bodies. It was irresistible. We hurried back to my room in order to satisfy our intimate needs.

When we reached my room, I pulled her towards me, held her tight and hugged her tighter. I kissed her forehead, her rosy cheeks, her sensuous lips while undressing each other. The fire within us had become more intense; the hunger more violent. Our naked warm bodies were wildly brushing against each other. Our breath was uneven and heavy. Everything was happening too quick; our lovemaking was more of emotional satisfaction than the physical one. It defined the way we felt for other. After some time, we lay next to each other, staring deep into each other's eyes.

"I have to go now. My hostel gates close in half an hour," she whispered, kissing my forehead and standing up. I clutched her hand, pulled her towards me and requested her to stay the night.

"Arnab, I would love to stay, but, you know the rules and you know how much it means to me to follow them," she said.

"Yes, I know. Thanks for everything, sweetheart," I said and started dressing up.

"It was all worth it," she said.

"You are beautiful," I said, seeing her red lips and cascading hair.

"Now don't you start all over again! Drop me to my place," she commanded and moved out.

We reached the hostel but stopped at some distance so that no one could identify us. She opened her bag and took out a huge card from it. It was decorated with hearts and flowers and had 'Happy Birthday' written in the centre in beautiful calligraphy. I opened the card and read the beautiful poem Jahnvi had penned down for me:

"When I see you, my face glows.

All other activities, seem to go slow.

When I am with you, I feel pleasure,

As if you are the world's most precious treasure.

I feel like talking to you hour after hour,

About all things, whether sweet or sour.

I love you from my heart's core,

I have craziness to love you more.

Memories we share together, good or bad,

Enlighten my heart, but never make me sad.

Of all the people who had come and gone ,

You are the one who is above them all,

You are my life's sweetest and melodious tone,

I am living with the colors which you have shown,

Promise to be with me in life's twists and turns,

Because with you I am surely the happiest one.

To expess the feelings I have for you,

I just have to say that I LOVE YOU."

"This is amazing, Jahnvi." I was speechless now. "Just when I was beginning to think the surprises were all over, you come up with something else. You are unpredictable," I said and clutched her hands tightly.

"It's not over yet!" she said, creating suspense. "There," she said, giving me a small heart-shaped box. I started to open it.

"No!" she exclaimed. "You can't open it before 11:50 tonight."

"But why, what is it?" I asked.

"Another surprise. Now go and remember your promise," she said and marched towards her hostel. She turned back half way, pointed her watch and mumbled 11:50. I drove back home, holding the box and wondering what could be in it.

A ring, I thought, but she did not know my size, or maybe she did. I shook the box, but no sound came. May be it was empty and that was what the surprise was all about. Could I open it then? No I had promised Jahnvi, my inner voice replied.

I reached home and found Rishi was sitting on the sofa, watching television.

"So how was it?" he asked.

"It was like never before. It was a blissful day," I said and showed him the box.

"What is it?" he asked.

"I have no idea. Jahnvi gave it to me and asked me to open it at 11:50 p.m.," I told him.

"May be it is a bomb. She must have set a timer in it," Rishi joked and gave it back to me.

"May be," I wondered.

I sat down beside him, waiting for it to be 11:50. The seconds seem longer when you are waiting desperately for something. There were only five minutes remaining. My hands became sweaty and I felt nervous as if it was some kind of an examination I was appearing for and I knew nothing. My phone started to ring. It was Jahnvi.

"Are you ready?" she asked.

"Of course, I am more than eager to know what it is," I replied.

"Okay then, on the count of three...hey, wait a minute; please give the phone to Rishi," she said

"But why?" I asked

"Just do as I say," she ordered. I looked at Rishi suspiciously and gave him the phone.

"Yes. Hmm...hmm. Okay. Cool," that was all he said and giving the phone back to me, went into the room.

"On a count of three..1..2...3...open it," Jahnvi said.

I opened the box. At first I could not make out what it was. I saw a triangular structure. I was still wondering what this structure would be when suddenly I heard a loud cry from Rishi. I ran into the room. It was dark.

"Rishi?" I called out. He switched on the light and there on my bed, in front of my eyes, lay a guitar. Now I understood what the triangular structure was. Rishi came to me and hugged me.

"With love, from Jahnvi," he said.

I was holding the box when I realised Jahnvi was still on the call. I was not able to respond after seeing the red guitar lying on my bed. There was a heart-shaped cake nearby. I gathered all my strength and shouted out at the top of my voice, "I love you." This was the most unexpected gift and it also became the most precious gift. She knew I always wanted a guitar. I don't know how she collected the money for everything or when she bought this or how it came to my room. The only thing I knew was that I was the luckiest person in the whole universe.

"Remember this afternoon, you called me and I said I was with my friend?" Rishi asked. "I was with Jahnvi. We looked around and bought the guitar. Then I dropped her to our flat," He continued, "And when you both left for CCD, I came into the room and hid it under the bed."

"I can't tell you how happy I am," I said, holding the guitar.

"You don't need to. I can see it all over your face," he said.

I literally started crying and thanked him and Jahnvi for making my day so special. I wished every day to be my birthday, but true love needs no special occasion to express itself, I thought. I'll make every moment of her life special.

I remembered Jahnvi was still on the line. "Hello," I said. "Words are not enough to explain how much I love you and how thankful I am to you. I want to celebrate every birthday of mine with you."

She simpered and said, "It would be my pleasure."

We talked for some more time before she said that she wanted to hang up since she was feeling very sleepy. I could imagine how tired she must have been after planning so hard and who knows since when. I put the phone down and closed my eyes. I began re-living the day's events again and again. This was one of the days I could never forget till my last breath.

When asleep, the two things that accompanied me the whole night were my dreams, which obviously had Jahnvi and the other thing was a huge smile pasted on my face.

The day had started and ended on a surprising and pleasant note and it had also made me more confident and sure that Jahnvi and I were meant to be together, forever and forever. She was my "Chocolate Sauce in life by now."

Chapter-13

Full Stop

The amount of sleep required by an average human may be just five 'more' minutes, but Jahnvi's seemed never ending and I say that for I had been waiting outside her hostel for almost twenty minutes to drop her to college. When I called her to say that I had left, she sounded drowsy but she convinced me that she would skip her bath, which I was sure she would not and get ready in the next fifteen minutes. As expected, I had to wait for half an hour before I saw her coming out in her night suit.

"Wow, a new dress?" I jested.

"I don't want to go to college today. All I want to do is just sleep, eat and sleep again," she said, modulating her childish voice.

"Oh my baby! It's okay, don't go. From next time, just try to share your decisions with me," I teased her.

"Are you equating my sleep to laziness?" she asked.

"Lazy and you? You are the most active person I have ever met," I retorted.

"Shut up! Let's have tea at Ranade's," she suggested.

"Where is that?" I asked.

"Oh, it's a new place I have discovered. It's a canteen with an open space like a tapri and they make the best tea in Pune," she said and took me to Ranade's canteen near her hostel, on F.C. Road.

The place had a peaceful ambience and was surrounded by trees, giving it a forest like feel. She ordered two cups of special tea. We chatted for about two hours and had four cups of tea each. It was certainly the nicest tea I had ever had. Since then it became our new hangout. Although it was no match to CCD, it still had its own attraction.

We spoke about how quickly time had passed and how our equation and relations had evolved over time, transforming us from strangers to acquaintances to lovers to soul mates. How every tiff had only brought us closer every time!

Our courtship was about to complete a year, which had passed very fast. Our stay in Pune was to mark the celebration of one year of 'us' being together. 31st December was the D-day and our friends had asked us to join them for the New Year bash, but neither of us wanted to be a part of the loud crowd. Instead, we wanted to relive our past moments and weaving new memories. We spent the end of the year with each other, visiting our favourite places and talking to the hilt, only to start our new year with new beginnings.

❖ ❖ ❖

My internship had come to an end and it was time for me to go back to Indore, leaving Jahnvi alone. The thought itself gave me a strange lonely feeling. I knew I was going to miss Pune a lot. I also knew that I would miss my friends I had made here and most importantly, I was going to miss Jahnvi and the time I had spent with her. I promised to come back to be with her again. We laughed, we cried, we consoled each other and we parted ways. My friends came to the station to see me off. It was an emotional sendoff. I was sad that I was leaving Pune and my loved ones, but I was also happy that I would now prove myself and chase my dreams. I would be again with Jahnvi soon and share more special moments.

It had become a habit to be with each other – a habit that we loved.

❖ ❖ ❖

On a happy note I left Pune and moved back to Indore. Jahnvi was still in Pune for completing her post-graduation in the next year-and-a-half. Then she informed me about ill health of her dad one day.

It was a month since I had got back from Pune and was preparing for my exams; it was a month since Jahnvi had called me last. Her Dad was doing well now, she had said when she had last spoken. He was back on his routine and going to office every day, but she still sounded tense. After the many events that had transpired in the last few months, her tense voice could give me goose bumps, especially when she was at home.

Exam times were one of the several occasions when in the past when Jahnvi and I had tried to study together at C.C.D. Apollo Square. Once again I was reminded of the time I spent with Jahnvi and how much I missed her presence and so was Aditi, of the time she had spent with Virat.

Now it was just Aditi and me who would follow this routine. We were back. As usual it started with the plan to study but ended up on a disappointing note when Aditi, out of the blue, asked me the reason behind the tense look on my face.

"Something is wrong for sure, Aditi, otherwise she would have called me up," I said looking away to avoid direct eye contact with her.

"Don't worry Arnab, she must be busy with something else. That's why she hasn't called you," she ended, trying to put it simple, but nothing was enough to convince me.

"Anyway, this is not the first time it's happening. Remember last year? You were so worried even then, but whatever happened was the best that could ever happen," she added, trying her best to convince me.

"Okay, agreed, but doesn't she have even a second to spare and send me a message? Can someone be so busy?" I wondered, scratching my head. "Something is fishy. I still remember our last conversation when I asked her about her strange behaviour."

And I replayed my entire conversation with Jahnvi to Aditi when Jahnvi had said, "Look Arnab, we can't behave like kids all the time or take things lightly. We need to put in our efforts for the things we want to achieve. I am trying to behave more mature because I think it's enough of childish behaviour with you and all my friends, including family. At least, now I talk more sensibly with my parents. Otherwise from you, I hardly have anything to learn. My Mom scolded me today, saying, I have done nothing in the twenty-one years of my life. All of her friend's daughters were working at some M.N.C's or the other.

"So, I suggest you be a bit more serious about your life now. Okay? It will help you sooner or later."

"Jahnvi, I am pretty serious about my life and I am doing all the things I can possibly do at this time. If I am nice to you all the time, it doesn't mean that I am running away from my responsibilities. Right?" I told her.

It was shocking to find Jahnvi talk all this and that too all so suddenly, when I had not done anything to let her down.

"Sagittarians just talk; they don't do much. I actually wasted a year with you. At least I could have done something productive," she had mumbled.

This completely shocked me. I became numb and could not talk at all. The only thing I knew was that my sight was getting blurred every passing second, what with the tears slowly making their way out.

"Forget it. I have other things to do. Mom is expected any time. I'll call you later. Please don't call or message me and for God's sake, behave maturely. Be mature Arnab," she said and hung up without waiting for my response.

"You never told me all this Arnab!" Aditi finally said after recovering from the shock.

"Yes Aditi, I know, but there are some things which can't be shared with anyone. They become too personal for a couple and letting them out means breach of trust. I did not want to add to these many issues at hand, but now I can't take it any more," I paused to gather my thoughts. "I am not holding her responsible for anything. What I want is just a clarification about the situation, Aditi, so that I can stop thinking so much about it. I can't concentrate on anything when my love life is not perfectly fine," I finally tried to open up.

"Nobody else but you are to be blamed for this. You have mollycoddled her enough, Arnab. That's the reason why she is taking undue advantage of it. Seeing all this, I just wonder if she cares at all about you," Aditi lashed out and was very direct and open with what she had in her mind.

"Let it be the way it is. I think we should leave now," I said and started gathering my books that were lying on the table, untouched.

"Yeah, you had better leave. You are not sounding too well anyway. Just sit here and I'll take care of the bill," she said

"No please, let me pay the amount," I said as I put forward my hand to collect the bill.

She pushed my hand away to stop me from paying the bill.

"You have fever; you are shivering too. Can't you even understand such a simple thing? Why should you always be the one to cry?" she said, still holding my hand tightly. I could now not look into her eyes, so I just put my head down, staring blankly at the wooden table.

"Forget it. Come with me. I'll take you to a doctor. I can't imagine how you can be such an idiot," she said and pulled me with her towards the door.

"Let it be Aditi. You are just over-reacting," I said and let myself free from her grasp.

"I don't want to hear a single word. Just come with me. I am dropping you and I don't need your suggestions," Aditi said stubbornly. Holding my hand tightly, she took me along.

While driving, Aditi said, "Look Arnab, I understand your situation, but it would be better if you behaved in a little more mature manner. Let her meet you first and sort the situation out. Don't jump the gun. God sometimes approves even the bad things we say."

"Our exams are nearing. You can't afford to take any chances at this point. It's just a communication gap between the two of you, which is creating these negative vibes. You have to be positive and give Jahnvi a chance to explain her side of the story."

She dropped me off at my residence. Don't worry. Everything will be fine. I trust you."

❖ ❖ ❖

The problem was that everybody trusted me, whereas I couldn't trust anybody. I lived my life like a social worker. Life would have been so much better if you could have an affair with every girl who fell for you. Unnecessarily, I thought, I had proposed to her and created tensions for myself for the rest of my life. The problem was that now I could neither live with it nor die without it.

❖ ❖ ❖

One and half months passed and one fine day I got a call from Jahnvi, "Hello!"

"You finally found time to call me?"

"Not really. I have just reached Indore and going to Shruti's place now. I just thought of telling you this," Jahnvi said.

"But Jahnvi, at least meet me first. It's been more than one-and-a-half months since we last met. There are so many things to talk about. We need to meet."

"I'll meet you later. Got to hang up now since I have lost Shruti's address and I need find her house."

"What? Look Jahnvi, it will only take some time. Let's meet first and then, I'll drop you. I want to meet you sweetheart," I was almost pleading my way out to meet her.

"But I don't want to meet you. Please don't irritate me now. I'll call you later and don't try to call or message either because Puja is also coming. I don't want to make an issue in front of her," she said rudely and hung up. (Puja is her childhood friend).

Her hanging up the phone abruptly made me go worried. Again I was unable to figure out the reason for her strange behaviour; it only made me more anxious. Yes, love is tough, I admit, but it is even tougher to control your anger when your loved one avoids you without giving you any reasons for it.

❖ ❖ ❖

The day passed but Jahnvi never called. I waited like a bloody slave for his master's instructions. I finally called her after two days, "Hello baby."

"Yeah, what's happened?" Jahnvi said dryly.

"Nothing; called just like that. Where are you?" I asked.

"I am in Treasure Island with Puja," Jahnvi replied.

"What the hell? Is she going to stay with you forever?"

"Mind your language, Arnab. She is my friend and I won't listen to anything about her. So it would be better if you keep quiet. Whenever you open your mouth, you sound totally ridiculous."

Her words hit me hard and drained me of my emotions momentarily. I was stunned at her unreasonable behaviour and I knew that this time this was not just any fight that we have had in the past. it was bigger and worse and it was not going to be as easy as the other times we had fought.

"Are you alright, Jahnvi? There is definitely something wrong. You are not in the best of your moods these days. I have been asking you consistently for the past few days but you neither want to clarify things nor talk to me," I said keeping my anger in check as much as I could.

"Just go to hell, Arnab. Don't irritate me. Leave me alone and let me spend some time with my friend. Why are you disturbing me?" Jahnvi asked.

"Disturbing you? Are you in your senses? Have you gone mad or what? If this is the way you behave, I don't think it is going to work positively for our relationship in future," I said dryly, trying to hide my anger.

"Whatever, I'll call you later," she said and obviously she was in no mood to talk.

I was hardly breathing. I noticed the mirror against which I had hit my hand two years ago when Jahnvi had ignored me.

❖ ❖ ❖

She kept disconnecting my calls and I kept calling her. She switched off her phone. An hour passed by. Finally in the eleventh attempt she answered, "What in the hell is wrong with you? Can't you understand a simple thing that I don't want to talk you? I am simply cursing the moment I accepted your proposal," Jahnvi said. That was the final nail in the coffin.

"Listen to me first, you can curse later. You have the whole of your life to do that. Why are you acting this way? Have I done something wrong?" I asked.

"Did I ever say so?" asked Jahnvi in a strange tone.

"Is there someone else in your life now because of whom you are being so indifferent towards me?"

"Unfortunately not."

"Then what is it? Look, I am not mad. I can understand and feel that there is definitely something wrong. Just tell me what it is and I'll hang up. Don't be too stubborn," I said.

"Listen Arnab, you are no one to teach me how to behave. Okay? And if I ever feel like sharing some matter with you, I'll do it. And if I don't, I won't. Do whatever you want to do," Jahnvi said indifferently.

This left me with no other option but to scream at her, "Jahnvi, I wish I could kill you. Go to hell with your attitude problem. You needn't share anything with me. For two months I have been tolerating such kind of behaviour from you. You are testing my patience to the extreme. You do not realise but every day you fight for me with me."

"Then why don't you leave me? Leave me and be happy," Jahnvi screamed back at me.

"Be happy. I was a fool who loved his girlfriend like mad and has now been dumped without any reason. You have given me tears from day one till now. It was my mistake. I shouldn't have proposed to you at all."

"Arnab, Arnab," Jahnvi said after she heard a sound as if some hard solid thing had broken. It was due to my pulling out a two-pin plug and breaking it into pieces as it fell on the ground.

"Arnab!!!Arnab!!! Say something. Are you alright?" Jahnvi asked frantically.

"Why are you so bothered? Stop pretending that you still care for me. You have left me with no other option but to destroy myself. You have tested my anxiety levels and now you will see how I destroy myself and you. You really don't have any idea how bad it can get. You can then enjoy your life."

"Listen. I'll tell you everything. Let your exams get over, okay?" she said. I could sense her getting worried and concerned.

"No, you have to tell me now," I said, expecting to receive the worst pieces of news.

She kept on arguing for some more time as the balance in my prepaid card kept on decreasing as I pressed on.

"Listen, Arnab, I called you back so that you could concentrate on your studies, okay?"

I wanted this matter to be closed once and for all and begged her to answer my question.

My intuitions had never failed me, though I seriously wanted them to ditch me this time. I screamed out like a maniac, without realising I had injured my hand. I further acted more impulsively and banged my head hard on the door of my cabin. The thick iron key struck my head and felt blood flowing down my forehead this time.

"Don't act insane and listen to me. Everything is not fine in my personal life," she said.

"Speak out everything," I said, rubbing the blood off.

"I mean it's something to do with my Dad and Mom," Jahnvi said.

"Is everything alright between them?" I asked quickly.

"Yes, but..."

Now I was even more worried on seeing that her father had not been in the best of health since the past few months.

"What? Is uncle okay?" I asked her.

"Yes, he is fine, but my Mom and Dad are not happy with the choice I have made," Jahnvi said.

"What choice?" I asked her even though I knew it had something to do with me.

"Regarding my life and the person I have chosen for my future life. It's regarding you, Arnab!!" Jahnvi said.

"They don't like you. They have asked me to stay away from you and most importantly, they want me to get married to one of their friend's son."

She continued to speak, explaining the ways in which we could distance ourselves. I was totally numb on hearing her but not caring to hear what she was saying. Nothing that she said got registered in my mind. I mean I could not believe she was even talking about going away, lest stand by my side and fight together.

I went partially unconscious for a few moments. There was hardly any future left for us after listening to her reasoning. Illogical rejection was painful, sudden and heartbreaking. Tears started rolling down my cheeks. I felt as if I had lost somebody for whom I had cared all my life. I suddenly realised that even Jahnvi had stopped talking and the silence was shouting a thousand words on behalf of us, and none of the words were enough to convince either of us.

"I knew that you'll not be able to cope with this. That's why I was not revealing all this to you. Why did you force me, Arnab?"

Jahnvi asked in a depressed voice. Her voice was choking but this time I made no effort to cheer her up. How could I when even I myself was getting weaker with every passing second?

"Baby, can't we do anything? There must be something. Please don't do this, please. Please don't leave me. I'll talk to your Dad and Mom. I'll convince them. Give me a chance," I begged.

"Arnab, I have already lost all hopes. I've been leading my life as a stranger in my own house. Do you think I haven't tried to talk about this with my parents? I tried for two months to convince Mom and Dad but you can't even imagine the pain I have been going through. It's easy for you to ask for one more chance, but it's not that easy for me. Try and understand, Arnab, it's tough for me. I have confronted this most horrible situation and time of my life. It would be better to create differences between us and be away from each other. Time is the best healer and life will walk its own gradual pace. Let's face reality and accept the situation. We have had a good time all this while and may be, it was destined to be over. I am happy that we shared some beautiful moments together and I am going to cherish every moment I spent with you."

"There must be some other way out, baby. I'll do whatever you want me to. I'll prove myself, Jahnvi. Please, please, please, I beg of you, please don't lose hope. I can't let you go away like this." It took more than a couple of minutes to speak this much.

Tears were still on rolling down. She didn't cry a bit; probably she had been doing so since the past two months with no one to stop her or maybe she thought that if she started crying with me, then both of us would become emotionally imbalanced, there would be no one to comfort us.

"Arnab, please, if you respect me, take your exams seriously. We can talk about it after your exams. Please don't cry like a small baby and listen, if you spoil your exams, you can forget me. Never ever call me if you fail to comply by this. You know that I am very good at not answering calls and don't irritate me by calling me again and again. I am mentally prepared to call off our relationship. It would be better if you did so too at the earliest," she said. I could not utter a word as I was silently sobbing.

"I had to make a choice and I chose my parents, Arnab," she spoke again and broke the awkward silence.

I hung up, expecting her to call me back and ask for forgiveness or laugh it off as some prank she was playing or simply tell me that whatever happened, she would be with me always. I waited for her message. I waited for her to call. I made no move this time. All I did was to wait and wait for long.

But she didn't call back this time.

This was the worst manner in which one could have been dumped, I thought. Flashes of all the beautiful moments of togetherness darted before my eyes. I was going to lose them forever this time. My life had collapsed; destiny had played its game and cheated me, leaving me lonesome and forlorn.

God can give you anything you want and he can also snatch it away from you any moment. Sometimes you wonder if something is happening for real in life or it is just a bad dream. I did it hundreds of times till I reached the pinnacle of insanity. I had lost the person with whom I had planned spending every moment of my future. I had simply lost my love and probably my senses too with it. I could not tell what was worse: losing someone who was alive and loves you or someone who is dead and leaves you forever.

When bad news is what you have been hearing for some time the numbers just don't matter. I was ready to do anything to get Jahnvi back. I was trying hard to think of every possible to win her back and cursing the moments when I had unknowingly behaved badly with her. I felt love for her like never before. I could do anything to see that cute smile on her face. The phone call had disturbed my life badly. I was expecting a marriage invitation from her any day now and that made my knees go week.

"Arnab, what happened? I can't see you cry like this. Arnab, please tell me what's happened?" Aditi asked, worried on hearing me cry on a call.

"Aditi, I have lost my love. I have lost Jahnvi." Aditi was the only one who I thought could understand my pain.

"What happened Arnab? What are you talking about?"

"Aditi, her Mom and Dad don't like me. They want their daughter to get married to some well-settled boy they already know," I told her between sobs.

"But her mother used to like you, isn't it? Then what happened all of a sudden?" Aditi asked, perplexed.

"I really don't know what happened. Jahnvi and I thought so too. Perhaps she is still feeling bad about the November 2007 incident."

"Arnab, just wait. I am coming to meet you now. Please I can't see you like this. I know I can't do much about it, but let's meet and think over it," Aditi said.

"I can't meet you now. I would suggest that you too go away from my life. I am nothing but a loser," Arnab said.

"You want to cry? Spare your tears. We'll cry together. I am coming," Aditi said and hung up.

I cursed myself for what had happened on the 24th of November 2007. It all happened in front of Jahnvi's Mom because of which my life had now shattered. I never knew she could make such a huge mountain out of a molehill. She would take that one innocent mistake of mine so seriously that I would end up paying such a heavy price for it.

Aditi reached my place. She tried her best to pacify me since she wanted me to do well in my exams. She tried to look at the positive aspects of the incident but deep within, both of us knew it was a hopeless situation.

"It's the last exam tomorrow. For now on, just study and clear them. I promise we'll do something and extract Jahnvi and you out of this precarious situation. Don't spoil your year like this. You are a strong guy and brave enough to fight and come out of this mess," Aditi said encouragingly.

"I told you how it was but you were not ready to believe me see now, what's happening? My intuition can never deceive me," I said while sobbing.

Aditi stayed back and heard my entire sob story I had been telling her. She was with me, for me, supporting me and explaining me. She was my pillar of strength then. Not even once did she flinch when I was crying my wits out. It was getting hard to breathe. Fond memories were making me weep. Aditi didn't leave me till I had cried myself to sleep. She woke me up the next morning, telling me to study and messaged me questions which could be asked in the exam. I had hardly glanced through any notes, least of all read them.

I kick started my bike. One thing I was sure of was that I was going to fail in the exams since I hadn't studied anything.

It was 5:45 a.m. The streets were dark and deserted. A few stray dogs, regular joggers and morning walkers were the only company I had at that time. Memories started flashing before my eyes yet again. I wished Jahnvi was there with me this time. I would make her realise how much I loved and needed her.

The early morning rain was no longer special without jahnvi. I was cursing myself for telling a lie in front of her Mom. If she was not happy with me, why did she lie to her daughter? And even if I had lied, it was to my parents. What did it have to do with them? I only tried helping and impressing them because I liked their daughter. What was wrong with that? I wondered if her parents had never told a lie even once in their lives!

Why do parents forget that they too could have done the same things during their youth? Why did they consider it a crime now? I've never seen parents reacting so strongly on such a small issue. Why did they think that if somebody loved their daughter, he must be a rogue.

I have been a shoulder for Jahnvi whenever she needed me and now she was just not there when I needed her badly. I loved somebody who couldn't stand by me in times of need. It was just my luck and I couldn't blame her or anyone at all. I took a 60 degree turn on the single-vehicle lane and didn't notice a group of stray dogs fighting under the truck. To avoid hitting them, I pressed the brakes and my Pulsar skidded, throwing me a good ten feet away.

I bruised my knee, knuckles and legs. My shoulder too was badly hurt. I bled a lot and the road was covered with my blood.

There was nobody to come to my aid at that time. I wished I had hurt my head instead as that would have been the end of all my misery, my frustration. Unfortunately, I was still breathing and my bike was as fine as it could be.

I reached Aditi's flat to pick her up to go for the exams. Seeing me bleeding all over, she forcefully took me to the hospital. I got my wounds nursed and my hand bandaged. Aditi couldn't see the flesh coming out from my shoulder and hand. She almost fainted. The nurses helped her. She looked grim and so did the doctor. I was smiling.

"You think this a joke?" the doctor admonished me.

"Oh, no, no, I am an object of joke. Worse jokes are being played with me since yesterday."

"Come for a dressing daily for the next fifteen days. Don't forget or else the infection may spread all over your hand and things may get worse for you."

I nodded and we left for the examination centre. We reached the hall and were handed the question papers. Some of the questions were the same as Aditi had messaged the previous night. I didn't know the answers to any. I wanted to leave the hall, but every time I tried doing so, Aditi signalled me to complete the paper. We exchanged our answer sheets. That was the only saving grace in my otherwise problematic life which gave me some hope of passing the exams.

I switched on my cell after the exam. I received a message from Arush bhaiyya: "Congrats, your results are out and you've been selected by IBS, Mumbai. It's a decent college for freshers. I would say 'yes.' Now make your choice between Pune and IBS, Mumbai. It's your call."

It took me less than a second to make my decision as to where I'd be spending the next two years. I was never a poet, but I penned down some lines that day.

Hui hai khata phir mai tujhse yun chalte dur chala!

Kadam kadam ke faaslon se thehar gaya hoon ab yahaan!!

Mai yoon chala, yoon chala, yoon chala sabse dur!

Wo waqt tha kabhi apna, jo waqt sang kafoor ho chala.

Kashti me duba har sapna, ek aahat apni chod chala

Yaad aayein, ab rulaye, bite wo pal jab the muskuraye.

Teri palkein meri baatein, badla sab kuch, badli raatein.

Sannate ki tikhi chikhein, ujale ke gehra andhera.

Jeete jeete ab hai marte, zindagi ka bura ye pehra.

Hasi hai rulati, aansu hai hasate, tute sapno ki aandhi kehlati hai yaadein.

Na hai koi thikana, na hai koi manzil, bitte hain lamhe, aur jalta hai yeh dil.

Me yoon chala, yoon chala, yoon chala sabse dur!

Hui hai Khata phir mai tujhse yun chalte dur chala!

Kadam kadam ke faaslon se thehar gaya hoon ab yahaan!!

Chapter-14

Hypnotism

We reached the airport and Aditi parked her car. "Are you all right?" she asked before opening the door.

"Yes, very much," I smiled.

"You look cute when you smile half-heartedly. Smile with your heart and you might just look handsome."

"I don't think this is the time for jokes, Aditi. Sorry!" I said.

"Smile always. Things may just fall in place. Remember Dr. Raghubeer's magical words?"

"Yes, I do."

"I hope you don't need him any more. Do you?"

"Even if I were to need him, he's not there to help me now. He's dead," I said morosely.

"What?"

"Yes, he passed away a month back."

"Well, keep his words in your mind. You know they have helped you in the past and they will, even in future. Anyway, you're getting late. You better leave. Here's your ticket," she said, handing me the ticket before hugging me. Her hug was a little longer than required. "Bye, dude! All the very best for beginning a new phase in your life," she said, still holding my hands.

"Thanks for everything."

She smiled and whispered, " Love you."

I smiled and collected my luggage and then moved to the ticket counter to get my boarding pass. Aditi was still waiting outside. She smiled and gave me the thumbs up, wishing me luck. I could see tears in her eyes and how I wished I could console her. But before I could even gesture to her to stay calm and not worry, she turned and wiped away her ears. After few seconds, she faced me one last time, waved and was off.

❖ ❖ ❖

I completed my graduation successfully and for further studies in management, I received offers from a couple of top colleges of Pune and Mumbai. Since studying in Pune would have made it even tougher for me to get my life on track, I chose Mumbai.

Memories, they never leave you and if I had selected Pune, I knew that place would have reminded me of Jahnvi and our good old days and I would have led a dead and miserable life. Every place there held memories for me; every spot there had Jahnvi's essence; everything, each and every small place and thing would haunt me and make it more difficult for me to stay there.

I chose IBS, Mumbai after getting short listed in the IBSAT exams. I shifted to a new address in Hiranandani, Powai as it was close to my college campus.

One cigarette remaining, last half filled vodka glass, a dark room with just a small bulb illuminating little amount of light, a brand new laptop of Dell.

A youth with long shoulder-length hair of 1980 standing stood with his beautiful wife and two sons, aged five and eight years approximately as per the picture. One boy looked fair and the other had dusky complexion. And they seemed to be a happy-go-lucky family.

A fully drunk young man in his early 20's tried to capture the picture in his memory in a single look. He smiled and suddenly started searching something in his laptop, but it had got discharged. He somehow managed to stand up and get it charged. He sat down on the carpet and started searching for something again on his laptop.

Suddenly he saw something and started smiling and bent down to kiss someone's forehead.

What he saw was a picture of a beautiful girl with a fair complexion and with a height of 5'3". He clicked the next photo in which he was expressing joy wholeheartedly with that girl. It had to be clicked when this guy was enjoying his once-upon-a-time happy days.

Something fell in his half- emptied vodka-filled glass.

The thing which fell in the glass was nothing but his tears. His face still showed no expression. Tears continued to flow at a regular pace, yet no expression was noticeable on his face. His face was blank; his expression dead.

He was none other than me!

When I checked my mail that day I saw the chat dialogue-box flicker with a message from Jahnvi. "Come online," was all that she had written!

She and I were begun communicating after twenty days after I had made close to a thousand calls and lost a lot of weight due to worrying incessantly. I logged in and she asked, "Yes, tell me what happened?"

"Call me. I'll tell you," I said.

"No, I can't call you, Arnab. Tell me now," she wrote.

"How are you?" I started formally.

"I am great. Is that fine?" she said.

"What is wrong with you? You never answer my calls, never reply to my messages or my mails. Do you even know what I have been going through?" I asked.

"As if you don't know what I am going through. Okay, take it like this – I was in no mood to talk to you. Is there a problem? Do I always have to talk with you?" Jahnvi asked.

"Do you realise you are not in your senses?" I said.

"Mr. Arnab, I am very much talking sense. Can't you stop irritating me?" she said.

"Jahnvi I am lost; I am a regular patient of hypertension now. My blood pressure fluctuates like an old person's due to hypertension. Jahnvi, I need your support please. Please don't do this to me; please don't throw me out of your life in this way," I pleaded.

"Is there anything else you want to say?" she asked bluntly.

"I guess this much was not sufficient for you. Soon you will read the news of my suicide because I am anyway not able to survive now," I typed my sentence in BLOCK letters to show my anger.

"Do whatever you want, but please don't pull me into this," shc said and I was shocked at her callous statement.

"Are you already engaged to someone else? Your attitude is unbearable and unexpected, Jahnvi."

"Why the hell should I tell you this? You are no one for me now."

"Where the hell was your attitude when we were busy making love?" I typed.

"Shut up; else I'll kill you."

"Then why did you accept my proposal if you were going to leave me this way?" I continued.

"Remember Arnab, I never promised you marriage. Rather, I told you that if my parents were okay with you, I would not have any issues. You are good at remembering sentences. I hope you remember this too. You took me for granted."

"And what about the relationship we shared for seventeen months? It means nothing to you?"

"I told you I tried my best. I cannot go against my parents, Arnab."

"That's great! Now I'll actually kill myself. I don't need anyone in my life. I am finished with you. Because I started it, I'll end it also by putting an end to my life. I won't forgive you, Jahnvi, not at any cost."

I had completely ignored the change in her tone. She was getting weak with every sentence. My frustration was at its peak and I blabbered some nonsense to her.

"Can't you understand a simple thing as to why am I ignoring you?" she asked.

"Why?"

"Nothing. You go away, please."

I saw the sentence below the chat box. Jahnvi was typing the message which was visible to me for almost a minute and I knew she was longing to send threatening sentences to scold me. But her next sentence took me by complete surprise when I read it: "Arnab, please do something. I don't want to marry anybody else but you. Please do something so that I can live my life happily with you as your wife," she typed and I could sense that she was in tears.

"Tell this to your parents, damn it!! Wait. I am coming to your place tomorrow to talk about this, Jahnvi," I said.

"No, no no. You don't do that please. It will only make the situation worse. I can't make my parents unhappy, Arnab. They were very happy when I accepted the proposal they had in mind for me."

"Then tell them that Arnab is struggling to do the best he can. Ask them for some time or tell that guy about us. I hope he'll understand."

"I can't do that Arnab. You please sign out of chat now," she said.

"I am not going anywhere. Listen Jahnvi, please don't lose hope. And there is still a one per cent chance of us getting married. Be mature and think positive."

"I can't dream anymore, Arnab and it was just an emotional outburst. Don't take my previous statement seriously," she said, referring to her words about wanting to marry me. "I merely care for you. You should be happy and work well and remember one thing, I can't be happy if you are not happy. If you want me to talk to you further, you better be happy." And she gave me no chance to get a word in between.

"No, I can't please; not this time. I can't behave like a puppet all the time, Jahnvi and please don't show me your false concern for me, Please mind your business and live a happy married life. I know what I have to do with my life."

"Okay, then go and act insane."

We both were still online, waiting for each other to say something. A couple of minutes passed and both of us kept on writing something and erasing it before entering it. Finally I gave in to her demands of being happy and studying well while not contemplating any rash step. I agreed to her not because I was her puppet, but because I loved her immensely.

"And if possible, forgive me for the mistake I made, Arnab and for the very last time in my life I want to say, 'I love you.' I am signing off. Bye."

❖ ❖ ❖

"Arnab, don't sound so forlorn and helpless. You are not alone in this world; we are here for you always," Aditi consoled me.

"It's easy for you to say this!!"

"Arnab, I have gone through a similar phase in my life. You are not the first person to face this. Try to take life realistically," Aditi said.

"You are saying this because you are probably one of those who have never been in an actual relationship," I replied in total frustration.

"What? I was not involved…Do you have any idea what you are talking about? I loved a guy for two consecutive years, but he died. I acted normal after a year's trauma and fell in love again. One fine day I caught him making love to my best friend. Can you beat that? Go to hell when you have already decided not to understand me. Why should I even bother to waste time over you?" Aditi said and disconnected the call.

"Tring...tring...tring…"

"What's happened now?" I asked when Aditi called back.

"Nothing, sorry for my behaviour. I can totally understand your mental condition. I just want it to be sorted out and see you happy," Aditi said. She was one of the few fools who cared for me beyond my expectation.

"That's the problem; everybody wants the same. I've no time to wait for things to settle down. Don't even try to help me out…all of you please go away from my life...I don't want any fucking help from you guys…from anyone," I said in despair, feeling completely disheartened. After a silence of fifteen seconds, I muttered, "Sorry for my words Aditi, I didn't mean that," I apologised.

"Apology accepted. Now, listen to me. The reason why I called you back is I am sending you a tarot card-reader-cum-psyschiatrist's contact address. I took this person's help before and believe me, it works. Please seek an appointment with this person," she pleaded.

"Aditi, I don't believe in tarot card-readers. You believed them because you didn't have any alternative. In your worst time, if someone shows you hope, you blindly believe them and that's where tarot card-readers come in," I said.

"You had no one with you. I always have you till the universe exists. Is there anything wrong in trying it out?" she asked, ignoring my comments.

"Yes there is. They charge a huge amount of money and I don't have the money to give to that psychic," I responded with a lame excuse.

"He'll charge Rs. 2,500 only as consultancy fees. And that psychiatrist is not psychic. If this is the case, then I can contribute some amount for you," Aditi offered.

"Oh man…these girls. Do they have a solution for any and everything?

"No...no, they don't."

"Leave the money aside," I said. "That's because I know that bullshit. The tarot card-reader can't change my fate. He doesn't know anything about me…any situation. So it would be better if you stopped giving me such crazy ideas. Now please allow me to do what I like…isolation. Leave me alone," I yelled and cut the call.

Why the hell they thought that a psychiatrist could change this situation by some cards. What the heck…could he? Should I call him? No, I don't need him, I thought. I was in a dilemma, but I did not let even a slight positive thought enter my mind for more than a second.

After whatever had happened, I was nowhere near working and achieving the aims I had in my life. I had lost all possible hope of getting Jahnvi back. Indeed I was struggling to get myself back to the kind of life I had wanted for myself. My family tried every possible way to make me happy and they probed and prodded to find the reasons for my sorrow as it was troubling them no end. I had not answer to give and so they got no answer from me.

"Arnab, it's more than enough now. I can't see you like this, beta," Mom said to me once day.

"Okay then, better leave me alone...Please don't look at me...I can't act like a joker and smile all the time," I responded rudely.

"Who is asking you to act like a joker? At least tell me the reason for this behaviour. I am your mother, beta...you can share your problems with me." By now my mother was distraught and confused.

I didn't reply.

After some time, she asked again, "Is it something related to Jahnvi, is it?"

"Why do you think my life always has something to do with her?" I replied angrily. My anger was enough to prove to my Mom that she had been right in her guess.

She put her arms around me and said calmly, "Just because you are best friends and have a good time with each other. I am sorry if that hurt you."

"Why are you sorry, Mom?" I said and realised Mom had already begun to cry.

"What is it Mom? Am I not crying enough?" I asked, vexed at her concern. "Listen Mom, I am passing through a difficult time now. There is nothing much to worry about. I promise you; I'll share it with you some day, but this isn't the right time. And I'll be fine soon, okay? I just need some time to myself to think and re-shuffle my friends' list," I said.

"What live 'my life?' What reshuffle friends; list? Arnab, should I talk to Jahnvi?" Mom said, while wiping away her tears.

"Mom, why are you irritating me now? Did I ask you to help me out?" I replied though I felt sorry for being sharp with her.

My mother was by now playing the drama queen to the hilt. It was a full-fledged soap opera in my room that day!

"Oho my drama-queen mother, your son is perfectly fine. Now please go and prepare some good food for me. I am starving," I said to make her happy and desperately wanting to be alone.

She wiped away her tears and said happily, "I'll just go and prepare your favourite dish. You just wait for half an hour. Love you beta."

"I love you too Mom...and no more crying...or soap opera dialogues!" I said, trying to make her smile.

I had not given anything away but managed to save the situation somehow this time. I did give some serious thought to Aditi's message after this and decided to try my luck one last time in life.

"Hello sir, this is Arnab. I got your number from one of my friends," I said, speaking to Aditi's reference, Dr. Raghubeer.

"Yes, please. Go on," I heard a soft voice at the other end.

"Sir, I would like to fix an appointment for tomorrow," I replied.

"I am afraid my appointment book is full for tomorrow. How about the day after?" Dr. Raghubeer replied.

"Alright sir, thank you," I said, already feeling pretty calm. There must be something more to this man, I thought.

❖ ❖ ❖

I found his place in the midst of a filthy area, where the roads were narrow and could not even accommodate two two-wheelers at the same time. The people I bumped into on the way seemed to be pretty hot headed and impatient and cursed aloud at each other across the street. Was this the same scene every day or was that day special?

I parked my bike 200 metres away from his office and turned towards Dr. Raghubeer's office to reach which I had to climb many steps.

"Hello sir," I greeted the doctor.

"Yeah, Arnab, come in. Have a seat," He said, without even looking at me. "So Arnab" and he looked up "…oh you look younger than I thought you would be…"

"Thanks!!"

"So, should I ask or you will tell me your story yourself?" he said affably.

"I'll tell you, but I have a question for you. Could you please answer it before I pay my fee?" I said and he nodded in agreement.

"Sir, how can this tarot card reading change your future?" I asked.

"First of all, stop worrying about the fee. When you take an appointment with me, you should end all your worries. Relax. My fees, payments, etc. are matters we can always talk about later. Secondly, who said that tarot reading changes your future?" he asked, looking at me in a friendly manner.

I immediately liked this guy. "People say so and that's why I am here I suppose," I said.

"If you are here for this sole purpose, my son, then I would suggest you need not waste your money," he said.

"So, if it's not true, how does tarot card reading help?" I asked.

"Now there you go, son...as you just said, it helps you to know about certain causes which are responsible for what is happening to you. It shows you the way to move ahead while avoiding tension in your life. It shows where all you may be fortunate and helps you avoid situations that may potentially be problematic for you. It also gives you an idea about what may be the right time and the right place for you. It guides you, directs you to the right track."

I guess I had understood something told to me by someone after a long time. He told me about some general things and asked me to choose ten cards out of a kit. "Don't think too much, just take any ten cards out of this pile," he said, while watching my anxious face.

And I did as he said. I chose ten cards and handed them to him. He looked at the cards and began doing some calculations. He seemed to be lost in the cards. Ten minutes elapsed but he didn't utter a single word. I concluded that this old man was a waste of time and that I had come to the wrong place. I was literally thinking of running away with my money.

"So, what do you think about your life?" he asked, breaking his silence.

"I? Me? Let me tell you something about myself first and sorry, if I use unpleasant words…without them I won't be able to define myself…I am a big time asshole with no potential and I strongly feel that I am a person with no capabilities, A big-time failure...a Sagittarian, who only knows how to speak, but doesn't try to implement it. I am a person who is useless, ineffectual…worthless...hopeless...lifeless.

"I am unlucky for everyone. I was born to face insults, to be abused, to be thrown out of the lives of others. I can't take my own decisions. My life is dependent on others...a bloody useless life, full of tears, I don't want to live. I am a bloody fucker, allowing everyone to kick my ass whenever they want to," I concluded, realizing that I had spoken non-stop for five minutes.

"Hmm....is that all?" he asked casually.

I laughed ironically with anger and said, "My life is totally done for, sir and you are asking if that's all?"

"No Arnab, I asked this because your cards are showing you have much more potential and much more in terms of capabilities. You can face much worse situations with what you are facing now. It shows you have emerged as a winner all the time in your life till date and you are not the one who loses heart easily. I doubt my reading now, which I did overseas to understand a person's psychic and mental conditions," he said, while analysing my cards.

I didn't want to listen to him any more, but sitting there in a 100 square-feet room with an air-conditioner that was furiously buzzing and thinking of the money I would have to shell out, I decided to sit back.

After making some odd faces, he said, "So, It means your love-life affects you more than anything else?"

"I don't know that. I think we are over it now," I replied, avoiding his question.

He looked into my eyes and I into his. He knew he was right, I could gauge.

After fifteen seconds, "Yes, this is all what affects me and hits me badly," I yelled and decided to share my feelings with him.

He studied the cards for some more time and asked me gently, "Arnab, have you been in a relationship before this?"

"This was my first ever relationship, or I would say the last one too," I said, avoiding any eye contact.

"Don't tell me that. Your card shows that you are a person who has girls all around you," he said excitedly and looked slyly at me as if he could feel the girls dancing around me.

I was wondering and looking at the card which was responsible for this statement. I wanted to tear it and fling it out. The devil, the love, strength, the hang man – these were some of the names I wanted to call out. He gave me the impression of being some devil who had the strength to spoil my love life and hang me. "I won't tell you to act superstitiously, Arnab. What I would suggest to you is to keep yourself busy with things that you like to do. Do you follow any sports?"

"Yes, I do."

"Keep yourself busy with that. Try things you always wanted to try in your life. A second affair is always advisable."

"No, I can't make it worse."

"Who is asking you to get serious about it? Talk to those girls who love you or fall for you. I am sure you must be having enough options."

"I don't know. I am just not prepared for anything."

"Take the frustration out of you. Act villainous sometimes, flirt with girls, have a great time painting the town red with them. Enjoy your days because once youth goes, it never comes back."

I was amazed at this old man who surprised me no end.

"Thanks doctor, but my situation is worse than it sounds. I am not out of my breakup and you're asking me to do crazy things."

"Don't get me wrong. My motive behind all this is to distract you from Jahnvi's memories which keep on distracting you all the time."

"That always will be."

"It may sound bit weird to you, but having seen so many patients till date, I must say it's only with you that such depths have been touched. It's really important to cure you as soon as possible, else things can get worse for you."

"And how I can be cured?"

"If you don't find the above suggestions suitable, you need hypnotism."

"Are you crazy, doctor? I am just twenty and you're asking me to get hypnotised. I'll be a regular patient of hypnotism throughout my life then. Instead of helping me fight my problems, you're trying to make money," I said nastily. "Sorry, I shouldn't have said this. See...this is how I react these days, Out of the blue, I start shouting at anybody."

"I understand. There is no need to get upset and with hypnotism, I don't mean to take you to a different world. There are different ways to heal the mind. I'll hypnotise your memories in such a way that they won't irritate you every now and then; they won't distract you from your life and happiness. You'll definitely be in a better state than this."

"I need time to think over this."

"Take your time and call me when you trust me. All I can say is it takes time to come out of memories – it may take months or years, but this will help you to a great extent. I treated my son for a year. I saw him crying, beating himself and killing himself when his girlfriend died. I wouldn't have suggested it to you if it wouldn't improve your condition. One more thing: I have earned enough money in my life. I won't extract the last rupee from you for this. You do not have to pay my fees today, nor do you need to pay me for any of the treatments. Love yourself. There's enough love left in your life. You can do wonders. Take care."

"Thanks doctor," I replied.

I thought over this and felt that maybe it was not a bad suggestion. I could give it a try. The man also did not seem to be a cheat or one out to make a fast buck. I decided to go in for the treatment he had suggested, but for only once a week. I paid him a counselling fee, forcing him to accept it.

During those sessions, he had a number of questions to ask about Jahnvi, our relationship, how we met, how long we stayed together, how we separated. I could hear the voice, but could not sense anything else. I could feel and see the pain simultaneously. Memories were running in flashback yet again, I smiled when we met...I cried at her ignorance, I smiled at her acceptance, I laughed at the jokes we shared, I felt the love we had between us, I cried every time she hugged me, loved me, kissed me. I was amazed how she could be so easily surprised. I was heartbroken with shock when we decided to end it. I could not bear to let her go. I wanted to keep her with me. My throat was getting dry, my hands heavy and I could not get a hold on her. I wanted to take her to my own world where nobody apart from me could see her... I wanted to say something, but I could not say anything...I was helpless. I was useless...everybody was laughing at me as I was crying...Jahnvi was going away...going away...forever...

I was drenched in sweat when I opened my eyes. My hands were shivering and I had to struggle to breathe. When I came to my senses, I checked my watch. I was feeling groggy. I had been hypnotised for only five minutes but it seemed like a lifetime.

Dr. Raghubeer gave me a glass of water to wash my face. For some unknown reason, hypnotism made me feel lighter and relieved.

"Feeling better?" he asked.

"Yes, feeling relieved now."

"I liked the surprise this girl planned for you."

"Oh, she is a mastermind; she had mesmerised me on every special occasion," I smiled.

"But, one thing that I noticed was your expectations from Jahnvi were sky high."

"One tends to expect things when is in a relationship."

"One thing I am sure of – Jahnvi surprisingly is not as expressive as you are. She keeps it to her heart while you vomit it out on somebody or for that matter on her too sometimes."

"You see any hope of us getting back together? I need a frank answer."

"It is as impossible as a corruption-free India. You want her back in your life?"

"Absolutely, but that's not possible I suppose."

"It's still possible till the time she does not marry someone else. It may take months, a year or two. You are not facing anything that cannot be mended. You still have the situation under your control. Just don't go by what her parents say. They are here to fulfil their duty. You can still cast your magic. Don't waste your time, concentrate on your studies and find a good job, get settled and show them your capability and worth. Do the best you can. At worst, even if she does get married to somebody, she won't be blaming you for the rest of her life for not having tried to win her parents' trust."

The doctor made me feel positive for the first time in the past few months, but for how long could this positive attitude last?

"Smile always as things may fall in your favour," he said and I left.

I had a hint of a smile and a glimmer of hope for the first time since the last few months. I was happy that I had visited this doctor. I thanked Aditi again in my mind and heart. If it wasn't for her support, I would have drowned in deep depression. Here I was smiling again; feeling alive again.

Chapter-15

Drunk, Kissed and Cried

It had been six months since my college had begun. I had been trying to come out of the past through Dr. Raghubeer Yadav's help and his treatment. My progress was evident. The frequency of hypnotism sessions had reduced from once a week to twice a month due to the physical and mental improvement. As per the doctor, I was now beginning to concentrate on things I liked. Travelling was one of them and I travelled a lot.

I explored new places with Rishi. He had taken up a job in Mumbai and we shared a room. On the terrace of our building, we would drink when the world slept. Half our salaries would be spent in meeting our day-to-day expenses and on buying booze. We cared about nothing; we had become careless and carefree. We had practically become alcoholics; we partied without reason. Rishi broke up with Resha for her being disloyal to him and I had already broken up with Jahnvi for no reason. We still had our occasional phone calls though, which would end up in fights - fights that had often ended with sex earlier, now ended with tears for her and alcohol for me. And trust me, both were equally intoxicating.

Jahnvi had always been calm and composed while I was the outspoken one. The more she asked me not to drink, the more adamant I became and continued drinking to my heart's content. We stopped interfering in each other's lives after some time, although I kept track of her movements silently. After our breakup, many of Jahnvi's male friend had tried minor affairs with her, all of them wanted to try their luck. They were the ones I had always warned Jahnvi against but she had never given a single thought to my words. Dominance in a relationship affects seriously and she had always been the dominant one.

A man becomes lively when he has enough money in his pockets. I had more than enough to make sluts dance to my tunes, but why should I spend on them, when they are easily available?

I had the job of an assistant writer in a new production house. Although not as respectable a job as that of a banker, but it was definitely something I loved doing. I got a decent salary of fifteen thousand a month for working four hours a day and that was enough to take care of my expenses. I earned extra by supervising the sales of our family business in Mumbai. I got a share in my Dad's business as an incentive. I rented a 500 square-feet godown in Mumbai to store goods.

I came across a bunch of talented but frustrated individuals, the 'so called' intellectuals in college. People who joined the college with a "committed" status were either single or in an open relationship or committed to someone else. The ones who did not fall into any such category were happy to lead their lives like bohemians, sleeping with anyone, anytime and anywhere.

It was time for the first semester exams. As always I was not prepared. I studied only the night before as was the habit with me. I missed Aditi on this occasion. She was doing her MBA from Indore. I performed miserably in the exams and as expected, got lousy grades: 6 'C's', 1-'D' and 1-'A'. My parents were cool. Instead of scolding me for my C's and D, they appreciated my effort and were quite surprised that I had managed an 'A' in one subject.

The second semester began and I become a familiar face on the college campus. They saw me playing music, shooting films, acting and having sex with the best of girls in college. I was open and so were my intentions. I did not spare even my seniors, classmates, batch mates, friends' girlfriends. Nobody doubted my intentions. I was happy 'making out' with girls – left, right, front and centre. They all had their own charm. My frustration would ease out, though for a while, when I was busy giving my bottoms a nice time. I had seen the same girl sleeping with two of my roommates at different times and promising love to somebody else over the phone. A bunch of mediocre 'wannabes' were the future managers in the country.

Though I made some good friends in college I never 'belonged' to any one particular group. Faculties interacted with me for only one reason – they wanted celebrities from the television industry to put in an appearance during college functions, without asking for any money or at least someone who could fit their budget.

However, soon I found that the rules in college had become stricter. Individual attendance in every subject was compulsory and supplementary exams were being held. There was a test once every two days and submissions had to be made within the stipulated time. There would invariably be somebody crying even after getting 90 per cent, while there would be somebody partying at merely clearing the exams. The strict professors reminded me of my mathematics teacher and the cool professors of my games teacher in school; the only difference was that we had to pay only a few thousand rupees per year in school while here, we had to dish out lakhs.

In the first half of the year, we went on some amazing trips from college – to Goa, Alibaug, Karjat, Matheran, Mahabaleshwar and saw it all. Girls called it a 'project'; I considered it an 'opportunity'. The feelings were mutual; the excuses were different. There were enjoyable rides and stays at hotels. I was always lucky enough to be in the company of beautiful girls in their 'live' projects. If any other guy accompanied us, he would be treated as a piece of junk and banished. Girls were willing to put their virginity at stake while I had nothing to lose. I was a master at the game. I stopped using trial packs of condoms; I now used the super large pack – I called it 'family' pack.

"Hey Arnab, what are you doing this evening?" Whenever a girl asked me this question, she would end up in bed with me. Whether it was a bed or my car parked somewhere in the middle of the long highway, it did not matter. What mattered was what happened.

It was exam time once again. Once again we studied at the 'nth' hour. Only the 'geeks', as we called them, buried their heads in books all the year round, aiming at scholarships. I called them 'nuts'. Wasn't it ironical that they were wasting lakhs of rupees over college fees just for a scholarship of a few thousands? They would eventually be the ones to get better salaries, no doubt, but why did they want to take on responsibilities so early in life? All this was beyond me. I cleared my exams with grades not too difference this time as well: 4 'C's', 2 'D's', 1-'A', 1-'B'. My parents were astounded, and so was I. My results made me more confident about my approach to studies. I probably had an advantage in my internals which reflected in my overall grade sheet.

A year passed in a similar manner and it was time for a session break of ten days. Thereafter would begin the four-month long internship. Tearful farewells were exchanged by those who would be away from their forever changing 'bed partners'. I didn't opt for summer placements but continued with my previous employer Outlook, but this time at their Mumbai office. I was still an assistant writer, but worked on a part-time basis for five days a week and full time over weekends. The off-season sale in Dad's business was taking off very well. I was earning better money now. It was a cool twenty grands from the business per month. That coupled with my salary as an intern, was by no means less than what a good management postgraduate would earn from his first job.

I was working as a management trainee in the Relationship department of Outlook India. There were a couple of girls with me. The office was simply awesome. We were treated as fair as any intern should be. Our training lasted for two days and we were told about our responsibilities. I was provided a subject for my research for the next four months. I had to find out about customers' potentials, their preferences, their choices, our competitors and their strategies, options to expand the business, locations feasible for expanding the business or not and so on.

South Mumbai, Pune and Indore were under my team's coverage. It would be fun, I thought, as it meant frequent flights at company cost and a monthly stipend of thirty thousand rupees. What more could one ask for? Mom was bound to be happy to see me fly in and out of Indore twice a month.

Pune still occupied a special place in my heart. There was an emotional side of me that this city had witnessed. I was scared of it starting all over again, if I went there. Fond memories never leave you. I hired a cab to Pune for a client's meet and started out on the Mumbai-Pune expressway. In no time I reached Lonavla Food Court, where I had shared some of the most beautiful moments of my life, done crazy things, eaten often and then run away, acting like a ghost in the middle of the night, shivering in the cold and taking shelter in the rains. We had planned our lives at least sixty years ahead. I smiled to myself as I recollected those moments.

People had started identifying us and calling us by our names. I stopped there and ordered a cup of tea.

"Where is ma'am? It's been a long time. Seems like you don't miss us any more," the waiter commented.

"She is ill; will bring her along the next time. She too has been missing this place," I smiled and left.

"Take care of her and one more thing, I always wanted to say is that you both look very nice together."

There were tears in my eyes which told a different story. A tall, tough-looking man, formally dressed in a black suit, had no right to shed tears. It was quite unnatural and unimaginable.

"Are you alright, sir? Would you like some water?" the driver asked.

"No, thanks. I am fine. This place makes me so nostalgic. It is close to my heart."

"I am so sorry. Had I known it would upset you so much, I wouldn't have stopped the car here at all," he said apologetically.

"No problem. I really wanted to remember my good times. It was good that we came here," I smiled and gathered myself. Just then I received a message from Jahnvi: "Long time. You haven't been responding to my calls. Is everything well? Plan a trip to Pune and let's meet. It's been almost a year."

I never respond to her occassional messages earlier. I didn't respond this time either.

The roads were clear. We were in Pune in the next forty-five minutes. It had taken us only two hours from Mumbai. My colleague Aakriti joined me some time later. Pune was her home. We planned to meet at 'The Great Punjab' restaurant over lunch and asked our client to meet us there. As expected, this beautiful girl with me turned the meeting into a deal worth five lakh rupees which was a new business opportunity for us. Our efforts bore fruit. The client was visibly impressed with the layout we had planned exclusively for his company.

I had never seen such convincing power before. "You almost sold me your company at a huge profit," the client said.

We smiled and thanked him for the compliment. Our manager declared an individual bonus of ten thousand rupees for this achievement. He had almost accomplished one-fifth of the target with this deal. "You are one of the best interns I have ever come across," were his words. It glorified the moment and we basked in its glory.

Within an hour the money was transferred into our accounts and then it was party time for both of us. We went to 'Jazz by the Bay' to celebrate. I chose the safest place since Jahnvi was a teetotaller and we had never been there.

If I drank like there was no tomorrow, I would begin to cry on remembering the past. It would definitely spoil the mood for the evening.

"One 750 ml. bottle of Tru Organic Vodka and then buffet will follow," Aakriti ordered for the two of us.

We raised a toast to our success and had our drink. We discussed our respective lives for quite some time. She bitched about her boyfriend and the story seemed like something I had heard before from every girl I knew. "We were introduced to each other by a common friend. We started chatting up regularly. He was the first to propose. I ignored, but he persisted. I had to give in. We were in a relationship for a year. Then he ditched me. I caught him sleeping with my friend. I dumped him. Now I am free to do whatever I want."

I was reminded a lot about Aditi.

"We did a wonderful job didn't we?" Aakriti asked.

"Sure, this is definitely one of the best days of my life. I feel like I've done something useful finally."

"I agree. I feel like we have conquered the world – a good start to our career."

"And I am no more a useless fellow. I have proved myself."

"Oh, but you never were. You are quite good at whatever you do. What makes you feel so?"

"Nothing, it's just that I have a point to prove to somebody."

"Girlfriend? Don't tell me!" she looked at me with eyes wide.

"Why, am I that incapable of having a girlfriend?" I asked.

"Oh! I am so sorry. I didn't mean it that way. I mean you are not like the 'falling for a girl' type of guy."

"Hmmmm..."

"What happened? Not together now?" she asked.

"Forget it. It will spoil everyone's mood. We are not together any more and I am actually happy about that."

"Come on, bitching about your 'ex' is always such fun. To prove your 'ex' a jerk gives us immense satisfaction, you know."

I started narrating my tragic tale right from where it all started. I began with how it happened and as always, didn't quite know where it ended. Many drinks followed after that. The last thing I can remember about that night was that the bouncer and Aakriti helped me to her car when I saw Jahnvi from a distance with a man, coming out of the 'E-square Multiplex'. They were coming towards us and my doubts were confirmed. She was with Rajiv, one of her friends. Tears started rolling down my cheeks. Aakriti mistook it to be the sweat on my body. She hugged me and said, "You are looking sizzling hot. I wish we could make out here. I so want to feel you burn."

We were drunk way beyond our limits.

I was too numb to react, so I pulled away from her. Jahnvi drew nearer and noticed me. She was seeing me in a state she had never seen before. She stared at me in shock. She saw how Aakriti had held me tight, how my feet wobbled, how my eyes were blood red, how everything seemed like a nightmare for her. It had been a year since we had last seen each other. She was no more the fatso she used to be. She was looking dull but beautiful, innocent but mature, happy but lost. She looked surprised and shocked. I wanted to grab her, cry on her shoulder and ask why she had left me a year ago. I wanted to hold her like a small baby and cuddle her cheeks which I had kissed the most. I wanted to kiss the lips that had made me realise that kisses are special. I wanted to live with her. I want to love her again...forever...and ever.

"Why are your eyes fixed on that girl? She's not your kind. Doesn't look like it," Aakriti said as she lit a cigarette.

"She's Jahnvi, my 'ex' girlfriend," I said in a broken voice.

"Oh, so she's the one who is responsible for your condition? Let's end it here itself," Aakriti said, and saying this, she grabbed me and kissed me. She came over to me and dug her nails into my back.

Jahnvi saw it and tears swelled up in her eyes. She gave us a disgusted look and ran away. Rajiv turned and raised his middle finger at me.

I slapped Aakriti and this stunned her. She came back to life. I hired a rickshaw and went to the hotel. The same night I hired a cab and left for Mumbai.

The next morning I saw there were twenty-two missed calls from Aakriti, five missed calls from Rajiv and three messages.

"I am really sorry for what happened last night. I don't know why I did so. If possible, please forgive me," Aakriti.

"This was not expected from you Arnab. You have no idea how much you hurt her yesterday," – Rajiv.

"Now I know why you don't reply to my messages any more. You could have told me that there was someone else in your life now. You've changed a lot Arnab and so have your choices...

Thanks for proving my parents right. You lessen my guilt," – Jahnvi.

I didn't respond to any of them. I explained the events to Rishi and even he did not have any consolation to offer.

Aakriti requested for a change of location thereafter since she was embarrassed at what had happened at 'Jazz by the Bay' that day. She tried getting in touch with me a number of times, but I didn't respond. She was posted to Pune. The day she left the Mumbai office, she messaged me: "Shall never forgive myself for that night, miss you."

I tried calling her back after a couple of days, but she had already changed her number. I felt guilty at having hurt her and being stubborn. The next two months were quite uneventful. I would go to office at 9 in the morning and come back at 7. I landed a couple of good projects too and one of them was in Indore. When I visited home, Mom was pleased to see me and so was Dad who felt I had become a responsible person and Swapnil sir was happy at my success.

He invited me to the Renaissance Annual Fest the same day and praised me in front of thousands of "Renaissance and Indore Indira" students. I was happy and on the top of the world when people clapped to welcome me on the stage. I shared my experiences with the juniors and the response I received was overwhelming. I took the flight back to Mumbai the next morning. I was returning richer, what with all the love and appreciation that had been showered by my friends, my graduation college and my family.

Internship taught me more about life, most importantly on how to react when you see your 'ex' and how to keep a tab on yourself when you are drunk and with a beautiful girl.

I secured an 'A' grade in my internship programme which raised my CGPA to 7.8. I was no more a mediocre performer. I was given a pre-placement offer too but the compensation package was to be disclosed only during the campus visit. I decided to try my luck in the main placement season, and so I kept my acceptance at the PPO on hold. I wanted to keep all possible options open.

❖ ❖ ❖

The third semester began shortly. I chose marketing and advertising as my major-minor areas of specialisation. Number crunching experts, accounting souls and commerce graduates unlike me, landed up in core finance, for better placements. It was an accepted fact placements in the finance field were always better than those in marketing.

About 30 per cent of our batch opted for finance. They were the ones who had taken loans of eight lakh rupees. They had no other option but to get a better placement and repay the loan. About 40 per cent were the meritorious ones and the remaining 30 per cent wouldn't take marketing as they thought it to be below their dignity.

The students of marketing had no reservations; they were not eligible for finance and had no great interest in IT. They were not aware of other fields. Somebody came and remarked, "To know the real market, one needs to start from ground realities. One needs to do sales. Let's take a challenge and opt for marketing." So we joined the gang for this with one solid reason.

The new session started and so did the threats from the placement cell. They were often found saying, "Placement is not your right. It's just a facility we are providing, so don't take it for granted. If you are serious, we can push the numbers in good companies but if you are not, we are hardly concerned. Try to secure the placements in the first phase. Tone down your expectations. You are just a fresher. Beggars cannot be choosers. And if you act choosy, there are insurance companies waiting at the gates with a truck. They can take as many numbers as they want. One student one offer – that's what we have decided on this time. Welcome to the party."

Students were worried regarding the placements and so were their parents. Some talked about joining their family business, but nevertheless opted for companies secretly; some were busy badmouthing the placement cell and the TPO; some were desperate to take whatever they were offered while some intellectual souls tried to put up a fight for their rights, by saying, "We are entitled to receive two offers from top companies and nobody can stop us from that. We should fight for our rights. We have paid lakhs of rupees for this course and they should try their best to get us placed. Other colleges are also providing students with such options. We are not going to tolerate this injustice." They were also the ones who were seen as placement co-coordinators. One moment they would side with the placement cell and at the other, they would be seen badmouthing them. When questioned about their behaviour, they said, "We need to be a part of the system to change the system and that's what we are doing." They were often termed "frustrated manipulative souls."

The placements were open and nobody including the companies cared about the results in the third and fourth semesters. They just wanted comparatively better results. Students were excited, nervous and anxious about the months ahead. They made many attempts to groom themselves as professionals by styling their hair, wearing branded formal clothes and tight-fitting business suits, as if companies would select them solely on the basis of their appearance.

Placements began with the finance giant J.P. Morgan offering a one-and-a-half million rupee package. This was the one company which every finance student would give his life for but which rejected 75 per cent of the applicants on grounds which were not disclosed. The remaining 25 per cent participated in the interview. Only eleven students were lucky enough to grab the package. The celebrations started in the campus itself and with that IBS, Mumbai was off to a flying start in placements.

❖ ❖ ❖

Aditi called me once to explain how her 'ex' wanted her back in his life. She said she missed me. I had no different story to tell. We discussed our college life and remembered many of the incidents very clearly. You can never have everybody forever in your life, I thought.

Rishi would speak to Jahnvi quite often. This was a deliberate ploy so that I could keep a watch on her life. No matter, how worse the relationship had got in the last calendar year, I still wanted to see her life going smoothly.

Aakriti had managed to get hold of Jahnvi's number through her sources in Pune. That would not have been too difficult considering I had told her almost everything about the two of us, including some very personal details.

She met Jahnvi on one occasion where she explained everything about how we had met, what had happened that night and how deeply hurt I was after the incident. She also told Jahnvi how much I still missed her. Aakriti however did not tell me anything about her meeting with Jahnvi, neither did she contact me after that night. All possible contacts were broken. It was Rishi to whom Jahnvi mentioned about having met Aakriti and admitted that it was a big mistake she had made. She was sorry for the way she and Rajiv had behaved that evening with me.

"Don't worry. He's a man who has seen a lot in life. He has come out of this one too," Rishi had replied.

I received a message from Jahnvi saying: 'Sorry'. But I didn't feel like talking to her that moment. I missed all four of her calls that day. No matter, how strangely we had parted ways, I missed Aakriti sometimes. We shared a good bond. We would create magic with our management acumen. I had slapped her that night just because she had kissed me in front of Jahnvi, but that had happened out of our pent up anger and our decision that if we saw either of our 'exs' in the next two days, we'd kiss each other right in front of them. What I had never imagined was that we would actually bump into Jahnvi and that Aakriti would really kiss me. Her kissing was spontaneous and so was my reaction.

She was definitely not the only one with whom I had spent some intimate moments after my break-up with Jahnvi. There had been many more with many others. All these memories, all this nostalgia was taking a heavy toll of me as it was again draining me off emotionally. I was lonely and helpless again. Suddenly I could see the ray of hope in my guide, my philosopher, Dr. Raghubeer.

I visited him and as always, after the treatment, I felt relaxed. I would worry sometimes if I was doing justice to myself by undergoing these hypnotism sessions, then I would tell myself that as long as it was Dr. Raghubeer, I could trust him that nothing wrong would happen to me. He had helped me come out of the worst situation in my life; now nothing more was left to happen.

Half the students found placement before the third semester exams itself and with this, the first phase of placement came to an end. The exams were approaching and placements were kept on hold for a fortnight. The ones who were already placed did well but the others ruined their papers as for them, these were the last thing on their mind when one could not find any placement. I was one of them and didn't expect any better results.

Everybody else was back after a short five-day break. I didn't go anywhere mainly to avoid being asked the same question at this critical stage of life. "Placed? Why not?" And I didn't want to answer any of them.

I was shortlisted by a multinational company which offered 0.8 million rupees as CTC. After waiting for two hours, the names of some candidates were announced. I was one of them. Generally, the names of the selected candidates would be announced, but this time, they announced the ones who were out, since their number was comparatively less than the ones who had been selected. I had missed out on this and once again I was sad at being rejected.

It was already three months into the fourth semester and I had still not managed to get a decent placement. Nearly 80 per cent of my batch-mates were successfully placed. Anyway, I was shortlisted by four companies – they were banks, FMCG companies or from the entertainment industry. I was out either in the group discussion round or at the presentation stage. I never went up to the personal interview level.

Outlook was expected to arrive on campus, but they were not very sure of their visit this particular year to our college. So they offered me a PPO outside the campus route. I was disappointed with the offer they made. I had gone with huge expectations; it was disappointing.

The pressure was mounting. Threats from the placement cell became louder and clearer. The defaulters were given a last warning and reminded about the insurance companies visiting with their open trucks.

The third phase began. I received a mail and I was among the ones shortlisted by HDFC Bank. The test, presentation and interview were scheduled for next Monday at nine in the morning. There was one more unread mail. It made me flinch, but it made me smile too. It was from Jahnvi. It read:

'Arnab, I tried calling you a number of times. I guess you've changed your number. For the last time in my life, I am asking you to meet me. It's important. I would appreciate if you could take some time out from your busy life and meet me. I'll be waiting for your mail. Take care'

Her message sounded both hopeful and sorry and revealed love as well as hatred, care as well as sarcasm. "Love you and miss you" had been deleted long ago from our conversations, mails, messages and calls. I sat there, reading her mail again while contemplating if I should reply, but what could I reply. I continued thinking, deciding, re-thinking and re-deciding. I finally took my decision.

Chapter-16

CCD Pune, Old Monk & Rhea

I was waiting at the airport for the boarding announcement. Memories of the time when Jahnvi and I had flown to Pune during our "Plan Pune" came to my mind and I was taken to the period past. What fun it was, such adorable moments, such unconditional love it was!

I wanted to talk to her. It had been more than a year now. We had been in a relationship for three years and had spent the best of times and the worst of times; worst they were only when Jahnvi would not talk to me for days on end.

I looked at the people sitting around me – some looked happy, probably excited about their journey, while some others looked sad possibly because they were leaving behind a near and dear one.

I had mixed feelings. I couldn't help but recall the moments spent with my love, and that brought a smile to my face for a few seconds.

Jahnvi, oh Jahnvi...I made a sincere attempt to love you and you broke my heart.

I called Jahnvi.

The Airtel subscriber you are trying to call is not responding. Please try again later.

Beep...beep...beep!

Beep...beep...beep

As I approached the CCD – F. C. Road, I called her again. She as usual didn't picked up the call in the first attempt. I decided to do what I had been doing for years – wait.

I agreed to meet her on Sunday, after she told that she had something important to tell me. Rishi had already told me it was about the marriage proposals her Mom and Dad were considering for her and she wanted to meet me once, before that.

I was shocked, though I knew very well this was bound to happen some day. That it would happen so soon, I had never visualised. Rishi convinced me to meet her and I booked a cab to Pune once again. It was a difficult moment for me as numerous thoughts came flooding my mind. And these thoughts only made me more anxious.

I was overcome with a strong feeling of depression as soon as I reached Pune. It had been a long time since Jahnvi and I had last met. The eagerness to meet had been replaced by an unusual awkwardness. The last time we had seen each other had been a chance encounter – it was the night when I was with Aakriti and she with Rajiv. She had been horrified to see Aakriti and me kissing. Thereafter she had messaged me saying she had not expected such a thing from me. However, she had apologised later on learning the truth from Aakriti herself.

What will I talk to her? It's been a long time, I thought.

The place I chose to meet was C.C.D., hoping that Jahnvi recall the pleasant moments we had spent together there and wish to come back to me. I knew that was wishful thinking, but how could I prevent such thoughts from haunting me no matter how silly they were.

I was lost in my thoughts when I saw her marching towards me. She had lost weight and looked fragile, I thought. Earlier it was a routine for her ask me whether she had put on any weight or not. I would simply smile and say, 'Yes baby, you look slim. I was not even able to recognise you.' She would then break into a very broad, cute smile, so typical of her.

"Hi!" I said when she came to me. "You are looking quite slim," I complimented her, expecting the same cute smile. Her response was one of indifference.

"Thanks. Shall we go in?" she said and entered the cafe. We chose a place to sit.

"Well, what would you like to have?" I asked. This was the first time ever that I had asked this question.

"Is there any need to ask such a question, Arnab? Of course, our usual masala and Darjeeling tea," she said, in a tone which was full of shock and disappointment.

"No, I just asked since preferences tend to change over time. It's always better to confirm," I said, almost holding her responsible for the situation we were in. Then I signalled to the waiter to take our order.

"A litchi chill for me and masala tea for the lady," I said, changing my preference this time intentionally.

"Sir, please try today's special. You'll like it," the waiter suggested, offering his 'special' for the day.

"No, thank you, just get me what I ordered," I said without responding to his smile.

"Sir, it's a combo pack and money saving too," he explained.

"Have I asked you for your suggestions? Are you going to pay our bill? Do I look that miserable? I earn enough and can afford anything on your menu. I am not in that miserable condition," I gave vent to my anger at the waiter, my eyes fixed on Jahnvi. Jahnvi indicated to the waiter to leave.

He apologised profusely, his head bent low.

"How about an explanation for what you just did?" Jahnvi asked me in a sharp tone, raising her eyebrows. "He was merely telling you about today's special and this is part of his job. What the hell has happened to you?" she asked angrily, as if she didn't know why I reacted that way.

"Don't you know why?" I said meaningfully, avoiding direct eye contact with her.

The silence was gloomy and awkward. The waiter served us. I apologised to him. He acknowledged me with a smile and replied, "Sir, I can understand. You need not be sorry. Please enjoy your order. Thank you."

"So, how is everything with you in Mumbai? What's your schedule like?" she asked after almost half the tea was over and in an apparent effort to change the topic.

"I have my college from seven in the morning to twelve noon; then from one in the afternoon till ten in the night. I work for a production house, as an assistant writer. I also manage Dad's business for half the month," I said like a reporter reading the news. I was still avoiding eye contact.

"That's quite a lot of work. I mean what's the need to do so much?" she asked.

I could see she was still concerned about my health. She was like a dietitian, always advising me on what to eat and what not to and preaching about the health benefits of different kinds of food. But I must admit her tips had helped me a lot. Headaches were not so common when we were together, but by now I perpetually lived with one.

"I am doing it for myself and my family. I have actually learnt a lot about work in the past few months. It's not true that Sagittarians only dream," I said, reminding her of the words she had used for me once. "Actually you know what? I want to prove you wrong this time, Jahnvi, who thinks that people like me are only good at star-gazing and hardly make any effort to achieve things."

"Well, it's not as if someone rejected you, Arnab. It's just that may be they got a better option than you," she replied as calmly as possible.

"Better option?" I asked, staring at her this time to show my anger and frustration. "What better option? Just because someone is earning more than me doesn't make him a better person? Just ask him if he is ready to make all the sacrifices I made and struggle as much as I did to get you back."

Jahnvi chose not to respond and preferred to stay silent. She was not even looking at me.

"Is he ready to work fifteen hours a day for you? I bet he can't even do half of the things I have done," I said, almost screaming with a rage in a most unusual way of behaving.

"Money was never been an issue, Arnab, and my parents never had any personal grievances against you. But they would naturally want me to settle down in a family which is well known to them," she said. "There is something called 'relations.' He is my Dad's best friend's son and he is well settled too in his business," she said, when I abruptly interrupted in between.

"Oh! Don't tell me all this bullshit about business. That guy is just carrying on his Dad's 'already settled' business at the age of 25 and you call him well-settled?" I asked, holding my glass tightly. My litchi chill was actually 'boiling.' "I am running my Dad's business in another city single handedly, having a good job and also pursuing my MBA simultaneously from one of the best B-schools in the city. All this at age twenty and I am not settled? Is that what you are implying?" I had thrown an unexpected question and before she could answer I continued, "Jahnvi, let's try and clarify what you and your family are looking for in your husband."

I valiantly tried to control my tears and did succeed to some extent. However, one tear betrayed me and came down. Soon others followed as if a dam had burst. "I am a professional now. I work, I study and travel for 18 hours a day. I hardly get any time to rest. If you don't believe me, just pay me a visit once and see how I live my life," I said.

She offered her sympathies for my situation but did not utter a word.

"You know what my colleagues call me? They call me a psycho. But I don't care. They are just jealous of my work," I said, sobbing now. "I am not happy Jahnvi and you know why. It's only because you are not with me any more. I wanted to always share this happiness and success with you," I said, not realising why I admitted the fact. So, as if to correct my previous statement, I said, "Well, if you take me seriously, then, mind my words. I am happy, very happy," I said, behaving like a psycho. "In fact, I am very happy to be dumped by you in the midst of my life, Jahnvi. Thanks a lot for all you did to me," I said and my glass of litchi was again full die to the melting of ice.

"Don't misunderstand me or my family, Arnab. I know no one will love me as much as you do. You are the best person I could ever get as a life partner but I am not good enough for you. One needs to fix one's priorities in life. My parents are my first priority," she explained as her eyes turned wet.

"Priorities? What were your priorities when we were making love? You never discussed anything with me then," I said, making the situation worse.

"Forget it, Arnab, you won't understand this. You have asked me this hundreds of times before and I could not succeed in providing you with a convincing explanation," she said, ignoring my statement.

"All I asked you to do is to try and convince them and give me one single, fair chance," I said. "Can't you see how well I am doing for myself now?" I asked her, hoping that she would change her mind.

"Yes, I can see that but it's too late now. You took things too lightly when you shouldn't have done so. You would only build castles in the air and do nothing about it. You started taking me for granted, didn't you, Arnab? It was only after things went out of hand that you pulled up your socks and that's why we are in the mess we are in now," she fired back.

"Oh! So, now you hold me responsible for this break-up? Dreaming high can't be the sole reason for the break-up. I dreamt at twenty. Who doesn't? Twenty is no time to chase things. Let me remind you, you were the one who always encouraged me to dream. You never stopped me from doing that in the past. Then, why are you holding it against me now?" I said breathless with anger. "Why don't you admit that you never had the courage to approach your parents?" I began to lose my cool and failed to realise what I was saying was not the right thing to say.

"Oh, if that is what you want to listen to then well, so be it. I don't have the guts to talk to my parents about you any more. And one more thing, I don't love you, Arnab. Your behaviour in the last few days has made it easier for me to come to this decision," she said in a cracked voice and took her eyes away from me to hide her tears.

"Thanks for everything, but first thanks to your 'great' parents," I said, still not able to control my anger or my tongue.

"Don't you dare say anything against my parents. I'll kill you mercilessly and I mean it" she said with all possible anger in her eyes like a mother protecting her child. "It's a lot that I've heard from you against them. I will take it no more."

She would have actually killed me, I was sure of that. The conviction in her tone complemented the look on her face.

"Okay then. If this is all you had to say, then you may please leave and do whatever your parents want you to," I said. I am sure she was aware of the ire in me. "I'll do something very significant in my life to show you and your family what you have lost," I said.

I ignored her warning. She remained silent, seeing me boil with anger. Deep within me, I was crying from the bottom of my heart while still speaking. "Your Mom hated me for no reason. The only reason I can see is probably my age. Twenty years only and she had a daughter, six months elder to me, and many 'well-settled' guys earning millions and ready to lose their virginity to her."

She was speechless. All I could see were the tears in her eyes and crashing hopes. For a moment I thought I was seeing myself in a mirror. I began to realise how badly I was behaving. I hurt her by saying so many things, but most of all, I hurt myself with my words. She was looking down and crying. I was the reason for tears in those beautiful eyes – the eyes which meant the world to me.

I knew she still understood and loved me more than anyone else and yet, I said those harsh words only to make it easier to break-up, which was very harsh on me, since I was still deeply in love with her, and she knew it. It wasn't easy for her as well, and I could see that she was still finding reasons to support her decision. I was the best man she could ever get, but she would not make such a selfish move and hurt her parents. It was just not in her nature to do so.

And I respected that, but then either it is justice or it is love. I'd go with the former. Only God knew how much I loved her, but given the present circumstances, my faith was waning.

❖ ❖ ❖

It was Sunday evening and the young crowd was there as always. Travel agents fleeced tourists every weekend at Parihar Chowk. I was waiting for a seat in a cab while Shivneri was teeming with visitors as always.

I was left with only 500 rupees with me. In a hurry, I had left all my credit and debit cards back in Mumbai and I had nobody else in

Pune now to turn to for help. I would rather beg than borrow from Jahnvi.

"Excuse me," I heard a girl say from a distance on seeing me wait for a cab.

I confirmed if it was me she was talking to.

"Yes, you," she said, waving her hand.

I walked up to her. She was beautiful and looked sexy in a light blue outfit. She was quite fair, with dark pink lips, dark hair and brown eyes. Her voice was sweeter than a koel's.

"Yes, please?" I asked.

"Are you waiting for a vehicle?" she asked.

"Yes. I want to go to Powai. Do you know anybody here?"

"There is an Innova standing there. We are already three of us and are looking out for one more person. Would you like to join?"

"How much is he asking for?"

"Eight hundred bucks."

"Sorry, I just have 500 with me. I think I had better wait for some other cab."

"No use. The fares will reach 1,000 by midnight. Don't worry, I'll pay the rest. Anyway, nobody else is coming. They are expecting a cab at 200 rupees per seat at this time."

"Are you sure you wouldn't mind?"

"Yes. Now don't waste any more time. Let's go."

I had to take a cab anyway since I had my interview scheduled at nine the next morning and I didn't want to be one amongst the defaulters. It was thanks to this girl that I could find a seat for 500 rupees.

I paid the money to her and she gave me a hundred back, saying, "You'll need it. This cab will drop you till Andheri flyover only."

We started moving and a lively conversation began between the four of us in the car.

Ranjeet was a senior chef in a 5-star hotel at Mumbai; Kunal was the owner of a restaurant chain and had just opened a branch in Pune. The most-awaited introduction was that of Rhea. She was a radio jockey in Mumbai and a struggling television artiste. In comparison to them all, my profile was the least impressive.

The driver too narrated his life in half an hour. Kunal, who was sitting on the front seat, beside the driver, interrupted and said, "I don't know why the hell he is narrating his life to us. Is anybody interested?"

"No," everybody replied in unison and burst out laughing.

The driver realised he was the subject of the joke and kept quiet thereafter.

Ranjeet opened a bottle of Old Monk and everybody, other than me, had a gulp each.

"Why, don't you drink?" Rhea asked.

"No. I don't."

"Come on, don't lie, Arnab. I don't believe you. You don't look like someone who has never had a drink," Rhea said and winked.

"I have been noticing this from the time we started our journey. There's something that is bothering Arnab. He's very quiet. Open one more for Arnab and let's see him on a high," Ranjeet suggested.

"Nothing like that, guys. It's just that I end up on a drastic note when I drink. I have had some nasty experiences in the past."

"Don't worry, Rhea won't rape you Arnab." Kunal said. Rhea smiled naughtily.

"You can't trust me, when I drink. Beware," I replied.

"We would love to see you drink – a drink in the name of Arnab," Rhea said and opened yet another bottle of Old Monk.

"So what do you do, Arnab, apart from pursuing MBA?" Kunal asked.

"I study, I do a job and manage the family business."

"And what does that mean?" Ranjeet asked.

"I am an assistant writer working for a production house these days. I have a business in Mumbai and I am in the final year of my MBA course."

"Great genius. That's fantastic. What made you come to Pune?" Rhea asked.

"I was here for six months doing my internship. Right now I came here to meet my ex- girlfriend."

"That sounds interesting, but isn't it ironical that you are meeting your 'ex'?"

"Had some old issues that needed to be sorted out. Now we can move ahead."

"Not every love story has such a good ending. Are you happy now?"

"Yes, kind of."

"It sounds as if your love life has not had a happy ending."

"We are not that old. You can talk to both of us. We are in our 30's, but that doesn't mean you need to feel shy in talking to us. Right, Kunal?" Ranjeet said and laughed.

"Agreed Ranjeet. Who knows these two might turn out to be a couple and we might see them making out somewhere," Kunal said.

I felt embarrassed for myself and for Rhea too.

Surprisingly, Rhea was really cool and said, "Shut up guys. Can't you see him turning red?"

For the very first time in my life I realised why girls grow up faster than guys. I was turned on the moment I saw her. She was making it more difficult for me to control myself. I could pay the whole cab fare and ask to be left alone with Rhea, I thought. This made me smile to myself.

I began narrating my story about how I had spent my life so far. With the first peg I talked about the 'Renaissance Rooh' musical band I was part of. By the time I consumed the sixth peg, I was telling them all about how my love life.

We crossed Lonavla. I noticed tears in Rhea's eyes after I had finished my story.

"Why are you crying champ? You've got better things to do in life and I am sure enough girls must be waiting in line for you," Rhea said and I realised I was crying too.

Ranjeet offered me his shoulder and I wiped off my tears. "Sorry guys," I apologised for spoiling their mood.

"Don't be. It's better to speak out, rather than keep things to yourself," Kunal said and went on to say how just for his child's sake, he had kept quiet even on seeing his wife having an affair with another man.

I was the only one who looked shocked; the rest of them took it as an unimportant matter.

Ranjeet told us how he survived terrorist attacks in his hotel. He said, "Life gave me a second chance and I'll live it to the best."

Rhea then went on about her life and struggles, and how difficult it was for a small-town girl like her to make her mark in the radio industry.

We seemed to share a similar story as far as our love lives were concerned, the only difference was that her boyfriend was a television artiste. He had set his own principles and turned a four-year commitment into an open relationship asking Rhea to do the same. According to him, it was boring to see the same face for so long. Wasn't that cool? He had a brief affair with his co-actress. When that came to an end, he was left with nothing and asked Rhea to come back.

Rhea was not the one to give in easily and gave it back to him in his own way. She got the satisfaction she was looking for.

Our cab then came to a halt due to a flat tyre. We were completely drunk. We came out of the car and sat along the Pune-Mumbai expressway.

"You want to pee?" Ranjeet asked on seeing me dance around.

"No, I am actually enjoying this moment. I don't want to be normal," I said. Rhea smiled.

I fell in love with Rhea's smile. Her teeth sparkled like diamonds. I wondered if she could look prettier than this. She was so full of life even after a break-up. Her brave attitude was inspiring. It looked like we had been friends for years.

"What plans for tomorrow? Come on air them with me. We are looking out for musical talent and I can see one in you. Give a 30-second bite."

"I have my placement interview tomorrow. What about the day after?"

"We have the competition lined up for tomorrow only. Why don't you stay the night at my flat? We'll record your bite at six in the morning and I'll drop you back at your college. Powai is not too far from my office. I hope you don't need to prepare before you go for your interview."

"No, not at all. I've faced enough interviews till date. The sad part is I was never selected," I smiled. "But will it be okay if I stay at your place?"

"Come on, I wouldn't have asked you otherwise. It's my flat. Be assured. We'll have fun. We'll get drunk. I'll record your voice and drop you off at your college. Simple."

"Done. It'll be fun to attend an interview in a drunken state of mind."

"You have enough reason for everything; you're different Arnab," she said.

Ranjeet called us once the puncture got fixed.

We sang songs, exchanged jokes, drank some more and enjoyed the next half an hour before we reached Mumbai. We exchanged numbers and promised to meet up soon.

"It's difficult to see you leave. You got us so addicted to your company in these three hours," Kunal said.

"We'll meet soon. It was nice to be a part of this journey. Thanks guys. See you."

And they departed.

Rhea took me to her home. Her flat was a beautifully well furnished one with neat curtains, a beautiful swimming pool and other luxuries. On one of the walls I saw a picture of Rhea with four different men and on another wall was a sad picture with a guy on either side.

I racked my brains but couldn't understand the reason behind the arrangement of pictures on the walls. I then asked Rhea about it. She replied, "He's the guy who made me sad, my ex-boyfriend, Robin. And they are the ones who made me happy, for a month, day or even for some moments."

I was visibly flummoxed. On seeing my expression, Rhea said, "Let me explain. With these pictures I console myself that I have a greater number of people who have made me happy and less number of people who have broken my heart. Whenever I get weird ideas, such as wanting to commit suicide, I see these pictures and feel happy that I have many who fall for me and still love me." As an afterthought, she added, "You can't always trust yourself."

"I know. I agree and am quite impressed by your logic," I said and she thanked me for this.

"Feel comfortable. Would you like a drink?" she asked.

"Anytime," I said.

She opened a bottle of IS VODKA - England and a bottle of wine. I saw her cupboard had a collection of Vodka bottles.

"Cheers," and our glasses clashed.

We talked about each other's lives, fantasies, wild dreams and almost everything under the sun. And I heard her say, "We got introduced through one of our mutual friends. We started meeting up. He proposed, I ignored. He proposed again. I couldn't resist and agreed. We shared a bond for four years. He ditched me and I ditched him too." From then, I've been in many brief relations and flings.

It reminded me of Aakriti, but this night was not meant to remember the past. It was meant to live every moment of the present with a smile on our faces. No matter how sleepy I felt, I told myself not to sleep. I made myself a promise.

"The latter part of your story was not good for your image. Everything else sounded cool," I said.

"What's wrong with that? One need not be in love to fulfil sexual desires. I feel sex is just another need of the human body: the more you hold back, the more frustrated you get and spoil everything you do."

Though I argued with her on some points, I was mesmerised on seeing her. I thanked God for giving me this opportunity to spend time with her. We came closer. She smiled.

"Which wall will you put me on? Happy or sad?" I asked.

"I'll put you on a different wall since I have never ever seen a guy like you." There was something different in her tone and I could not make it out. Was it love? Or lust? Or simply an invitation?

I thought for few seconds over it and then told her: "You are turning me on," and smiled wickedly.

"This is not the first time. I'll take it as a compliment."

I lost my balance and fell on the floor. She helped me sit up. This time she sat just next to me on the balcony. It was a feeling I had never experienced before, not even with Jahnvi. But I knew what Jahnvi was for me, Rhea would never be that. Jahnvi was my love, my life. while Rhea was a friend I had been lusting for since the moment I had set my eyes on her.

"It's getting impossible now. You had better not try to move away from here now."

She switched off her mobile. "Here we go," she said.

We came closer to each other. Mumbai rains come always as a shock. This time it was a pleasant surprise. It made us both wet.

"Is it getting uncomfortable here?" she asked.

"There is always a sense of pleasure in being uncomfortable when there is a beautiful girl with you. Do you need a blanket?" I added.

"It can't get any warmer than when we hold each other closely."

I blindfolded Rhea. She took a good hold of me. We undid each other's hurdles - clothes.

She was the beautiful fairy, I was the horny devil.

She was the innocent soul and I was the lusty cock.

She had intentions to keep it just right; I had my motives to spoil everything that night.

She removed the blindfold. She looked. I caressed her breasts. I was crooked.

She bit me on the shoulder. She bit me on my back.

I bit her under her lips, and she was taken aback.

She didn't lose the fight, she held on her breath.

I held her bums tight, and slept beneath.

She was shy, she was afraid.

I didn't ask why, it was just great.

She looked into my eyes, and I bent forward.

I looked back into her eyes, and I conquered the whole world.

It was fantasy, it was ecstasy,

I made her scream, I never was that cozy.

I made her cry, I made her shout.

She didn't ask me why, I was the one to be allowed.

She was pleased, she was mesmerised.

I was amazed, I was satisfied.

She was breathing hard, she was the beauty.

Evil intentions on the cards, I had not yet finished my duty.

She calmed her nerves, her eyes were venomous.

I started it again, this night is wondrous.

She scratched by back, she scratched my hand.

I was full on sweat, I held back her hand.

She had gone crazy, she again came from the back.

Smoother and greasier, and she was again awake.

Sex was in the air, we saw it everywhere.

Under her lair, we did it everywhere.

We played a lustful game not in the balcony but in the washroom, with every combination possible. Sex feels good when you have it with a loved one, but it feels better when done to get rid of frustration. I released my frustrations and so did Rhea. Thanks to Mumbai for its unpredictable climate, it made life more pleasurable.

We slept. We woke up early and recorded music in her studio. She dropped me back at my college for the HDFC Bank interview. She kissed me and wished me luck.

The only thing I was worried about was the love bites on my chin, upper neck and ears. I didn't want love bites to be the reason for being rejected at the interview. I could almost hear the placement officer saying: "Placement is not your right. It is just the facility that we provide you. Join the insurance truck or else go away. Happy placement day," Horrifying, it sounded.

Chapter-17

Money, Respect and New Job

I reached the hall well before time. The students milling around were either nervous or afraid. I had mixed feelings this time too. The placement coordinator appeared and announced, "We shall start the process in a few moments." This increased our heartbeats threefold. Everyone knew that banks did not subscribe to 'bulk recruitments'.

Then, they arrived – a man in his mid-thirties, a lady in her late twenties and a girl just a couple of years older than her. They seated themselves on the makeshift podium. They were welcomed by the placement cell's members and the man rose and introduced himself as Rohit, the cluster head. Then the trio launched into the company's history and everything else which this class must have crammed a number of times before. They proceeded to the company's mission, vision, and goal. Finally, they came to the critical part which we all had been waiting for.

The Deputy Manager's profile conveyed that he would be based in Mumbai and the package would be one million rupees CTC. I noted a 20 per cent improvement in the package from the previous year. We were amazed and we were happy souls though only for a moment. Our dreams were shattered when they announced that there were only three vacancies for which they would select candidates from this college. Most of us had expected at least eight vacancies, similar to the previous year. This time there was to be a test which was to serve as the elimination round and would comprise of questions on Maths, GK, Reasoning and DI. It was to be an hour long.

We sat for the test. Within half an hour the results were declared. I was among the shortlisted 50. My batchmate Gaurav cried his heart out at being eliminated in the first round itself. The next round was the presentation round, where five of us would have to team up and present a case on banking. The topics would be written out on chits of paper and we had to pick up a chit, discuss and place our case together. We cursed our luck since banking had been one class most of us had bunked throughout the semesters.

We were given an hour to prepare the presentation and all of us managed to do it within the stipulated time. We shared our roles and everybody asked me to introduce the case. I agreed, since introducing the case did not ask for too much and everything else was proving to be difficult to comprehend. When the panel called out my group first, we panicked. Since I had to introduce the case, I stepped on to the podium first. I was so scared and nervous that I was sweating. I held the mike and greeted the panellists with a "Good morning" instead of a "Good afternoon". The gaffe was obvious. I could see many in the audience smirk; my groupmates shaking their heads sideways which showed their disappointment. But the panellists remained pokerfaced.

I don't know if that was a good thing or bad, but now I had to immediately cover up this blunder so as to save my ass. I smiled and said, "I am still feeling as fresh as dew in the morning. Apologies if the rest of you do not share my sentiments," I replied and everybody laughed.

"Shoot!!" Said the cluster head and gave me a warm smile. I introduced the case and as it was based upon relationship management, I explained the roles and duties of the manager.

"Wait, wait, wait!! What are you doing? What you are saying about the role is actually listing out the duties and what you are saying about duties is actually the role of the manager. Do you want to reconsider what you have just said?" the girl from the panel asked me.

Almost everyone jeered at me at this turn of events. I apologised for the mistake and revised the introduction.

"Why should you keep your HNI clients satisfied? Is it mandatory?" Rohit asked.

"It's because they are the ones who have tried almost every product when you earnestly wanted them to buy those and if they are satisfied, it means a lot to the bank," I replied.

"Why does it mean so much to the bank?"

"Because a happy customer will spread positive words, which will increase our market share for obvious reasons and a negative customer will say the wrong things and take customers away from us. So it depends on who we select for the role."

"Yes, that's what I was looking out for. That's the line I wanted to hear from you. Great, excellent," Rohit said and I gained back my lost confidence with this.

Everybody who had been jeering at my gaffes had by now fallen quiet. I completed my part and handed the mike over to the other members of my group. The presentations were completed in three hours. My group members were not too happy about the introduction but I had nevertheless brought them back into the reckoning or I at least I thought I had.

We took a break for lunch and the panellists said they would put up the selections post-lunch. None of us ate much; everyone at best gulped down energy drinks. The results were announced soon after and in this round, 20 people were shortlisted. I had made the cut...albeit just by a whisker. I was number 19 on the list. Payal, Jimmy, Piyush, Harsh...and a few more known names completed this bunch.

I had by now visited the washroom thrice in the last one hour as I was so nervous. The time had come for the final interviews. I was once again the first one to be called inside. There were two panellists taking interviews. The first round was by Rohit, the cluster head and the second by the older lady. We were divided into two groups of ten members and each member was to be quizzed by both panellists. This was the time when I sent across urgent messages to God. praying fervently and hoping that I would steer clear of the hurdles.

Then I saw the placement coordinator smile at me. She was already placed with a media company and so smiling was not proving too much of an effort for her.

"Arnab, it's your turn. You may go in," she said.

I froze when she asked me to move and my hands began to tremble involuntarily. My throat dried up but something from deep within made me stand up and walk the few steps to the place that would open many other doors in my life.

I knocked on the door and heard a muffled voice say, "Come in."

I sat down in front of the panellists. "So, Arnab, this is obviously not your best day! How is it going?" I was asked.

"Not really, ma'am. I started on a wrong note but I am back in the game and not a coward to run away and not face the challenge. So it's been pretty interesting," I replied.

"Sounds confident. Introduce yourself," she continued.

I went through the motions just as I had rehearsed.

"You are into music, writing, travelling. So why a bank?"

"I took it as challenge to clear a bank interview and I did that. I always try my best to work upon the things I like."

"If you get a chance to work in the music or writing industry, would you leave us and join that assuming you get through our interview?"

"No ma'am, the reason would be that I believe in working at one thing at a time. And I have a passion for banking."

"Your father has a business, your brother did get a job here in Mumbai, but quit in a year's time to join your father. It somehow doesn't look good on the charts. You've got all the facilities to lead a luxurious life, so why are you making your life miserable here?"

"My Dad's business is quite seasonal. My brother and he are able to handle it very well amongst themselves. There is no need to introduce another family member in the same thing. Hence, I decided to work what I thrive for, for what I am passionate about."

"You didn't answer the first half?"

"Oh, yes, my brother. He is a different person and has different priorities in life. I am a different person. Both of us have our interests and capabilities, our dreams and aims. We have always been different. I cannot do what he does best and he can't do what I am good at."

"Hmm...are you flexible with the location?"

"I think it's for Mumbai only."

"If we put you elsewhere, would you have a problem with that?"

"No ma'am, I would still work with you."

"We have been in the recruitment field since the past decade and have seen enough attrition on issues of location to last us a lifetime. You do not hope that we would buy your 'yes madam' thing?"

"I totally respect your point, ma'am, but I am flexible enough to go anywhere."

"If you were based at Satara, is that fine?"

"Being a fresher, I don't expect too much of a say in the choice of location, ma'am. I should not expect this either. Even if you send me to Antarctica, I shall be ready to start as soon as you give me an offer letter. Yes, provided, the place you send me to, will take care of food and shelter for me."

She smiled, asked me some more questions and signalled me to leave.

"All the best!" she said as I left.

I was happy with my performance and satisfied with the way I had performed. I was in a good mood and smiling. A small voice cautioned me, "This is not going to work for you."

I silenced this voice and did not let it dampen my high spirits. Seeing the transformation in me, the others waiting for their interview, felt a bit threatened and nervous. Half of them asked for water while the other half seemed to be holding up well on the outside though seemed dead scared from within.

Once the first round of interviews ended, we got ready for the second round. It was 9 p.m. and we waited for the results.

The HDFC officers soon left but not before handing a sheet to the placement coordinator. "So guys, tell me who all are genuinely interested in getting placed with HDFC bank?" he asked.

Everybody raised their hands.

"But everybody can't get it. They have only three vacancies." He went on and on about the kind of reputation we had to uphold given the college had always given HDFC bank the best professionals – people who had worked their way up the rungs. Nobody was interested in this speech.

"Results please!" said a girl from amongst us.

"Yes, of course."

I always hated it when somebody created suspense for much longer than necessary. Why prolong the agony? The coordinator took out the sheet and said, "There are three students and these three have made the panellists very happy. Congrats to those who are selected, and all the best to the rest. Don't lose hope as this is not the end of the world."

He did not announce the names of the lucky three. Instead, he called out everyone's names and suffixed them with a 'selected' or 'not selected', thus making all of us irritable.

"Harsh- not selected. Payal- not selected. Jimmy- selected. Expected and he was happy. Anish- selected. Arnab..." He said and then his phone rang. He fished it out and answered it. I cursed the person who had called and could feel all eyes bore into me.

"Selected" he said. I had been sitting with my eyes closed all this while. I heard him announce and jumped up.

"Am I selected?"

"Yes," laughed the coordinator.

I jumped up and down and hugged everybody who happened to be standing next to me. My friends congratulated me and patted me on the back. I shouted out aloud and fell on my knees to thank God. I had proved myself. I was selected for a post that would pay me a million rupees per year. What a stroke of luck! I was happy and at the top of the world. I rushed home with the news and my Dad was the happiest. His voice choked with emotion but he fought back his tears and hugged me. My brother did the same. My mother could not hide her tears. Rishi called me and on hearing the news, declared a late night party over the weekend. Aditi was happier than me. She said, "I so want to hug you. I wish you could be here with me."

I messaged Rhea. She called me back and said, "See, I told you. You are so different. You won two battles within 24 hours. Meet me this weekend; let's have fun and you owe me a treat."

I agreed. She was on for a show, so we couldn't chat longer. "Miss you," she said.

"Bye," I replied.

This was the time also to get in touch with the one person who had helped me when I was down and low and who had given me the strength and courage to make it to this point. Dr. Raghubeer Yadav. I had to visit him. I went to his clinic early the next morning but did not find him there. The clinic was shut, which was odd because it opened pretty early. I went on to his apartment and what I saw there broke my heart.

Dr. Yadav had apparently died of cancer the previous night – the night when I had celebrated my selection. He had been in the terminal stage but seemed to be in the pink of health in spite of the chemotherapy. He had told me he was going to the US for a holiday. Apparently he could not handle the last round of chemo. It was very painful and he had asked for death this time. I was shocked, stunned by his sudden demise.

Seeing his family totally distraught, I broke down too. My mentor, the person who had changed the course of my life had left me. He had been a living legend for me. Unlike other psychiatrists, he had been a man with dreams, hopes and energy. I would miss him; this void in my life would always remain.

"Dad had kept this aside to be given to you," said Dr. Yadav's son as soon as he espied me.

I opened the envelope and pulled out a sheet of paper. "Hey Arnab," It read. "Sorry champ, didn't tell you about this. You must be wondering why? It's just because you needed to complete your treatment first. It could have been bad for your health otherwise. You are a true fighter beta. You are one different patient that I have ever seen in my life and I am happy to die after having met you.

You've cried a lot. Now is the time to move ahead and make your own miracles. You are meant to do that. Never neglect the signals God is giving you. You are smart enough to understand that.

"Always remember to 'smile' and things will fall in your favour. God bless you with a happy life ahead."

Tears welled up after reading his letter. He was the one who had shown me the path to walk, been with me through my thick and thin; he was the one who had showed confidence in me and my abilities. I was going to miss him badly.

❖ ❖ ❖

It was 1 a.m. and I had still not slept. The joy I had experienced at having been selected had now been replaced by sadness at the sudden demise of Dr. Yadav.

Rhea called me a number of times but I didn't respond to any of her calls. She messaged: "Arnab, the results are out and I am so happy for you. Muuuaahhh. Call me when you read this, darling."

Her message didn't distract me either.

I had moved to Pune and Mumbai for Jahnvi. She would have felt good had we been together. She would have demanded to be taken out on a shopping spree to celebrate this. A big chocolate cake would have been cut to make the event memorable. We had enjoyed so much as a couple about two years ago. Those times were magical moments; her smile was all that I demanded. Why she didn't give me one fair chance? It could have got better, if handled in a better way, I thought, holding back my tears.

'Rhea is right when she says you don't need love to have sex and you don't need sex to prove your love,' I thought. 'Things have changed to a large extent now. She is getting married soon, but I still miss her. I love her so badly that I want to make her parents realise that I have proved myself,' said a little voice inside me.

I messaged her:

"I loved you to the heart's core, but I can't take it anymore.

I thought you would come back; I waited till sea-shore.

I hate the moment, I loved you and love the moment I hate you.

I doubt the love we shared, I doubt now if it was you.

You knew me inside out, you didn't trust me either.

I battled and alone fought, I was the broken feather.

You kissed me on love, I hold you on trust.

You smiled and just said- it was emotional outburst.

We walked away in life, we enjoyed till last moment,

I was still enjoying, I still beg and bent.

You cheated me on love, you cheated me on life.

I was kicked alone, you meant me a life.

I cared you till death; I cuddled you till last breath.

I am living die; you laid a coffin under the wreath.

I loved you to the heart's core, but I can't take it anymore.

I thought you would come back; I waited till sea-shore."

Rhea and I met twice over the weekends as we enjoyed each other's company, but that was it. I flew back to Indore after my exams got over in a month's time to spend some time with my parents and old friends. I needed a break from life and what could be a better way to spend the break?

Chapter-18

Dream or Reality?

It was a dark and gloomy night and everything was blurred. I was feeling low, immobile, motionless and lifeless. I had again fought with Jahnvi near 'Hiranandani Galleria.' She was crying and I had left her in the middle of the street, alone and helpless. She was trying to talk to me but I had been ruthless. I had hired a cab and moved away.

I was sitting in a cab with no idea where I wanted to go. I was replaying the entire evening with Jahnvi and sulking. I knew what I had done was wrong, but I had no will, no guts to resurrect it. I could feel someone sitting besides me in the cab. I turned to my right and couldn't believe my eyes for what I was seeing.

I was surprised to see my Dadaji in the cab with me. He looked different; in fact he looked a lot younger, as young as my Dad perhaps. He said, "Arnab, I have little time. I know that all is not well with you. Just pay attention to what I am showing you. This is the time to act and more importantly, to understand something."

"Dadaji, how do you know everything? And how are you here?" My eyes were still wide with bewilderment.

"I came here for you and I know everything, Arnab; everything. I just have limited time with me, so try to understand what I show and tell you." Saying so, he took my hands and clutched them and asking me to close my eyes. I was blank for a few seconds. Then slowly the uneven and blurred image appeared in front of me and I saw Jahnvi crying in front of her parents.

"How can you say that Arnab is not the guy for me, Mom? He's just 20. How can you expect him to become a millionaire at such a young age?" she was asking her parents betweens sobs. I could see her eyes were red with crying for hours together.

"Jahnvi, we have seen enough of him. That guy has nothing impressive to show. He's just another fellow and we can't let you marry a useless fellow."

"Give him some time. Give him one fair chance in life. I am sure he won't let anybody down," she was begging.

"Jahnvi, the guy who lies to his parents can do nothing better. The poor parents don't know how often that guy lies to them."

"He lied for you Mom, not for any other reason. I saw him preparing to teach you. He did everything possible to impress you and you saw nothing special in him. He lied because his Dad is a heart patient. He didn't want to make him anxious. Unfortunately, everything went wrong at the time; wrong place it was," she explained.

"Whatever. Your Dad and I don't like that guy; he's not as good looking as you. In fact there is nothing that I can recommend about him," her mother said.

"You shouldn't have married Dad then!"Jahnvi fired back and was slapped by her Mom.

"Young lady, you had better watch your tongue. Don't you dare compare that good-for-nothing chap with your father, who has proved his mettle early and has garnered a lot of respect in society."

"I am sure he didn't gain this same respect you talk about when he was in his early 20's," Jahnvi said, sobbing.

"I need not answer everything you ask me. We have Malhotra uncle's son, Sahil. He wants to marry you and he is gearing up to handle his Dad's oil business. We have matched your horoscope and the compatibility levels between you and him have made us eager to go ahead with the match. If they also agree to this, I would not want you to create a scene but simply agree to the marriage," her mother said point blankly.

"How can you take any decision regarding my life without even asking me? Now, are you not cheating on my life? Where's Arnab wrong now?"

"Don't shout. We have had enough of this blabbering. Please call off this relationship between you and Arnab and settle down with the boy we choose. It's a question of our standing in society." With this Jahnvi's Mom left, leaving her to cry her heart out, with no one to console her.

She brought out the picture we had clicked at the Sarovar and hugged it tight and cried uncontrollably. I don't know how Dadaji managed it, but he showed me some more images of Jahnvi being screamed at by her Dad. She was pleading her case but her brother and father argued her into silence. Everyone at home seemed to have stopped talking to her, making Jahnvi lead the life of a stranger in her own house.

The situation took a turn for the worse when Jahnvi's father was diagnosed with a critical heart ailment. The pressures he had undergone suddenly seemed to take a toll on his health and this made Jahnvi relent to their wishes. Everyone seemed happy with her decision but I noticed that Jahnvi had completely lost herself. Her figure had begun to droop and her eyes carried a far away look. She was with people but still away from them. She was lost in a world of her own thoughts and remorse.

I had doubted her, doubted her intentions. It was right that I did not deserve her. I was shown some more moments where Jahnvi missed me, cried for me, called me to convey what all she was going through. She wanted help in resettling it all between us and every time she called me, I disconnected her call or nailed her, abusing her family.

I lost myself in the thick of things with girls after I had broken up with Jahnvi. There was Rhea, the one whom I bedded even as Jahnvi was admitted in the hospital because of a nervous breakdown and fluctuating blood pressure. When I was drinking myself silly, she was the one struggling for her life. When I was earning thousands per month, she was the one who was alone between a thousand souls. Her friends made it miserable for her as some of her so-called friends bitched about her behind her back and demeaned her in front of others. With so many unpleasant events conspiring against her, she had to pass two miserable years, though they passed in a jiffy for me. Poor Jahnvi died a hundred deaths in those two years!

Dadaji showed me how those two years had been for Jahnvi. She had become a recluse, lost all her friends and stopped going out. She tried to communicate with her family, but they were invariably rude to her and rebuked her. She cried every time I disconnected her call.

She also tried to end her life but what stopped her were thoughts about me and how I would react to this news. Though she maintained a calm exterior, I knew there was a storm brewing inside her. I realised how rude I had been to her each time she called. I had left no stone unturned to make her suffer and regret her decision to let go of me. And now, thinking of all this, made me feel worse and worthless.

I saw everything right from how she stopped celebrating her birthday and how she would to go to the church, sit there for hours together, praying silently with tears rolling down her cheeks; how she would visit CCD to experience and relive her memories of the times we had met there; she would often walk on the KNP-Pune Road and had once even visited Lonavla to plant a sapling near the bus stop where we had kissed for the very first time; she even went to Sarovar, Indore too.

The images were now getting blurred and very soon they disappeared.

My eyes were still shut and when I opened them, I realised that tears were streaming down my eyes. I began to sob loudly, not caring about the surroundings around me.

"How do you feel now?" Dadaji asked me, slowly patting my shoulder.

"I am lost, Dadaji. I don't know what I have done. I've hurt the girl who still loves me more than anybody else. She tried convincing her parents for so many days and weeks, and I badmouthed her. She cried every day, every night for me. She treasured the moments we spent and I was the one sleeping around with other girls! I am sorry, I am really sorry for what I have done. I didn't realise how I changed so much and became revengeful. I wanted to distance myself from her. I never wanted to hurt her. I... did no..." Leaving the sentence mid way, I broke down again.

"Say whatever you feel but you owe an explanation to Jahnvi. My sole intention in coming here has been to make you realise the mistake you were committing. You didn't come to my funeral and we couldn't meet before I died. I wanted to come and show you where you were going wrong, but now I need to go. I don't have much time with me. Never ever leave Jahnvi as she's the one you will need at every step of your life. She's God's child. I am afraid we can't meet any more after this, but always keep my words in mind. Go to the girl you have hurt. It's never too late to mend the differences. Don't leave her in the middle of her life. Go and apologise to her for the mistakes you have committed."

He hugged me and I felt a deep pain in my heart. He blessed me and disappeared. I was crying. Had that been a dream? Had Dadaji really come there and spoken to me or was my conscience playing tricks on me?

The taxi-driver now turned around. It was Dr. Raghubeer. He smiled.

❖ ❖ ❖

"Keep smiling always. You never know but things may just fall in place," he would have said. I was startled.

Was he for real? What was he doing, driving a taxi? I rubbed my eyes. Some more of what he always said echoed in my mind. "Never neglect the signals God is giving you. You are smart enough to understand that."

It took me a while to come out of what I was experiencing. Why were the two very important people in my life appearing out of nowhere and giving me valuable advice? There was definitely something in the messages these two people were giving me. They had unknowingly answered my unasked questions and given me the direction, the path to follow. I pondered over it for few minutes and made my decision. I opened my eyes.

I called and told Aditi about the dream and she suggested that I should call Jahnvi. She was yet again being my support and encouraging me to take the right steps and do it quick.

I pulled out my cell phone to call Jahnvi but stopped midway when a realisation dawned upon me. How could I call her? She had changed her number! I was perturbed about what I could do to contact her.

Chapter-19

Life 360 Degrees

Life is full of surprises and shocks and accompanied with all kinds of emotions. We all are beings of emotions, not logic. The little emotions are high post-captains of our lives and we obey them without any questioning.

In spite of doing well and having stood up to everybody's expectations, including my own, my heart was not contented and happy. It felt as if something was amiss. All were agog with joy and excitement but I was questioning myself the reason for my lack of happiness.

My parents were happy and so were the others, as according to them I had successfully ended a chapter of my life only to begin a new one. Everyone was thrilled and excited but the smile pasted on my face hardly reached my eyes or my heart, but no one cared to notice that. Life, for me, had turned gloomy; everything seemed vague and unsure. I thought perhaps meditation would help me ease off my uneasiness; but all it did was to make me more vulnerable as the universe had different plans in store for me.

I don't generally meditate because for me meditation brings along with it unpleasant memories and memories always won, leaving me with nothingness.

Frustrated with everything and nothing, I switched on my Laptop. Connecting device… authenticating… authenticated… and connected.

Beeped the dialogue boxes on the monitor. I logged into my Facebook account and was shocked. I saw the status update from Jahnvi.

It read:

"Last few hours in Pune."

I read and reread all the comments that were posted in her post. I did so only to come across something that would make me realise what her post actually meant. I finally came across a comment where a girl had wished her good luck and congratulated her for the next phase in her life.

So Jahnvi was getting married. I thought about it and my heartbeats trebled. I called Aditi and explained to her the situation. Even she sounded perplexed.

So that was why she had not been answering my calls. Now all the things were slowly falling in place; everything made sense now.

"Don't draw any conclusions and feel sorry; instead, do something," Aditi screeched.

"Aditi, call your travel agent and confirm my ticket on the next flight to Pune. I don't care how much it costs," I suddenly told her.

"Are you mad? Don't be so impatient and take decision in haste."

"Do as I say. I'll try calling her and if she answers the call, I'll....umm... congratulate."

"Shut up, nothing will happen. Be confident. I'll call you back in a while."

She called half an hour later. The tickets were reserved. She picked me up from my home, wished me luck and dropped me off at the airport.

And here I was waiting to board the flight for Pune; still hoping for the change; hoping for a fairy to wave her magic wand.

"Flight no. IT-2821 Kingfisher Red is boarding now. Passengers are requested to move to Gate 3."

The flight was uneventful. It took off and landed in an hour's time. I remembered how we had done the same route together when we had planned our journey to Pune the last time. That seemed ages ago now. Time was such a relative term. It would seem recent if any good event had occurred but it would become distant and age-old if it turned out to be a bad experience.

Things were different now. Jahnvi was getting married and I blamed myself. I simply hoped I could see her one last time. I wanted to apologise for all the ill I had said or done to hurt her or make her cry and would give anything at all to do anything to see her once.

By now many people must have come to know about her impending marriage and were probably congratulating her. She must naturally be quite happy. It was my ego and attitude that had messed up things and I was ready to take all the blame. No one else needed to be punished.

It took me half an hour more to reach the British library. My calls were still unanswered. I entered the street where I used to wait for Jahnvi in the past. It was pleasant and soothing to come to the same place. I wished I had the time machine on which I could rewind time to two years ago. I wished I could just fall off the bed and realise everything had been a bad dream and wished that Jahnvi and I could pick up from where we had left off. But then memories have their own rules – the sweet ones make you weep.

I reached her hostel. The watchmen stared at me and I felt uncomfortable. I waited for the next three hours and didn't move from my place. I called Jahnvi but she disconnected the call. Her disconnecting the call meant she still had saved my number. The Marathi announcement that followed post the ring tone meant she was still in Pune. I waited, waited and waited till I saw a cab driver ask for Jahnvi's hostel address. The cab reached the hostel and two girls started moving out with a lot of luggage.

I stood up and ran towards her but she didn't notice me. I fell down and even then she didn't notice. I ran hard to reach her before she boarded the cab and just then a bike came riding down and crashed into me on the road. I was badly hurt and began to bleed profusely. It was then that she noticed me. She came running towards me, her face worried and anxious. I was crying in pain and she was crying out of concern. We hugged and cried together. Her friend signalled to the cab driver to leave. Everybody present there was both surprised and shocked at the sight of two lovers, one bleeding and the other crying, embracing each other. I am sure no one would have witnessed this scene in reality, but only in movies probably. A couple of persons present there helped Jahnvi to carry me to the pavement. She washed and cleaned my bruises and finally when I felt better enough to walk, we headed to the closest CCD outlet.

"Can't you do a single thing right in your life?" she asked.

"I did; I loved you."

"Liar," she made a face and smirked.

"I swear on God, I wouldn't have come all the way from Indore otherwise."

"Look, I just told you. You are a liar."

I explained to her how I had waited to contact her and when I failed to talk to her, I logged on to Facebook and saw her status posted there. "I then flew down here to talk to you."

"What do you want to talk about now?" she asked dejectedly.

"Jahnvi, we can still change things. Please don't get married to anybody else. I know how hard it was for you and how much you fought for me."

"And how did you realise it after two long years?"

"That I'll tell you later but whatever made me realise this has changed me as a person. I have realised how badly I had behaved with you and how I was arrogant as to say so many humiliating things to you and about your family. Please forgive me for that."

"I forgave you the moment you said this, Arnab. I knew how hard it was for you to accept the circumstances. I probably would've done the same thing in your place. But yes, it did hurt me.... the words you used against my parents."

"I said sorry! I know how easy it is for the guy's family to accept a girl and how difficult it is for a girl's family to accept a guy. They have all the right to investigate your choice and comment upon it."

"Yes, they were wrong on some counts and I was tired of opposing them all the time. I tried hard for you, but even I had had enough, Arnab."

"Who's the guy you are going to marry?" I asked.

"And who told you that I am getting married?"

"People have been congratulating you on Facebook. You told me you were going to get engaged this year, so I inferred that you were getting….." I still could not make myself to say the word 'marriage.'

"They congratulated me because these are my last few hours in Pune," she said. Saying this she looked away.

"That's a …., you are moving back to your hometown, is it?"

"Hmm…" was all she said. I was still gazing at her, expecting something more for her to add, but she did not say anything. Instead, she started talking about life in Mumbai, my job, my friends there. I religiously replied to every single thing she had to ask me. Though her queries were not interesting, the fact that she was sitting in front of me was enough. I would cherish these moments for the rest of my life.

We spoke some more about certain random things – things we knew were not important to us, but still we spoke to hear, to see, to feel and to just be there. There was just one strange thing that happened when Jahnvi was with me and that was, she was constantly messaging someone and even excused herself once to answer a call. When I enquired who it was, she simply brushed it off, saying it was her friend from college. Her tone was enough to tell me not to probe any further.

A few minutes later I paid the bill and we left. I dropped Jahnvi to her hostel. I knew she wanted to say something but every time she was about to say it, she stopped and turned mute. She just smiled when she got off at her hostel gate and walked off, without saying a single word. I stood there for few minutes watching her till she stayed in my view. I then walked my way back to the airport. My flight was still two hours away, so I decided to sit in the café and kill time.

I was sipping my coffee and uselessly browsing through some magazines when someone patted me on my shoulder. I was startled to see what I had never imagined I would be looking at. Everything around seemed to have become non-existent. My eyes were wide with surprise and my jaw had flown open with bewilderment! My palms were sweaty and my legs were trembling. I stood rooted the spot for a few minutes, completely frozen. I wanted to talk, shout, shriek, but I had even lost that sense.

"Arnab…." the sweet voice said and prevented me from falling down. "I am here for you; for us."

"Jahnvi… what are you doing here?"

"I am going to Mumbai for my MBA. Didn't you know?" Jahnvi asked with a smile on her face.

"Mumbai? Really?" I asked her, still unable to believe that I was talking to Jahnvi; that she was standing in front of me, holding my hands; that she was flying to Mumbai.

"Jahnvi...Jahnvi...Jahnvi…!!" I suddenly started singing her name loudly. I hugged her tight. I carried her high and shrieked louder. I put her down and hugged her tighter, as tight as possible.

We were happy and glad. We were thrilled and excited. We were talking and laughing. We were hugging and kissing.

After we had expressed our feelings, Jahnvi told me everything – how her parents were seeing her plight over me, how they had to given in to their daughter's love, how everything had fallen in place, convincing her parents about our love and how Rishi and she planned to surprise me?!

Finally all was well. I had Jahnvi and Jahnvi had me. We were together again; this time forever. With this, I gave Jahnvi another piece of good news. I showed her my appointment letter from HDFC. She saw it; she read it and she began to dance with joy there and then. She was happy that I had landed myself a very good job with a fantastic pay. I was seeing Jahnvi this happy after ages and that made me happy too. She was thrilled with all the happenings, rather, we both were. We had not even for a second left each other free from our hand's grip and were consistently gazing at each other and smiling big. We started it at CCD; we ended it there before restarting it there again. I booked my ticket to Mumbai.

We did not realise when the flight landed in Mumbai and we were off at the airport, waiting for Rishi to pick us up. Suddenly I caught hold of Jahnvi's arm, pulled her closer to me and cupped her face in my hands. I leaned my head to right and she to left till our lips were just inches apart. "Arnab... what are...?"

I kissed her on the lips before she could even complete the sentence. Within seconds she responded intensely and passionately. By now we had become an object of shock and surprise for the people at airport. The 'oohs' and 'aahs' did not stop us. The shocked glares of the elders did not deter us. We kissed for more than a couple of minutes and finally when we stopped, I noticed Rishi waving at us. I waved back and smiled. We collected our luggage and I put my arms across Jahnvi's waist, looked at people around us who were still staring us and winked at them before walking off from the place.

I no more cared about what people might think. For all I knew I was happy that we were together again and this time for good. I smiled our way back to our flat. With Rishi around and him being a part of the plan everything was almost perfect. We talked, we laughed, we cried, we hugged, we kissed and we talked some more. Life and destiny had given us a second chance and this time we did not want to take any chances. We were with each other, for each other. We were in love once again; in love till eternity. We had hopes for a better tomorrow.

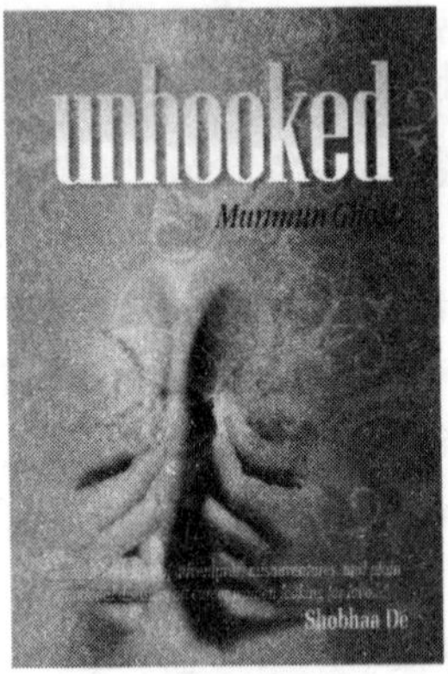

Unhooked

By Munmun Ghosh

Price : ₹ 150
Pages : 264
Size : 5 × 7.75 inches
Binding : Paperback
Language : English
Subject : Fiction
ISBN : 9788183520270

Love Destiny

By Murlidhar Srivastava

Price : ₹ 125
Pages : 208
Size : 5.0 × 7.75 inches
Binding : Paperback
Language : English
Subject : Fiction
ISBN : 9788183520218

I 'm Heartless

By Vinit K. Bansal

Price : ₹ 125
Pages : 184
Size : 5 × 7.75 inches
Binding : Paperback
Language : English
Subject : Fiction/Romance
ISBN : 9788183520966

The Fork & Spoon of Life

By Ankrish Khanna

Price : ₹ 125
Pages : 216
Size : 5.0 × 7.75 inches
Binding : Paperback
Language : English
Subject : Fiction/Romance
ISBN : 9788183520331

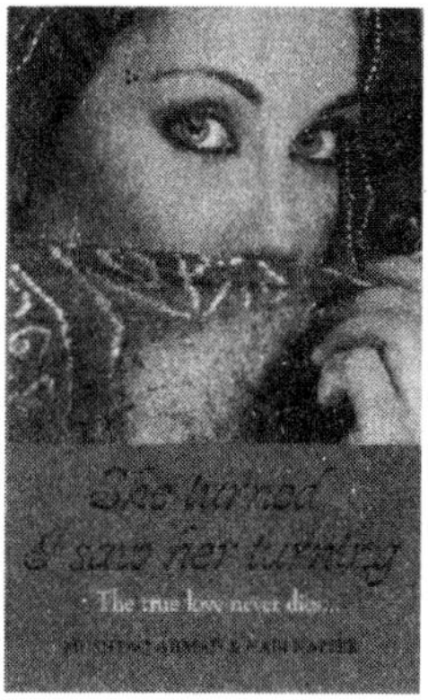

She turned I saw her turning

By Mushtaq Ahmad & Nabi Nazeer

Price : ₹ 99
Pages : 112
Size : 5.0 × 7.75 inches
Binding : Paperback
Language : English
Subject : Fiction
ISBN : 9788183520690

That's the Life Baby

By Priyesh Ranjan

Price : ₹ 125
Pages : 224
Size : 5.0 × 7.75 inches
Binding : Paperback
Language : English
Subject : Fiction
ISBN : 9788183520003

Love Me in the End

By Sonia Kundra Singh

Price : ₹ 125
Pages : 208
Size : 5.0 × 7.75 inches
Binding : Paperback
Language : English
Subject : Fiction
ISBN : 9788183520812

Let's Get Committed

By Smita Kaushik, Utkarsh Roy

Price : ₹ 125
Pages : 224
Size : 5.0 × 7.75 inches
Binding : Paperback
Language : English
Subject : Fiction
ISBN : 9788183520157

Take My Heart, Please!

By Gaurav Pandey

Price : ₹ 125
Pages : 182
Size : 5.0 × 7.75 inches
Binding : Paperback
Language : English
Subject : Fiction
ISBN : 9788183520829

Kiss Goodbye to..

By Manesh Pal Mrinamay

Price : ₹ 125
Pages : 192
Size : 5.0 × 7.75 inches
Binding : Paperback
Language : English
Subject : Fiction
ISBN : 9788183520904

Love Chemistry

By Shubham Arora

Price : ₹ 125
Pages : 186
Size : 5.0 × 7.75 inches
Binding : Paperback
Language : English
Subject : Fiction
ISBN : 9788183520898

Dear, I Love You

By Arun Sabtharishi

Price : ₹ 125
Pages : 208
Size : 5.0 × 7.75 inches
Binding : Paperback
Language : English
Subject : Fiction
ISBN : 9788183520874

Love in the Reality

By Hardik Dhamija

Price : ₹ 125
Pages : 188
Size : 5.0 × 7.75 inches
Binding : Paperback
Language : English
Subject : Fiction
ISBN : 9788183520850

Sorry for Loving You

By Abhishek Agrawal

Price : ₹ 125
Pages : 228
Size : 5.0 × 7.75 inches
Binding : Paperback
Language : English
Subject : Fiction
ISBN : 9788183520843

Trust Me, it'll Work!!

By Mohit Naryani

Price : ₹ 125
Pages : 244
Size : 5.0 × 7.75 inches
Binding : Paperback
Language : English
Subject : Fiction
ISBN : 9788183520836